BRIEF
ENCOUNTERS

BRIEF ENCOUNTERS

69 HOT GAY SHORTS

EDITED BY
SHANE ALLISON

CLEiS
PRESS

Published in the United States by Cleis Press Inc.,
2246 Sixth Street, Berkeley, California 94710.

Printed in the United States.
Cover design: Scott Idleman/Blink
Cover photograph: Image Source
Text design: Frank Wiedemann
First Edition.
10 9 8 7 6 5 4 3 2 1

Trade paper ISBN: 978-1-57344-664-8
E-book ISBN: 978-1-57344-685-3

"The Sensitivity of Skin" © 2005 by Shane Allison, reprinted with the author's permission from Savage Lust.com. "Safe Sex" © 2003 by M. Christian, reprinted with the author's permission from *Just the Sex,* edited by Jesse Grant (Alyson Books, 2003). "Drape It, Then Rape It" © 2003 by Robert Glück, reprinted from *Denny Smith Stories* by Robert Glück. "Switch" © 2001 by Daniel W. K. Lee reprinted with the author's permission from *Just the Sex.* "A Stolen Quickie" © 2010 by Christopher Stone reprinted with the author's permission from Velvet Mafia. "This Boy" © 2008 by Xan West, reprinted with the author's permission from *Frenzy,* edited by Alison Tyler.

Contents

ix *Introduction: Getting to the Good Parts*

1 *Hot for Teacher* • ROB ROSEN
7 *Senator Blanding Fucks Up* • JAMIE FREEMAN
13 *Red Bryce* • ROB WOLFSHAM
19 *The Lusty Librarian* • FRED TOWERS
23 *Jeff and Sam: After the Concert* • JEFF MANN
29 *Slicing the Knot* • KYLE LUKOFF
35 *Back Row* • LOGAN ZACHARY
41 *Mr. Popular* • JONATHAN ASCHE
46 *A Stolen Quickie* • CHRISTOPHER STONE
49 *Killing Time* • SHANNA GERMAIN
54 *The Sensitivity of Skin* • SHANE ALLISON
59 *Man, They Say Cutter's Gay* •
    JOHNNY MURDOC
64 *Diner Dick* • JAY STARRE
70 *Friday Night in Room 69* • JEFF FUNK
75 *Those Who Listen* • JAMIE FREEMAN
80 *Fucking Hot Daddy* • JAY ROGERS
85 *The XXXmas Gift* • MICHAEL BRACKEN
90 *The Coaster* • STEPHEN OSBORNE
95 *Drape It, Then Rape It* • ROBERT GLÜCK
98 *Two Men in a Boat* • M. CHRISTIAN
103 *Wrong* • SIMON SHEPPARD

108   *Archie's Tongue* • DAVID HOLLY

113   *Broad Strokes* • WILLIAM HOLDEN

118   *Making the Grade* • BRIAN CENTRONE

123   Pretty Boys Suck • DERRICK DELLA GIORGIA

128   *Justin from 360* • JONATHAN ASCHE

134   In Medias Res • PENBOY 7

138   *This Boy* • XAN WEST

141   *Room for Cream* • NATTY SOLTESZ

145   *Time Disappears* • ERIC K. ANDERSON

151   *Ain't Enough Time* • DIESEL KING

156   *Afternoon Delight* • L. D. MADISON

162   *Spurned* • SIMON SHEPPARD

167   *Jeff and Sam: Big Country Breakfast* • JEFF MANN

172   *Cocksucker in Jail* • BEARMUFFIN

177   *A Game of Shirts versus Skins* • GREGORY L. NORRIS

183   *Switch* • DANIEL W. K. LEE

188   *What Springs Up* • MICHAEL BRACKEN

193   *Sleeper Love* • R. TALENT

198   Alea Lacta Est • KARL VON UHL

203   *Show Dog* • DOMINIC SANTI

208   *The Highest Bidder* • GAVIN ATLAS

214   *The Wave Pool* • ZEKE MANGOLD

220   *He'll Suck You If I Say So* • JEFF FUNK

226   *Clown* • SLEEPY ACOSTA

231   *Out of the Shadows* • LANDON DIXON

236 *Opportunistic* • FOX LEE

240 *After Hours at the Gym* • JIM HOWARD

245 *Rush* • D. FOSTALOVE

251 *Primary Interaction* • CHRISTOPHER PIERCE

257 *Worth It* • CARI Z

263 *Under the Tuscan Sun* • D. V. PATTON

269 *One for the Team* • BOB MASTERS

275 *Night Sweat* • WILLIAM HOLDEN

280 *Friendly Fire* • GREGORY L. NORRIS

286 *Spit-Bubble and Snot* • LARKIN

291 *Good Vibrations* • R. J. BRADSHAW

294 *Talk to Me* • THOMAS FUCHS

297 *Waste Not* • TROY STORM

303 *As I Lay* • SHANE ST. JOHN

306 *The Masochists Among Us* • SHAUN LEVIN

311 *The Most Unexpected Places* •
     RACHEL KRAMER BUSSEL

316 *Good Buddy* • NICK GILBERTON MARENCO

322 *Safe Sex* • M. CHRISTIAN

326 *Midnight Decision* • JAY STARRE

331 *Ground-Floor Blow Job* • SHANE ALLISON

336 *After Hours* • C. C. WILLIAMS

342 *The Swimmer* • MIKE BRUNO

347 *Sock Fuzz* • GREGORY L. NORRIS

354 *About the Editor*

INTRODUCTION: GETTING TO THE GOOD PARTS

I could feel his eyes bearing down on me, sizing me up so to speak. I pretended like I didn't notice. I started massaging it, knowing full well what I was doing. He was tall and thin, the geeky punkster type, the type that I like. With his dick still hanging out of the zipper of his faded, brown corduroys, he moved closer over to where I was standing. I didn't really have to pee. I just like to stand at the pissers to check out other men's dicks. So there we were standing there, hot and horny, pleasuring ourselves. I boldly reached over and took his dick into my warm palm, wrapped my fat fingers around his shaft. He didn't mind. Our eyes didn't meet. I was nervous. I'm sure he was too. We took a risk of getting caught, but what is life without it? I was mesmerized by his thatch of red pubic hair, the hook of steel that pierced the bulbous crown of his slick, large endowment. I pleasured him until he came. Torrents of semen jerked against porcelain and yellow urinal water. I got a little of him on my fingers, but that happens during these sorts of situations. When I turned him loose, he tucked his dick back into his blue boxer/briefs, his tattered cords, and exited the bathroom without so much as a thank-you.

Brief Encounters: that's the perfect title for this anthology. I have always believed that the best sex is sex that happens in an instant, when we least expect it. An elevator ride, a late-night romp at a twenty-four-hour Laundromat with a tall, dark and...sexy stranger; or how about when your eyes meet across a crowded room or across a shelf of erotica in a bookstore, which is something I have experienced firsthand.

This anthology of fast, one-handed erotica will leave you clinching your sweat-drenched bedsheets for more. The following are sixty-nine of the shortest, hottest stories of gay erotica that I have had the pleasure of jacking off to—I mean reading. Some of the best erotic scribes in the genre are gathered here: Rob Rosen, Simon Sheppard, Gregory L. Norris, M. Christian, Jonathan Asche, Jeff Mann, Logan Zachary, Rob Wolfsham and a plethora of other stars. So without further ado, enjoy.

Shane Allison
Tallahassee, Florida

HOT FOR
TEACHER

Rob Rosen

P rofessor Johnson looked up when I entered, a slight
smile spreading northward. "Mr. Brown," he said,
deep voice tearing through my belly like wildfire. "What
can I do for you today?"

"Those marketing tests you're grading," I replied,
setting my backpack down. "I, um, need at least a B in
order to keep my honors GPA."

He rifled through the papers, tight sweater leaving
nothing to the imagination—pecs like granite, nipples
poking out—my cock throbbing at the sight of him.
It was no wonder I couldn't concentrate in class. And
then he found my test, his smile vanishing. "Guess you
should've studied harder." He flipped it over, my whole
world crashing in around me.

"But I can't afford a C-minus."

"Sorry, Mr. Brown, it is what it is."

Which was what I had figured, hence my reason for being there. He left me little choice. "How about some extra credit then, to help *get it up*?" I smiled, leaning in, bulging crotch now resting on the edge of the desk. His eyes quickly darted down, then back up, locking onto mine.

"Bit late in the game, don't you think?" There was a sudden edge to his voice, a nervous tic just above his eye.

"Never too late in marketing, sir. Always time to sell yourself, to get the public to buy what you're offering."

He folded his arms over his chest, the smile again evident. "And just what are you *selling* today?"

I leaned down, my hands on his desk, face now inches away from his. "A bj for a B-plus, sir. Seems an equitable trade."

He laughed, nervously. "Highly improper, Mr. Brown."

"True, but the only thing worse than not making a sale is not trying to make the sale in the first place. Besides, you always market your best product."

"Namely a blow job?" He stood, the tenting in his slacks clearly evident. "That the best you can offer?"

I backed up, my hands grabbing for the bottom of my jersey, which I hiked up and off, the cold hitting me in a wave, goose bumps running rampant down my arms. I flexed for him, pumped chest rising and lowering, then loosened my belt and pulled it through the loops, opened a top button to expose a flash of wiry bush. "I can throw in a little something extra, sir. To sweeten the deal."

He walked around to my side of the desk and put his index finger inside my jeans, pulling the waistband out and peeking in. "Nothing *little* here." He moaned, appreciatively. "Maybe we can work something out then."

I grinned and pushed down on the denim, seven steely inches springing up and out as my pants hit the floor. "But it takes two to tango, sir."

He took the hint and lifted his sweater off, triggering a lemon-sized lump in my throat at the sight of him. The guy was ripped, with a fine brown down covering the length and breadth of him, and two extra cans added to a fierce six-pack. "You like the merchandise?" he practically purred, running his palm across his chest and giving a tweak of a thick nipple, a fluttering of the eyes.

I nodded, sinking to my knees, hungry for what he had going on below the belt. "Nice packaging," I managed, sliding down his fly and reaching in to find a huge, hard lump waiting for me inside. The lemon grew grapefruit sized when it came flopping out, sausage thick, the shaft thickly veined, the wide head dripping. "No bait and switch here, sir," I moaned, downing him in one fell swoop, the salty precum hitting my tongue like a bullet.

He shoved it in, his hand running through my hair as he coaxed it down, my hands spreading his meaty cheeks, my index finger gliding down his hairy crack before zooming around his crinkled hole. Moaning while he face-fucked me, I decided to up the ante, pushing and prodding my way past his ring and up his chute, deep inside.

"Fuuuck," he exhaled, the sound ricocheting around the room, causing my cock to bounce and drip.

I popped his prick out, spit dribbling down my chin, my finger still entrenched up his ass. "You wanna?" I asked, my tongue moving down, circling his heavy nuts, my mouth taking each one in for a swirl and an eager suck.

"Oh, yeah," he moaned, head tilted back.

I jumped up and pushed him onto his desk till his body was prone, legs spread apart, asshole winking out at me and beckoning me in. Of course, I came prepared for, well, *coming*. The rubber and lube packet were yanked out of my jeans in the blink of an eye, sliding down and slicking up my dick even faster than that. "Now let's see if you feel just as good inside as you look on the outside."

He yanked on his thick nipples, sighing. "Feel away, Mr. Brown."

I lubed him up and slid it on home, his megatight hole fitting me like a glove, a million tingles riding shotgun through my gut and out my limbs. He bucked his ass into me, sucking me in like a Hoover, matching me moan for groan, sweat pooling between his chiseled pecs. I stroked his massive tool as I piston-fucked him, while he writhed on the desk beneath me.

With his balls banging up against mine, he shot like a rocket, cum spewing up and out, splattering his belly in a torrent before dripping over the sides. My own thick prick exploded a split second later, filling that rubber and his ass with ounce after creamy hot ounce of a hefty load, both of us gasping and moaning in sync.

"Now that's some extra credit," he panted.

But did I make the sale? I thought to myself, gliding out and helping him up.

He sat back down at his desk, my test paper in front of him, his red pen changing my grade as I slipped my clothes back on. Then I stared down, shocked at what I saw. "B-minus? Are you fucking kidding me?"

"What?" he replied, barely looking over at me. "You went up a whole grade. What do you want for a ten-minute fuck?"

"I want my B, sir," I grunted, clearly pissed. "I know marketing. I know how to step out of the box and grab 'em by the balls."

"Matter of opinion, Mister Brown," he said, dismissing me.

I grinned, despite his rudeness, turning around to retrieve my backpack and removing the video camera from within, my finger plugging the viewing hole he hadn't seen until that moment. "And my *opinion*, sir, is that I do, in fact, have you by the balls." I held the device in front of his face. "And all sales are final."

He returned the grin and changed the minus to a plus with a stroke of his pen. "You'll do well in the marketing world, Mr. Brown. Pretty on the outside, sneaky on the inside. The public won't know what hit them."

I turned and walked out the door, slamming it behind me. "There's a sucker born every minute," I whispered, "and no one sucks them off better than I do."

SENATOR BLANDING FUCKS UP

Jamie Freeman

Senator Charles Tolliver Blanding III has his big, sweaty feet up in my face. My hands are clamped around his ankles; he's squirming and groaning on the poly-blend bedspread. I'm slamming into him hard, watching the blood as he bites into his lip; watching the beads of sweat popping out on his forehead and running down into his thick silver hair.

A CNN anchor is stumbling through a story on the teleprompter and shuffling blank papers on his desk. "...Senator Charles Blanding is calling for public support for the Marriage Defense Amendment, which he calls a 'Constitutional shield against institutionalized immorality...'" I push harder, shoving a thick groan up through the Senator's clenched teeth.

"Yeah, baby, fuck me harder," he says. "Hurt me."

So I slap him hard across his face with the back of my hand.

He's startled, but I can see his cock leaping and bouncing with renewed vigor.

"Oh, yeah," he moans.

Three hours ago I was tending bar downstairs in the Dixie Ballroom, sneaking shots of Jameson and flirting with anyone who looked like he had something to shove in my tip jar. Strictly speaking, tips were donations to the candidate, but fuck that, I didn't see *her* pouring drinks for a bunch of hopped-up, alcoholic, homophobic, Old South, blue bloods. She was glad-handing like mad and when she ordered a chardonnay she looked a little too long into my eyes. It wasn't a fuck-me stare; I could see her flipping through her mental Rolodex. Blanding came up and distracted her, saying something stupid about "praying that dyke doesn't bewitch her way into the high court." They both laughed, talked for a while, and then the candidate drifted away.

Blanding tried to catch my eye.

I let him.

I dipped my head and flashed him a practiced look that started out doe-eyed and sweet, but ended up crazy and toothy, shy pretense overpowered by predatory glee.

It's a good look.

He laughed, but the sound caught wetly in his throat and I knew I had him.

"Get you something?" I asked.

"I know you from somewhere," he said.

"I don't think so." I knew him well.

"But you look familiar—"

"It's, uh…Hunter Parrish."

"Huh?"

"People say I look like him."

"Who's he?"

"'Weeds'?"

"I don't know what you're saying."

"The TV show…you know, Mary-Louise Parker—"

"Pornographic drug propaganda." He growled, but tried to smile. What a dumb-fuck. Hot as hell, but a complete dumb-fuck. He'd stayed at my parents' lake house dozens of times, but he was staring at me with the mute incomprehension of a priest making his first visit to a sex club.

Whatever.

But by the end of the night, Blanding was back. And he was just drunk enough to send his security team home and slide a key card across the bar with carefully manicured fingertips.

I dropped my hand on top of the key, running the pads of my fingers across his long, tanned fingers.

"Seven-twenty-four."

"Twenty minutes," I said.

And now he's naked on his back, his rippling abs and thunderous pecs sweating and flexing beneath me. His body's just like I remember it from the parties at the lake, hard and perfect as a Bianchi pictorial. Not a flicker of recognition crosses his glazed, dilated eyes.

He's jacking himself with his left hand, tugging on his thick cock and grunting as I pound him. I've been distracted by the television droning news of my father— "International Criminal Court, unable to indict John Hallowell, has issued a stern condemnation"—but the heavy smell of Blanding's body and the tightness of his flexing asshole are pulling me back into the moment.

My cheeks are flaming hot; sweat slips down my back. My cock bucks inside him.

"Oh, yeah," he says. "Deeper."

I glance over at the table where my uniform lies in a crumpled heap. I can't see the lens peeking out from my shirt pocket, but I know it's there. So I give him all I've got, pushing his legs back against his shoulders and folding him in half so I can shove my huge cock deeper inside him. When I feel my pubic bone pushing against his ass, I pull almost all the way out and then slam back inside him. This gets him going; he's a screamer. He lets out these deep, masculine groans that are intensely erotic, like music made of sex and thunder. His voice makes my pulse race. I slam into him again and again, letting the power build between my legs, feeling the burn in my arm and thigh muscles.

He's jacking like a madman now, his fingers slicked up with sweat and spit. Then he's shouting, "I'm gonna come!" over and over at the top of his lungs, drowning out the television and eliciting muffled bangs and thumps from the adjoining room. About five seconds after his crazed announcement, he lets loose, hosing himself down with explosion after explosion of cum. His chest is slick with it, his nipples frosted like melting cupcakes. When he slides his palm through the gooey mess and presses his hand to my mouth, I come too, shooting inside him in a trio of fierce bursts that leave me trembling and light-headed. I lick the spooge from his palm and he shoves the heel hard between my teeth. I groan and shake a little, biting down on the hot flesh and easing down from my orgasm.

"Shit," I say, sliding my cock out of him. I flex my chest and abdominal muscles, conscious of the camera to my left, thinking of my beautifully toned body moving through the frame.

"C'mere," the Senator says, motioning me forward. "Let me clean off your big dick."

I straddle him and crawl forward, lowering my long, limp cock between his lips and pushing it down until he is gagging on the flaccid bulk of it.

"This what you want?" I ask.

He makes a muffled sound and then nods his head, blinking at me and sliding my cock back and forth inside his mouth, cleaning me softly with his tongue.

"Yeah, baby," I say. "Clean up your mess."

There is something about my voice in that moment—perhaps I let my Carolina accent seep out between the wet little syllables—that causes the senator's eyes to snap into focus. "Oh, my god." His words—corn-holed by my fat cock—are nearly incomprehensible, but the look on his face tells me he finally recognizes me.

"Now he remembers," I say, pushing his shoulders flat against the bed, but letting him tilt his head and spit out my flaccid cock.

"Hallowell," he says. "What the fuck are you doing here?"

"That should be obvious," I say. I'm straddling him and I can feel his cock stirring beneath me, thumping in anticipation of another round.

"Fuck," he says, shoulders dropping to the mattress in defeat. "Your father's gonna kill me."

"I'm nineteen, Senator. It's your constituents who're gonna kill you."

"They'll never know."

"You ever heard the term 'live feed'?" I jerked my head in the direction of my crumpled uniform. "They already know."

RED BRYCE

Rob Wolfsham

The Red and the Black bar, Washington DC: cigarette smoke hugs the ceiling and strains Travis's tonsils. A crowd of fifty or so hipsters shift idly in the wood plank box of a room with bottles of Yuengling and cans of Pabst Blue Ribbon pressed to painted or scruffy lips. Bryce Samuels's band is playing tonight. Travis hasn't seen him in the seven years since they graduated high school in Texas and slid down different paths, Travis to the University of Houston, Bryce to Georgetown.

Bryce stands in a corner, protected by a troop of scraggly musicians. He stands six foot four. His orange curly hair sits lopsided in a messy fro. He wears a white-and-blue-striped tank top, loose and ruffled on his wide body—not fat, not muscular, utilitarian. Tattoos are stamped on his arms: a Virgo symbol on the thick veins of his left forearm, a blue Earth in chains on his right bicep and intricate Mayan glyphs spilling up his chest under orange scraggly hair from beneath the tank.

Travis ignores Bryce and his crowd, hoping to be noticed instead. He gazes attentively at the opening band onstage and sips his bottle of Yuengling to banjo playing, synthesizer landscapes and the warbling of a round-faced girl in a headband with a peacock feather like a flapper or a Lost Boy. Travis fits in but doesn't feel that way. A black V-neck T-shirt hangs from his short bony frame. Skinny jeans cut off circulation to his feet nestled in red Chuck Taylor high-tops. His brown hair is buzzed. The black frames of his square glasses are the right thickness on his long, sharp nose. His fuzzy brown beard wraps his jaw from ear to ear.

The last opening band shimmers away after thirty minutes, and Bryce's band scurries to set up. Travis walks up to his tall, redheaded memory, slices into his circle in front of the stage and gives him a side hug. Bryce grips the skinny boy around the ribs, unsure who he is grasping.

"Good luck," Travis says.

"My god," Bryce says, in slow realization, his round, turned-up nose points down at the boy beside him and his mouth falls open flashing bottom teeth. "Travis?"

The boy shrugs, grasping his beer bottle with both hands.

"What are you doing here?" Bryce asks.

Travis inhales, puffs up his V-neck and stares at the

redhead's chest. "I'm on a road trip," Travis says. "I was in DC and I saw on Facebook that your band was playing here tonight." He looks up and meets Bryce's shocked gray eyes.

"That's great," Bryce says, nodding, thin pink lips still agape, dimples pulsing with consternation as though he were grinding his molars. "How long is the road trip?"

"Indefinite. I quit my job, sold all my things on Craigslist and left Texas. I've been on the road for three weeks now. I'm a free spirit."

"That's big. Congratulations." Bryce reaches for a side hug with a gap between their ribs. "I can't believe you're here tonight."

Bryce kisses a girl before going on stage. Travis slinks away.

Bryce's band plays their forty-minute set of electronic folk. Bryce sings, masculine wails and growly poems. People shift in place, stamp their feet, spin in circles, holler at the end of songs as cymbals hiss. Guitars cut in and out. Bryce's MacBook freezes at one point, killing his synthesizer in the middle of a solo. Inebriated ears don't notice in the wall of sound slamming the wood walls and rafters. Bryce pours sweat, matting his red curls. He peels off his drenched tank top and wipes his forehead and nose. His shoulders are freckled. A red trail of hair from his prominent outie belly button dips into his khaki shorts that come down past his knees. His bare flat feet, large, monstrous, nearly trip on cords when he walks from the synthesizer to pick up a guitar.

The songs drift and seem to fall apart at each end. The guitarist and drummer exchange frustrated looks. The set ends. People shout for "Horticulture," a song for the encore, but the lights come up. The band is done.

Bryce storms from the stage, lugging his synthesizer case, muscles in his back twisting and bulging. He heads down a set of secluded stairs. Travis follows in the dissipating wake of chatting hipsters and catches Bryce in a dark storage room between the back of the bar and the van outside. Emergency lights above the exit sign cast two spotlights at each door in the small room. Stacks of boxes tower around the two, fracturing the spotlights with long shadows through the cityscape of cardboard. Travis says the music was great no matter what.

Bryce asks why Travis came to DC. The boy adjusts his glasses and says he was headed to North Carolina from Philadelphia, but the lie falls apart in his averted gaze. Bryce says the band is over and tonight was their last show. He's leaving DC. The city is toxic. He drops the synthesizer case and rolls his shoulder blades along the warm concrete wall, pushing out his taut orange-fuzzed chest, parting his pinkish knees. Travis walks between them and clutches Bryce's pearl ribs, kisses Mayan glyphs and pink nipples. Bryce pulls the boy's V-neck off. Travis's glasses clatter on the floor. He ignores them. Bryce grabs the boy's bony shoulders and pulls their chests together. He leans down and attacks the boy's thin lips. They twist tongues, gulp and flare hot air from their nostrils against each other. The boy grabs the tent in Bryce's khaki pants and kneads his hard-on.

Bryce's lips part against Travis's forehead and he moans, exhales.

Travis gets on his knees, pulls the musician's beltless khaki shorts down his strong thighs covered in woolly blond hair. Bryce's eight-inch cock bounces up in the air, pale like ivory. Thick long foreskin obscures most of the purplish head, revealing only a pink piss slit.

Travis takes it between his lips and shoves the sweaty cock down the tight folds of his throat, pulling Bryce's dangling balls against his chin.

Bryce grimaces with bottom teeth, grunts, takes hold of Travis's fuzzy head and fucks into it. The boy slurps, pulls Bryce's cock out with a wet pop, pulls the foreskin back on the purple head and takes it down his throat again. The boy's beard grinds Bryce's balls, and his long nose burrows in fiery pubes. It's seven years ago, the memory tied to the musky scent of uncut Bryce, high school bathroom stalls and music exchanging, cock-slurping sleepovers.

Bryce tugs Travis's ears and squats a little, impaling the boy's snug throat with his cock. Travis's face is rosy, nose scrunched up, eyes watering. Bryce palms Travis's head and cums down his throat. Hot semen gurgles back up as the boy gags. Bryce lets go of his ears and Travis ejects his cock with a gasp and a spittle of cum.

Travis sighs, smiles at the glistening penis and puts his glasses back on. He gazes up the ivory tower of Bryce's body and meets his eyes.

A rope of cum rests on Travis's shoulder. The boy swipes it with his fingers and licks them clean. He wipes his chin and stands. "Where will you go when you leave DC?"

Bryce pulls up his khaki shorts and tucks his waning cock in. "I figure I could keep you company on your road trip for a while."

THE LUSTY LIBRARIAN

Fred Towers

I may be straight and married, but I can't help myself. All I can think of is the new guy at work, while my cock throbs in my pants. He's tall and lanky, with a swimmer's build of lean muscle. As a librarian, I'm used to working mainly with women, so I've felt electrified since Greg was hired.

When he came out to me, I lost my struggle with my need for a man's touch. Since my wife also works at the library, I can't make a move, but I can't quit thinking of him. I've dreamed about finding him in the reference shelves, naked, waiting for me.

His long, thin cock stands against his stomach and begs me to lick up the precum glistening on the tip. I run my tongue over my thin lips as I sink to my knees and swallow his cock. When it fills my mouth, I sigh, realizing this is what I've missed in my life since that one time in college. After that night long ago, I rushed to confession, but this time I want this cock to fill me up like never before. I savor the salty taste of his precum, while I tease the spongy mushroom head with my tongue.

The ringing phone snaps me out of my daydream. I feel my cock pushing against the seams of my khaki pants. As soon as I've answered the caller's reference question, I ask another librarian to cover the desk for me and I escape to the restroom.

In the stall, I yank out my stout, throbbing cock for the third time that day. Since Greg, I spend a lot of time jerking off. I imagine sucking him or bending over to take it. I want him to spread my cheeks, spit on my asshole and shove his dick into my virginal ass. Sometimes, he eases into me, but other times he shoves it in. I want my ass to ache from him. I want to feel him in me long after he's gone.

I pound my cock fast and hard, imagining him plowing into me until his balls slap against mine. I bite my lip to prevent alerting anyone. As I roughly stroke my cock, my ass begs to be filled. A groan escapes me when my cum spews into the toilet.

That's how I ended up here, at the gay cruising spot. Slipping a finger into my aching hole isn't fixing my need anymore.

Ahead, another guy in a car flicks his lights. I return the signal. My palms sweat as he approaches. Once he parks his minivan next to my sedan, he motions his head toward the passenger seat.

I climb in. Before I can open my mouth to speak, I see the stranger's fat cock resting against his open zipper. I stare in disbelief at it. I wonder if my ass can open enough to accommodate it.

"What you looking for, buddy?" He strokes the massive dick. It appears to grow larger.

I open my mouth again, but still nothing comes out.

"Wanna suck it or fuck it?"

My twitching ass answers for me. "Fuck me." It barely comes out as a whisper.

The stranger smiles. "Get in back." He clears his throat as he motions to the backseat.

When I oblige, he bends me over the couch seat as he slides my pants down. He spreads a cool liquid over my virginal hole and fumbles at it with his fingers. As his meaty digits spread me open, I gasp. He roughly manipulates the small opening.

As he slides his cock in, I want to yell out from the intense sensations, a mixture of pain and pleasure. He inches in slowly at first, then, with a grunt, he slams into me. I scream. His huge cock impales me. With each thrust, he growls. I whimper. The pounding shoves my face into the back of the seat, and my glasses push against me in an awkward angle.

Even though my ass throbs from the pounding, my dick twitches like it wants to erupt. I close my eyes as I feel it build up from my balls to my piss slit. I shoot my load, cumming so hard I feel like I have released all my energy onto the seat. The stranger's orgasm explodes into the condom I didn't realize he'd put on, and he collapses against me.

A few seconds later, the stranger pushes himself off me and adjusts his pants. "Gotta go, bud."

On wobbly legs, I slide into the van's passenger seat. I see him toss the condom out the window. I struggle with whether to say something or just exit the van. Fearing my legs won't hold me up I slowly climb out and return to my car. Before I even plop into the driver's seat, the van speeds away. When my ass lands in my car seat, the twinge I feel reminds me of his presence.

I'm about to leave when another guy in a car flashes me. I think about ignoring him until I realize that while my ass is satisfied, my mouth craves the taste of a cock. I lick my lips and flash my lights back.

JEFF AND SAM: AFTER THE CONCERT

Jeff Mann

Sam's scent is strong. Again, just to please me, he hasn't worn deodorant. I shove him back against the edge of the dressing table. Kissing him, I unbutton his shirt, silk sweat-sodden with his concert exertions. Beyond this tiny dressing room, the applause is still thunderous.

"You sounded great tonight," I sigh into his ear, stripping him to the waist. "Your voice is just stronger and stronger."

"Your guitar was mighty fine too, especially on that new song," Sam says, squeezing the bulge in my jeans. "Ten years, buddy. Ten years of on-the-road secret sweet stuff. You gonna want me in another ten? Shit, my beard's going gray."

I shuck off my moist T-shirt, then caress the few

silvery streaks in his otherwise brown beard. "I love this gray. What do you expect, man? You're forty-two."

Sam laughs. "And it's getting harder and harder to get into jeans this tight."

"This help?" I unbutton and unzip his jeans, then mine. I pull two bandanas from my back pockets and lay them on the table.

"You sure we should? The guys'll want a few drinks before we head on out to the hotel. They'll be here soon." Sam tips back his black Resistol and kisses me again.

"Won't take long, promise. Door's locked." I jerk Sam's jeans and briefs, then mine, down around our cowboy boots. "The way you smell, all this sweat"—I run a finger between his smooth pecs, daub up the shine—"I got to have you. Now, Sam. And leave the hat on. I love you in it."

Sam nods, gripping my tattoo-sleeved forearms and grinding his stiff dick against mine. "God, I love your ink. And your big damn cock and your big fucking bulk." His lips brush mine, nibble my bearded chin. "Oh, fuck," he pants, "you know how much I love Hope and the kids, and I miss 'em like holy hell, but tonight, all through the concert, all I could think about was how much I need—"

My fingers stray over his bare ass, tickle his sweat-slick crack. "I got what you need. You want tied?"

"*Hell*, yes! But loose, okay? So I can get free fast if the boys get here before—"

"Sure," I say, grabbing a bandana. "Turn around."

As many years as we've been doing this—furtive quickies in back rooms across America—it takes me mere seconds to knot Sam's wrists behind him. As soon as he's bound, my tongue starts in on his torso. It's glistening, as if it were enameled with gold leaf. I'm eager as a farmhand swilling well water after hours in the hayfield.

"You know I like you hairy. When you gonna stop shaving all this?" I nip and nuzzle his chest's hard, gym-molded mounds, his flat, smooth belly. "I mightily miss that otter-pelt of yours."

"After the tour, I promise," Sam gasps, as I feast on one sensitive nip, then the other. "The publicist said that—"

"Yeah, yeah, those hungry hussy fans prefer shaved and buff. Stupid cows. At least you left me this"—I lap the fur of a smelly armpit—"and this"—I lick the pungent hair of his pubes—"and especially this"—I tug on the hair in his asscrack. "You're too cut, too buff, too lean. After this tour, I'm gonna plump you up on some pulled pork barbeque and country-fried steak."

Sam's groaning now, as I roughly chew a nipple. "You're just making noise so I'll do this, bud." I roll up the second bandana, push it between his teeth, and tie the ends behind his head. "I know what you want before you want it. Right?" I press a hand over his mouth. "You love gnawing a nice rag, don't you, boy?" I kiss his nose, stare into his wide eyes.

"Mmm." Sam blinks at me: long, almost girlish lashes. I knead his chest-meat, pinch his nipples and watch his face twist with pain.

"I could do this all night, but...ain't got time. You keep this gag in, okay?"

Sam nods. His obedience makes us both hard dicked and happy.

"Sucking and fucking you for a damn decade?" I chuckle. "I'm one lucky redneck! I'll bet all those bitches out there would love to do this." Without further delay, I drop to my knees, wrap my arms around his hips and swallow his cock. I mouth-pump him, tight and fast, till he's grunting and slamming my face.

"Again, I could suck you all night, but I'd rather ride you." I stand, grab his shoulders, turn him around and bend him over the dressing table. "You want it now?" I take his asscheeks in my palms, squeeze them and pry them apart.

"Umm!" Sam nods.

"I only got spit. Can't find the lube." I press my cock head against his wet cleft. "Brokeback-style? Might hurt some. Horned up as I am, it won't take long. You want it that bad? Think you can take it?"

"Ummm!" Sam presses his butt back against me.

"This should help open you up." On my knees again, I'm biting his butt, then lapping his fuzzy crevice, pushing my tongue into him. "Yum. All rich from your stage shenanigans, superstar," I growl.

Standing, I lube us with spit. I work the head of my

dick in. Sam winces, whimpers into his gag, gives me a little struggle and tries to rise. I should go slower, but he's too sweet and tight. I clamp a hand over his mouth, force him down, push into him full-length. Sam bucks and groans.

"Hurting?" I pick up the pace fast, from tentative thrusts to outright pounding.

Sam nods.

"Want me to stop?"

Sam shakes his head.

In the space of about thirty heartbeats, I'm shuddering and gasping, shooting up the tight clench of his ass. A few heartbeats later, I've rolled him over and am deep-throating him.

There's a loud knock at the door. Of course. Fuck. Glad I locked it. I hear a distant voice: Logan, the bass player. "Hey, guys, y'all ready?"

Sam grunts. His load floods my mouth. He fumbles loose his hands, pulls out his mouth-gag, grips my head, gifts me with another mouthful, and shouts, "Coming, man! We'll be right out!"

We stand, pulling up our pants, grinning like fools. "Jeff, hold on." Sam wipes his cum from my beard, tongues it off his hand. I tug on a fresh black T-shirt; Sam slips on a fresh gray one.

"We got adjoining rooms at the hotel, right? With a connecting door?" I pull on my rawhide jacket, then help him slip into his black leather drover.

"Yeah. February in West Virginia: good excuse for

you to sneak in tonight and keep me warm. I could do with some serious cuddling."

Our hands clasp and let go. I unlock the door and usher Sam out. The boys are rowdy and thirsty. After tonight's performance, we're all eager for a few beers.

SLICING
THE KNOT

Kyle Lukoff

I should have known that a July wedding was a bad idea.

It was the summer of 2004. My partner Jesse and I had been together for five years. When we met, Jesse was a campaign organizer for the Maine Marriage Equality chapter. When we started dating I got involved too. It seemed like common sense. If straight people could get married, we should be able to also. Right?

Imagine our excitement when Massachusetts legalized gay marriage. Jesse proposed immediately. I said yes, of course. We *worked* for marriage for Chrissakes. It would be hypocritical of us not to get married.

Wouldn't you know we broke up on the drive there? Our air-conditioning broke down halfway, and neither one of us deals with heat very well.

The real issue was that we hadn't had sex for a year. We were almost to Boston when Jesse joked about us getting the honeymoon suite.

"More like the Boston marriage suite," I grumbled. He asked what that meant, so I explained to him about those presumably sexless unions between two women in the early twentieth century. He grew tense, I egged him on, and before you could say Jack Twist we were screaming. I called him a castrated prude, he called me a greedy slut, and by the time we rolled into Beantown we were over.

I didn't want to endure another long drive with my now-ex. It was his car, so he dropped me off at South Station. I'd take the first bus back. Jesse's tires didn't screech as he drove off, but they might as well have.

There was a bus up to Maine the next morning, so I decided to make it a minivacation, get a hotel room for the night. I remembered a quaint little place in Back Bay and made my way there.

I should've been upset. We were going to spend our lives together in a happy, monogamous, state-sanctioned relationship. We had plans: a dog, a house, an adopted kid from some Third-World country. But as I sauntered up to the hotel reception desk, I felt giddy with freedom.

"Hi there," said the man behind the desk. "How can I help you?"

"I'd like a room for the night, please."

"Single?"

"Yes, I am." He looked at me with a confused half smile.

"My boyfriend and I came here to get married, and we broke up an hour ago."

"Oh, I'm so sorry!"

"Don't be. I feel better than I have in years."

"Well, good. We're usually booked up, but there was a cancellation so I can give you thirty-six-b." He handed me a key.

Before I could take a step he touched my arm. "Hey. I get off work in a few hours, at ten o' clock. If you want to talk…"

I looked him up and down. I liked what I saw. "Well, you know my room number," I said, and walked off.

It was a lovely evening. I strolled down Newport Street, browsed in the bookstores and had dinner. It was nice to make decisions for myself. If this was the single life, I could deal.

I made sure to get back to the hotel just before ten. I glanced at the desk, but there was some girl staffing it. I went up to my floor and grinned. The cute boy from the desk was there, leaning against the wall, expectation written all over his face. I unlocked the door, and when we were both inside I shut the door and shoved him down on the bed.

He was the first strange man I had touched in years, and our tongues tangled like clotheslines as we figured out how we fit together. Not wasting any time, we started ripping off each other's clothes. He reached down into the pocket of his jeans and pulled out a handful of rubbers and lube packets.

"Do you like to get fucked," he asked, "or do you want to do the fucking?"

"I want you in me."

He nodded, and without any hesitation I dove down and inhaled his dick. It had been so long since I had had a thick piece of meat in my mouth that I almost gagged, but then I remembered how to open up my throat and let it envelop him. I bobbed up and down, squeezing his balls with my hand until he was good and hard, and then withdrew. I rolled onto my belly, put my face down and waited.

I shuddered with delight at the first invasion, a long finger slick with spit. He prepped me for a long time, playing with my asshole until I was writhing with anticipation. When I couldn't take it any longer I lifted my head and gasped, "I need you. Please." He rolled on a condom, slathered it with lube and impaled me.

My hungry asshole swallowed him up, and I bit the pillow to keep from screaming with pleasure. Each downward thrust brought his smooth belly and pecs against my back, an intimacy I had missed almost as much as getting royally fucked. I heard him gasping too, and I felt a surge of joy that my body could bring another person pleasure.

His stamina was impressive—it seemed like he fucked me for hours. When he finally came he let out a canine yelp and writhed against me. Even through the condom

I could feel the hot semen pump out. When he was finished he rolled over and off of me, breathing heavily, and I propped myself up on my elbow to look at him. I put a hand on his chest.

"Thanks," I said, once he had caught his breath.

"Uh…my pleasure."

"It had been a long time."

"I thought you had a boyfriend?"

"Yeah. After the first couple years he just stopped wanting me, and then about a year ago we gave up on sex altogether."

The desk attendant shook his head and put his hand on mine. "You married types. You get so worked up about tax breaks and hospital visits that you forget about the important things."

"Huh?"

"Look, I'm a faggot and a slut, and I love men. I love the way they look, smell, feel…that's why I'm gay. I care about equality, sure, but marriage doesn't work for straight people. Why would it work for us?"

"But shouldn't we have the same rights as everyone else?"

"Everyone should have the same rights as everyone else, whether you're single or have a houseful of sex slaves."

I tried to remember some of the marriage equality talking points Jesse had drilled into my head over the years, but it was like they had been washed away in a wave of postcoital bliss.

After about an hour he got out of bed. "This was great," he said, "but I need to go home to walk my dog."

"No problem. Thanks again." I stretched out in the warm bed as the door clicked shut behind him. It felt nice to have a whole big bed to myself. As I drifted off to sleep, I decided not to go back to Maine. Maybe I'd stay in Boston awhile, maybe New York. It was time for me to rejoin the world.

BACK ROW

Logan Zachary

Don't waste that butter," a male voice said, from two seats down on my right.

I balanced my large popcorn container on my lap as I readied to wipe my hand on a napkin. "Where would you like me to put it?"

A smile twisted across his full lips. "I have a few places that would work." He stood and slid over to the empty seat next to me.

The beam from the projector flickered over our heads in the back row of the movie theater.

He wore shorts made out of T-shirt material. The elastic waistband was loose and hung low on his narrow hips. He pulled one leg up and reached inside to grab a rapidly growing cock. The outline of the fat mushroom head strained against the fabric as a dark, wet spot formed.

I followed his hairy leg up and saw his throbbing cock emerge. Without thinking, I reached over and smeared the butter on his thick shaft. My hand spread the grease up to the fat tip, feeling it throb and grow with each heartbeat.

His head fell back on his chair as I worked his dick, making it grow harder and longer.

My hand worked down to his hairy balls and back up to his uncut tip. As I pulled down, more precum spilled out of his foreskin and trickled between my fingers.

A low moan escaped from his mouth, as he licked his lips.

My hand worked back to his balls and squeezed.

"I know another place, a better spot," he said.

I released his dick and so wanted to lick my fingers.

He stood, slipped off his shorts, and turned his back to me.

A perfect ass glowed in the light from the projector. He pulled his fleshy cheeks open and winked at me.

I reached into my popcorn and rolled my hand around seeking more melted butter. As my greasy hand emerged, I touched a muscular cheek and massaged it. My fingers lubed his tight hole and greased along his crease.

He pushed his butt out, begging for more.

I leaned forward, guided his butt back, and ran my tongue over his tight pucker. I tasted and inhaled salty butter.

He moaned and pushed back on my mouth.

I thrust my tongue out and sought entry. The tip explored the tight hole and pushed firmly in. I felt his opening relax, and my tongue slipped in deeper.

He pushed back onto my face and rode my rough tongue.

My lips sealed around his hole and pulled hard on his opening. My cock ached in my pants, begging to be released. My nonbuttered hand opened my fly and searched for my cock. My underwear slowed the progress.

He looked over his shoulder and saw what I was doing. "Oh, yes," he hissed. "Butter it up."

The grease had a little gritty salt that tickled down my shaft. I lubed my cock and felt hot, wet precum ooze out my tip and mix with the butter. I jacked my dick and felt it grow thicker.

He gasped when he saw my eight inches approaching him. "You'll need a lot more butter."

I swirled my hand in the popcorn and collected as much as I could find. I applied more to my erection, pushed my shorts to my ankles, and moved my butt to the edge of the cushioned seat.

He backed up to me and spread his cheeks.

I lubed his hole and cheeks again. Butter glistened in the dark, as the beam of movie light swirled overhead.

He slowly lowered himself down and guided my cock to his hole.

I grabbed on to his pelvis and slid my fat tip up and down his crease, threatening to slip into the tight opening, but not entering, just teasing his ass.

More precum oozed out of me and mixed with the butter lubing my cock.

He found my tip with his opening and pressed down. He relaxed and slowly lowered himself onto me. He was tight and my mushroom head swelled as it tried to enter.

He pushed harder, and I felt it slide in, but the ridge refused to go any farther.

He inhaled deeply, and his butt relaxed.

I entered him slowly, inch by inch, until I filled his ass as he settled down on my lap.

He moaned as he landed.

"Shhh," a woman hushed us, but didn't turn around.

My buttery hand clamped around his cock, and he pushed forward and up. I jacked his dick as he rode me.

We started slow and easy, working from his tip all the way down to his balls. My fingers combed through his thick ball hair and cupped his testicles. I squeezed them and made him moan again.

He used his legs to increase our speed. My cock plunged in deeper and faster. My whole body tingled with the excitement of public sex. At any moment someone could turn around and see this hot guy riding my dick.

He thrust his cock into my hand as he bounced, adding more force and friction.

My balls started to rise as the sensation of pleasure grew.

The movie soundtrack sped up and intensified as if it had become ours. Images streaked across the screen as the scent of hot butter rose to my nose, mixed with sexy man sweat. Musky sex added to the joy.

I felt my cock jerk inside him as my hand filled with hot cream. It dripped between my fingers and down onto my hairy legs. His climax set mine off, and I exploded inside him—spurt after spurt as spasms took over my cock and drained my balls.

He continued to ride me, sending unbelievable pleasure over my body, and I couldn't take much more.

I stiffened, and he increased his speed as another wave of cum flowed out of his cock and splattered on the seat in front of us.

A huge explosion lit the theater screen and blinded me.

He stood and pulled off of me as a loud pop like a cork sounded in the back row. He bent over to find his shorts, showing his perfect ass dripping and shiny.

I wanted to lick him clean, but the credits had started to roll.

He sat down bare-butt next to me, struggled into his shorts and tried to slip them up.

I handed him a napkin before he finished.

He wiped his dick clean and adjusted himself in his shorts.

I cleaned and redressed before anyone walked past.

"That was great," he said. "I'm staying for the second film, are you?"

"Hell, yes."

"I'm going to run to the bathroom, and I'll be right back." And he disappeared.

I followed him to the lobby. Stepping up to the concession stand, I set the large popcorn tub down.

The girl at the counter picked it up and started to refill it. "Did you want butter?"

"Oh, yes," I said. "Extra butter. As much as you can give; I have a double bill today."

MR. POPULAR

Jonathan Asche

Most of the guys smiled—knowingly—when I stepped inside the club; a few said hello. The club wasn't the kind of place where everybody knew your name, but they remembered my face—and my cock and my ass. I made sure of that. One guy—midforties, short, solidly built, dressed like *The Wild One* was his favorite movie—bought me a drink. The man kept touching me, his hands sliding over my back and brushing my thigh before settling in my crotch. "You want to go in back?" he asked, eyes brimming with innuendo.

The back room was a dimly lit warehouse space, the only furniture a St. Andrew's cross in the corner and a padded horse in the center, over a drain. Only a few guys were back there when my anonymous friend and I entered: a couple making out—a hulking, bald, black guy and a slender white guy with a crew cut—and a bearded muscle bear watching, a hand kneading his hard-on through his jeans. But the room filled up once I was back there; guys following me, not wanting to miss a thing.

I liked the way Mr. Wild One's hands felt on my arms, the way he squeezed my biceps, the forceful way he pulled me against him. I felt the bulge in his crotch, pressing against mine. His eyes were expectant, and for a moment I thought (hoped) he was going to kiss me.

"Suck my cock," he hissed.

I waited a beat before dropping to my knees.

He had a big, ugly cock; it stretched my lips as I took it into my mouth. The man fucked my mouth deep until I gagged. Then he fucked my mouth harder.

Other guys closed in around us, caging me within walls of leather- and denim-covered legs. Cocks popped out, some guys standing so close I felt the sticky, blunt heads against my face, their owners ordering me to suck them. As much as they wanted me, I couldn't pull away from Mr. Wild One, not until—

A loud groan bounced off the walls. Cum filled my mouth, sharp, bitter—delicious. The man was still groaning when he pulled his cock out, batting its engorged, cum- and spit-covered crown against my face. I looked up, wanting to meet his eyes, maybe even get a smile, but he looked past me.

Hands grabbed my hair, pulling me toward other needy dicks. Long and short, thick and thin, cut and uncut—cocks in need of my mouth, men in need of *me*.

The men filled my mouth with their flesh, cum and piss.

I pulled out my throbbing cock and jacked off, shooting my load onto a black boot. A few of the guys ordered me to "clean it up." The owner of the boot, a stern-looking guy with a thick black mustache, waited for me to comply. I leaned down and started licking, keeping at it until his boot was shiny with my spit. When I was done there was a smile beneath the man's mustache.

A man in a jockstrap presented his ass to my face. He bent over and spread his round, muscular buttcheeks, exposing a hairy trench and reddish-tan pucker. Hands cupped the back of my head and pulled me forward, into that furry valley. I dug in, forcing my tongue past the throbbing sphincter. The crowd grunted encouragement: "Eat that ass!" Then I heard one guy say, "This guy's a total pig," a tone of admiration in his voice.

Admiring me.

My face was pressed into another ass—this one smooth, the hole shaved. I munched and munched, a pig at a trough. Some guys peed on the man I was rimming, aiming their streams at his ass. Piss sluiced down his asscrack, over my face and into my mouth. I sputtered and spat, but kept tonguing that hot hole. More comments were made about my being a pig, a *freak*. The men were amazed, impressed.

But they weren't satisfied.

I was lifted off the floor, confronting the faces in the crowd. There were all types—black guys, white guys, Latin guys; young and old; fit and fat; hairy and smooth. They all blurred together, but their smiles were clear.

The men stripped off my clothes, pinching my nipples until I cried out. An African American man with an imposing stare seized my balls in his hand, pulling until I begged him to stop. Some guys chuckled. The black stud smiled.

I was draped over the padded leather horse like a bag of dirty laundry. My asscheeks were pried apart; my hole attacked by probing fingers and tongues. A fat, drooling cock stifled my moans.

A thick stream of lube was squirted into my asshole, followed by the savage invasion of an anonymous dick. My muffled moans became stifled screams as the mystery cock entered me, stretching my sphincter wide, splitting me in two. It hurt, but it felt good, and when that pole was all the way inside it felt even better.

The unseen man fucked me hard, pushing my face into the crinkly pubes of the man stuffing my mouth every time he slammed into my ass. Loud, anguished cries announced orgasmic rewards. Cum flooded my mouth while the cock buried in my chute pumped out its abundant load.

Other men wanted me, and they took me. One after the other, they shoved their cocks into my ass, each one feeling different—some so huge I felt as if I were getting fucked for the very first time. While guys were taking me from behind, others lined up in front, fucking my mouth, jacking off on my face, opening their assholes to my searching tongue.

Then the noise died down and it was over.

I stood then almost collapsed. A heavyset guy with graying chest hair and nipples distended by large steel barbells helped me across the room to where my clothes lay in a heap. The crowd had thinned considerably; the guys who remained seemed to look past me, glassy eyed.

My shirt was ruined and my pants weren't much better, soaked in piss, spit and cum. I shook as I stepped into my jeans. I turned to thank the bear who had helped me, but he was gone.

And then I went home, alone.

A STOLEN QUICKIE

Christopher Stone

Shoplifting has always turned me on. The endorphin rush of fear turns my skin electric and pumps all my blood straight into my dick. I don't keep the stuff I take, but I love having some ill-gotten item shoved in my pants when I walk out of the store scot-free. It's almost as good as sex, though I'd prefer a hard man over a stolen "quickie."

I glanced over the wallets on the counter. They put them there to keep people like me away from the expensive spoils. I dropped two wallets on the ground and bent down to retrieve them. One was returned to the counter, the other nestled in my tight briefs, its thick leather making friends with my hard-on. I stayed for a moment so I didn't look conspicuous and then turned to leave. A large hand clamped itself to my shoulder and steered me from the counter into an office way in the back. He dropped me in a chair; I heard the door lock.

The man came around to face me and sat on the edge of his desk. His blue jacket had the word SECURITY stitched to the front pocket. He was built like a fullback: huge muscles and a lean waist. He had a sexy goatee that telegraphed an urgent message to my groin. "Let's have it," he said.

I claimed I didn't understand and he told me to stand up. When I stalled he lifted me out of my seat and dipped his hand down the front of my pants. His fingers searched my briefs. Rough fingers grabbed and dismissed my dick, then produced the wallet. He pulled it out, sniffed it. "Well, what do we have here?" The private cop told me to sit down, while his crotch hovered in front of my face. His thick muscle was barely concealed by the layer of cloth stretched over it. He adjusted his cock, massaging the lengthening shaft, then sat down on the edge of the desk, legs parted.

"What are we going to do about this?"

"Pretend it never happened." I opened up my own legs for him to get a nice view of my boner. I dropped my hand in my lap to outline the bribe for him. He smiled. "You kids don't have anything I want." He told me to get up and ordered me to take off my pants so he could make sure I hadn't stolen anything else. I did as I was told, lowering my jeans and briefs, my hard-on bouncing out against my T-shirt.

"That for me?" he asked with a smile. I nodded,

swallowing wetly. He asked me to turn around and place my hands against the wall. He massaged my ass, one globe at a time, then playfully ran his finger along the cleft, toyed with my hole and departed. "Nothing here. Take off your shirt." I dropped my T-shirt on the chair as he went around the desk and returned with a digital camera.

"What's that for?" I asked.

"Evidence." He knelt down in front of me and snapped a couple of shots of the scene of the crime. We reviewed the pictures of my boner on the little screen, while his free hand investigated my asshole. He put the camera down and pushed up behind me; his thick spike urgent to be free. The cop's heavy hand grabbed my cock and jerked me off quickly. I leaned back into him, parting my legs, dry-humping his crotch, and came with a violent shudder. He pulled away and wiped my spunk off his hand with a tissue.

"I'm gonna let you go this time, but if I catch you shoplifting again, I'm gonna go a lot harder on you."

He told me to get dressed and showed me the door. I'd already planned my next caper.

KILLING TIME

Shanna Germain

When it all started, it was just my cousin Rafi wearing my mom's lipstick: bright red and slathered on thick, just the way she wore it, so it made his teeth shine ultrawhite in the cigarette-butt dark. I was on my mom's bed with the whirring fan overhead that did nothing but tease the sweat on my skin, so the drops rolled around, streaks of mercury following the blades like they were magnets. I had nothing on but a rubber cock ring—something Gigi, my ex-girlfriend, got me before she was my ex-girlfriend for some little-dicked white boy, and now I wore it even when I wasn't masturbating, which wasn't often. I'd say she left me with a broken heart, but I couldn't tell beneath all the pain my dick was feeling. Finally getting to fuck and then losing it—fucking punch in the balls that was.

Rafi was sitting at my mom's dresser, picking through her smells and faces.

"That thing make your balls fall off, vato," Rafi said, eyeing me in the mirror. His street Spanish came and went, depending on who he was around and how much weed he'd smoked.

"Aw, Rafi. Didn't know you cared." I wrapped my hand around my half-hard dick, gave it a tug in his direction.

He pulled open a lipstick tube like it was a pen, yanking it until he sent the top flying across the room. I didn't know shit-all about makeup, but I'd seen my mom use it enough to know you kind of wiggled lipstick open, like a wine cork. The top clattered behind a chair in the corner that was piled up with her clothes.

"You better find that," I said. But my lips were around the cigarette that I'd emptied out and stuffed with dope, which was making it hard to care so much.

"It's cocksucker red, vato," he said, twirling the bottom so the lipstick rose up. I never noticed before how lipstick looked like a cock, long and skinny, with that little bulge at the end, from the way my mom closed her lips around it and colored both of them at once. "What's your mama do with cocksucker red lipstick? She getting down on her knees?"

"Yeah, for your mama," I said.

"My mama don't got a cock, vato."

I took another drag off the weed, let the heat burn my tongue and choke my lungs, words all coughed out hard. "She did last night."

He bounced over onto the bed, making bits of burnt paper and weed fall off the end of the doobie.

"Shit, Rafi." I brushed the blanket with the back of my hand, smearing the ashes. Fuck.

He took the smoke from me, inhaled. He wore nothing but tighty-whiteys, only colored blue, and his body hung dark and lean. Rafi wasn't really my cousin, but in a tio family like ours, everybody was your uncle, and that made everybody within five years of you into your cousin. We weren't even part of the tio family, not really—I'm white as unbuttered bread, so Rafi always said—but my mom and his mama been friends forever.

He sucked again, making the end of the doob light up orange. Then he took the smoke away and brought the lipstick to his lips, painted them red.

Rafi smacked his lips, turned on his side and grinned at me. "How I look?"

"You're supposed to use a mirror," I said. "You look like a clown."

"I'm gonna leave lipstick marks on your dick, vato," Rafi said. Like it wasn't nothing. Like we'd ever done something like that before.

"You go ahead and do that, cocksucker," I said.

Rafi leaned across me—his body was cooler than mine and my sweat sucked up to his skin, got stuck so our chests and bellies squelched and slid together—and then he stubbed the doob out on my mom's dresser.

"Fuck, Rafi! Goddamn it!"

But he slid down, skin along skin, and he put his mouth on my balls, tonguing underneath the cock ring, his greased lips sliding up the backside of my cock.

"The fuck, Rafi," I started to say, and then I was choked silent, my words all cut off by his mouth. The closed slit of his red lips opened as he pushed them over the tip of my straining cock, greasy and slow, so fucking slow I had to lift my hips off the bed, my hands digging into my mom's blanket, like I was trying to anchor some part of me to the bed. His whole mouth went up and down on me, leaving smears of red like blood, like the time I'd fucked Raquel and her period started in the middle of it.

So hot the air, and cool his mouth; the way he opened his lips, made them big and wet around me. His tongue curled along and around, soft flicks while his lips tightened and pulled.

"Faster, faster," I groaned. "Oh, fuck, faster." I couldn't say his name. Couldn't. I wanted to close my eyes and think it wasn't Rafi fucking me with his mouth, but I wanted to see too. So I just swallowed back his name and pretended that those lips, that mouth, belonged to someone else.

Rafi leaned back on his haunches, grinning at me; slicked the lipstick over his lips again, lube and saliva and grease and red. And then he sucked those lips down over me, harder and faster, until I was coming, big ropy strings that sprayed Rafi's chest and landed all over my mom's blanket.

"Oh, goddamn it, Rafi," I said later, when I saw the stains on her bed. I'd pulled the cock ring off my sore dick and wiped the lipstick off me with the darkest towel I could find.

"What?" Rafi said. He'd lit another pot cigarette and was leaving rings of dark pink around the filter. "I wasn't gonna swallow you, vato."

"Give me that." I took the cigarette out of his mouth, my hand only shaking a little. Rafi caught the inside of my wrist with his teeth, that cigarette burning dangerous between us, and us looking in each other's eyes without really seeing.

"We ain't gay, vato," Rafi said, his lipsticked mouth marking my veins. "We're just killing time."

His mouth moved up my arm and down to other places. Up. Down. Until there wasn't any lipstick anymore and there wasn't any pot anymore and there weren't any words anymore. Only minutes slowing down to the stroke of Rafi and me, marking each other, marking time.

THE SENSITIVITY OF SKIN

Shane Allison

The bedsprings squeak beneath me; the ceiling fan swirls from up above. I am clean but feel dirty tonight. I rub lotion on my arms and legs 'cause my skin dries out after showering. I can't sleep naked. I gotta put some clothes on after this. I haven't jacked off all weekend. Been too busy working, pulling a double at the drugstore. I could have met up with Collin, but all he wants is a blow job, and it's not worth the drive. He won't admit it, but he likes getting fucked. I recommend his place, but he says he doesn't want his neighbors to see me; doesn't want his wife, Sue, to catch us. We have phone sex sometimes in the afternoons when my parents aren't home, when he's out delivering drugs to people with mental illnesses.

This underwear's too tight. Too bad you can't try

them on in the store. I pull them off. There, that's better. My ass is so smooth. Hard to believe I've never been fucked. I'm an *anal virgin*. Where's that lotion? Here it is. Gonna squeeze a little here on my finger. It's cocoa butter, not my favorite, but it's good and oily. I need lotion that's oily for my dry skin. Deodorant soap makes me itch. My dick and balls are so hot right now. I smear the lotion around on the finger I'm about to veer into my asshole. The hairs on my head aren't as coarse as the hairs on my ball sac. Mark used to run his hand across my groin. It tickled, drove me crazy. We used to watch each other jack off behind cubicle desks in the library at my old high school. He wore glasses and had red hair. Mark had a cute butt, too.

I'm so happy I was born with a nice dick. There are times like these I have to pull it out and admire its size, its girth. Ron, who lives with his mother in a double-wide trailer, says I'm the perfect size. Not too big, not too small. I've used just about everything to jack off with: Vaseline, baby oil, lotion, cooking oil, butter, toothpaste. But I would advise against toothpaste. It stings. I'm thinking about getting one of those vacuum pumps they advertise in the back of porn mags. I could always make it bigger. Words can't describe how hard my dick is right about now. Wish Von was here to suck it. He gives good head. He's such a sissy. Von used to have orange hair.

Glad that I'm circumcised, though I don't have nothin' against an uncut dick as long as it's clean.

My slicked-up finger slides in so easily—unlike a man's dick, which never seems to have much luck getting up my ass. I might try a dildo. Start off slow with that, then try the real thing when I feel my butt is ready for it. Oh, man, this feels good. My knees point to the front corners of the room as I spread my legs. I wish my finger was a guy's dick. My eyes are closed. I think of James between these thighs licking my balls, rimming my asshole. I've just showered, so my ass is good and clean.

Sonny says he'll only rim me if it's clean. He gives good head. He blew me on the hood of his Cadillac in the park last weekend. Sonny really puts work into it when he sucks me. The next time I see him, I'm gonna let him eat my asshole.

My dick is so hard right now. Where did I set that lotion? I'm drying up. I'm gonna use my *fuck-you* finger this time. I'm really tight. Men don't believe me when I tell them how tight I am. Kenny, a Brit I met at a pickup bar, took me home and tried to get in me all night. "Let me in you," he kept saying. I tried to relax all my muscles, but it didn't help. I desperately wanted him to fuck me. He had a pretty dick. The shaft curved up like Von's dick, with a cotton candy-pink head. Wish I could snap my fingers, and Kenny would appear with that big, British dick in tow.

I pull my legs back behind the bedposts. That's better. Now I can see me fucking myself in the mirror I took from my roommate's bedroom. Jesus, look at my ass.

Look how easily my finger slides in and out. Where the hell are all the cute boys? My ass needs a dick in it. I'm thinking of all the men that have attempted to run their eager dicks up my ass, but with no luck. It tightens up when I'm nervous. I wanna get fucked. Who can I call? Not Marcus, he's outta town. He says his dick can bend up to his belly button. Damn! I just called Chris. He ain't home. He's a bottom anyway. I lose my hard-on when I wear rubbers. It tends to slide off in the ass of the dude I'm fucking.

Better give some attention to this dick of mine. The lotion's gotten cold. It can get much harder than this. Just need to massage the balls a bit. I caress the head of my dick with my thumb.

Oh, yeah, that feels good. I love jacking off. I think of Sammy, my neighbor, naked. I bet he's got a big dick. I know I'll never see it. His wife is such a lucky bitch.

Stay hard, dick! Stay hard! Wish Brian was here to fuck me while I beat off. Brian swears he's straight. Everybody thinks he's gay. I wish he was, so he could come over and fuck me.

I love jacking off. I do it about twice a day, sometimes three times when I'm really horny. I love it when I shoot, but I mostly ooze. I hate that. I like to explode. I shot all the way across my knee once. It feels like I'm going to come a big load. I gotta pee, but I'll wait until after I jack off. The room smells of ass and cocoa butter lotion. I wish Jeff was here to give my dick some attention. He, like Sonny, can suck a mean dick. He says he doesn't sleep with men anymore. Claims he's found Jesus, and that homosexuality is a sin. He says if I repent, I won't burn in hell. Jeff needs to have his ass here repenting on this dick of mine. I still got his name and number in my address book. He'll fall off that bible-beating bandwagon one of these days, and when he does, I'm gonna make him choke on this dick just for talking about all that God and hell stuff.

My dick is superhard right now. There's a little precum here. It tastes...salty. This is the first time I've ever tasted my own cum. Fuck, if only Oscar were here to watch me. His fingers felt so good up my asshole.

I gotta take my legs down from behind these bedposts. I can't jack off too good with my legs all up. This is the next best thing to getting my dick sucked and getting fucked.

More precum: I'm so close, thinking of Collin again going balls deep on me. I work the head. It's so sensitive. Here it comes. Gonna shoot a big load. I'm so horny; I wanna get raped by a gang of men. Feels so good. My ass muscles tense. I crumple the covers in my hand, sweating, heaving, breathing heavy.

I ooze. There's lots of cum. I wanted to shoot. It trickles over fingers. I walk across the green carpet with undies around my ankles. I clean up my mess, flush the stained tissue down the toilet.

I will wash the sheets tomorrow. I'm so sleepy. I'll call Ryan in the morning. He loves having phone sex.

MAN, THEY SAY CUTTER'S GAY

Johnny Murdoc

H He ain't gay," Mark says. "Ain't no way. Look at the man."

Truth is, I look at Cutter a lot. I watch him train, I watch him box. I watch him sit and read his book. Ain't no way Cutter's gay because that would be too much for me to take. Mark says, "Just look at him," and I do. I watch him move. I watch his feet dance on the floor. I watch his fists hover in front of his face as he works the speed ball. I watch him and I can't stop thinking about the curve of his jaw, the line of sweat that slides down from his armpit and disappears into his sleeveless shirt, the way his junk bounces when he jumps rope.

Cutter's the best thing that this gym has going for it. Cutter's the guy that all the other guys want to be. We want to move like him, we want to box like him and don't let anyone tell you any different, we all want to look like him. Cutter's fucking gold, man.

"Derrick!" I hear my name and look over to see Billy, the assistant coach, waving at me. "You and Cutter."

"Cutter's training," I say.

"Cutter's treading water," Billy says. Billy and Cutter spend a lot of time together. This morning they arrived together.

Boxing with Cutter isn't like boxing with Rico or Mark. Those guys don't hold back but they're not very good, either. Cutter holds back, I can tell he's holding back, but his blows are precise and quick and I don't comprehend how he moves. I can't focus, though. I swing at him and think about kissing him. When my fist connects, I think only of how much padding there is between my hand and his chest. How I wish it wasn't there.

I've been around guys and gyms all my life, and I have always been in love with everyone my eyes happen to graze across but not like Cutter. Cutter makes my heart want to explode, even when his fist connects with my face and my headgear doesn't stop him from almost breaking my nose. I taste the blood before I feel it. Billy calls an end to the session. I want to fight, but I can't. There are rules.

Cutter puts an arm around my shoulder and walks with me to the locker room. My nose keeps bleeding. Cutter wads up a piece of tissue paper and says, "Here, stick this up your nose. Hold your head back." I sit down on the bench and do as he says. I can hear him moving about the locker room, but I can't see what he's doing. After I sit for a couple of minutes, he steps behind me and looks down at me. He's just as beautiful upside down as he is right side up. His smile makes my dick hard. It strains against the warm hard plastic of the cup.

"How you doing?" he asks.

"I think I'm good," I say. Cutter steps around in front of me, looks at my nose.

"I think you'll survive," he says.

"I think so, too."

Cutter slaps me on the chest. "You're a tough guy. Good boxer. Sloppy, but you'll get there." As his hand pulls away it grazes my nipple and I nearly come right then. "Come on," he says. "Hit the showers. Get some of this blood off of you before you go home and your mom shows up to kick my ass."

Cutter pulls his shirt up and over his head and tosses it onto the bench across from me and sits down, pulling off his shoes. I catch myself staring at him, and I start to take my own shoes off. Cutter stands and reaches into his shorts and pulls out his cup. He pulls his shorts and jockstrap down in one swift moment and then I'm sitting only a few feet away from his exposed dick and I don't know what to do with myself. I wish I could smell him. My nose throbs. All I know is that my dick sure as shit won't go down now and there's no way I can strip off in front of him.

Cutter smiles at me and then heads to the showers. As soon as he's behind me I reach into my shorts and pull out my cup. My hard dick snaps up. I wrap a hand around it and squeeze, and I will it to go down but squeezing has the opposite effect. A small bead of precum forms at the tip.

"You coming, or what?" I hear Cutter yell over the sound of the water. I undress and decide to face the music. I can't just leave. No way Cutter's not going to see my stiffy, but I do my best to cover it up as I join him in the showers, first with my towel and then with my hands. I quickly turn my back to him. I fight the urge to watch him. Cutter is everything I have always wanted and he's showering four fucking feet away from me. I cover my face in soap and work to wash the dried blood off of my face.

"How's your nose?" Cutter asks, and he's standing right next to me. He puts a hand on my shoulder. "Here, let me take a look at it." He turns me so that he can see me face-to-face but he quickly glances down to look at my dick and sees it standing hard and proud. I do not feel proud. Cutter laughs. "I don't know about your nose," he says, "but your dick's definitely fine."

Is it just a joke or a come-on? Is it true, what the guys say about Cutter?

"I remember when every fight used to give me a stiffy, too," he says. "I spent so much time in this locker room trying to hide my erections from dudes, it wasn't even funny."

"So what'd you do?"

"Took care of it," he says, and he makes a jerk-off motion in the air between us.

"You never worried about getting caught?"

"Shit, ain't that half the fun?" Cutter smirks and my dick twitches between us. I want him to reach out and take ahold of me, to stroke me, to kiss me. I look down at his dick. It is definitely thickening. My knees are shaking. If only...

"You know, I been meaning to clean out my locker. I'll see what I can do about making sure nobody else comes in here." Cutter steps away and cuts the flow from his shower. He grabs his towel and disappears. For a moment it's just me and the sound of my shower. My thumping heart. My unsteady knees. My hard dick.

I listen to the sound of Cutter's bare feet on the concrete and I match my strokes to the rhythm. I think about his smell, his smile, his cock. I think about him standing here jerking off like I am, and I come.

DINER DICK

Jay Starre

On his way to El Paso, the truck driver struggled to keep awake. It was three a.m. when he spotted the diner on the lonely stretch of highway. Inside, the place was deserted except for a single sleepy waiter who performed double duty as cook.

One look at the hazel-eyed Latino was enough. Turning around, he switched the open sign to read CLOSED. He turned back to face the auburn-haired server.

"I'm gonna fuck your tight little ass. Right now."

Pretty mouth agape, Ricky stared speechlessly at the blue-eyed trucker. A T-shirt clung to broad shoulders and revealed muscular arms. He hadn't shaved in a few days, emphasizing a strong nose and chin. His baseball cap sat backward over curly blond hair. Rough, yeah, but he was hardly older than Ricky himself.

Luke smirked as he strode forward and launched himself at the mesmerized waiter. Slim and short, he was no match for the trucker's brute charisma. Before he knew it, he was spun around and bent over his own counter.

Big hands groped tight butt and boots kicked slender thighs wide. "Sweet," Luke commented, as he wasted no time in getting down to business. Pressing one hand into Ricky's back, he held him down as he crouched to inspect his ass. Tight jeans strained to contain firm globes.

He reached around to unsnap the waiter's fly and discovered a boner tenting his underwear. Laughing out loud, he hooked his fingers in the waistband of jeans and underwear. Yanking down, he exposed a honey-brown ass.

He spread the perky cheeks. In the center, a puckered opening twitched. He crammed his face into the fleshy crevice.

When moist lips and snaking tongue began running up and down his crack, Ricky finally managed to blurt something out. "Eat my ass, dude! Eat it like it's the best fuckin' meal you ever had!"

Grinning, Luke took his time to slobber all over that satin-smooth crack. Kneeling on the dirty floor, he lapped at the dangling ball sac before settling on the pulsating hole. Tight as hell, it took a few minutes for the slot to yield to his sucking lips. He spread it with his fingers and tasted the savory hole as he worked it with his tongue.

Ricky squirmed. Luke's wet lips were smooth, while his stubbled cheeks were rough. The contrasting sensations drove him crazy. He knocked ketchup aside as he reached down to peel off his pants and underwear. Kicking them aside, he raised one knee up to place it on a counter stool. His ass was wide open and that scratchy, sucking face was right in there eating him out. Luke's busy lips smacked. He loved opening a tight hole! The little slot had transformed into a vibrating maw by now—it was time to fuck.

He pulled away and surveyed the firm can. Hairless, even the dangling nut sac was smooth. The slot oozed spittle. He stood up and unbuttoned his fly, direct blue eyes on that juicy hole as he shoved down his jeans and stepped out of them. Ricky sprawled over the counter and continued moaning, his ass rising and falling. Eager!

Huge and solid under his stroking hand, Luke's dick bounced in front of him. The broad head would tear Ricky in two if he wasn't careful. He spotted a butter dish on the greasy counter and reached out to scoop up a handful.

The blond poked his fingers into the wriggling waiter's crack. He massaged the cleft with his greased fingers briefly before he abruptly crammed two fingers up the puckered hole. The hot flesh clung as he buried them past the second knuckle. He reached around to rub butter along Ricky's rock-hard dick, then pumped it as he corkscrewed his fingers up Ricky's ass until he found the prostate nub. He jabbed and Ricky squealed.

"Oh, fuck! So good!"

He gurgled, limbs quivering, mouth slobbering on the countertop, those fingers rooting up into his asshole. His hole hungered for more!

Luke laughed out loud. In T-shirt, boots and baseball cap, he rubbed his pink shank over Ricky's butt. The head left a trail of precum along the brown cheeks. It was time! He thrust into the crack, taking his fingers from the convulsing hole and replacing them with bulbous cock head.

He shoved. Ricky moaned. He shoved again, the head sinking beyond puckered lips and burying itself in asshole. Ricky pulled his thigh up against his chest and his tender hole opened as several fat inches of cock slithered inside.

Surrounded by clamping sphincter, Luke's dick was on fire. And Ricky thought he'd swallowed a baseball bat. Sweat dripped from their foreheads, down their armpits, into their crotches and butts.

Luke thrust deeper, banging Ricky's prostate. Luke's hands pumped his dick. He wriggled all over the countertop, but not to escape. He wanted more!

"Open up that tight little ass, punk," Luke hissed. The clamping hole squeezed his cock mercilessly. He'd never fucked such a tight hole.

"Just shove it up there!" Ricky challenged.

Taking him at his word, Luke fed him inch after

inch of stiff meat. He jabbed it in, pulled out, then jabbed deeper, each time impaling Ricky with more. Even though the waiter caterwauled like a gored pig, it seemed to work. The butter eased the way, dripping down Ricky's crack and onto his ball sac.

A final savage thrust buried Luke's pole to the balls.

Slot pulsed around his dick. His blond-furred nuts rubbed against Ricky's smooth buns. Stiff rod jerked under his stroking fingers. "You little fucker, now you're gonna get it," he promised.

Ricky didn't care that his hole strained to accept the monster cock buried up it. "I want it. Fuck me!"

Luke pulled out halfway. Anal walls clung to his shaft. He stared down at the juncture of dick and hole. The swollen lips stretched around his pink pole; butter glistened on the satin-brown flesh. Slowly, he pulled his dick out until only the head remained inside. The convulsing butt-lips twitched around his cock head.

He drove forward.

Ricky shrieked as fat shank rammed home. It was delirious pleasure. Luke yanked on Ricky's stiff dick as he pulled out and slammed back inside.

Ricky became a slobbering, moaning mess as Luke plowed him. He raised his butt to meet the drilling rod and bit his lip in a vain attempt to hold back near-constant squeals. Gigantic dick reamed Ricky's hole for a solid twenty minutes.

Finally, that dick pulled out and erupted. A stream of cum coated Ricky's heaving asscheek.

After that, Luke ordered the well-fucked waiter to serve him coffee and a hot meal. Dressed in only T-shirt, boots and backward baseball cap, he watched Ricky hard at work, wearing only his apron with Luke's dried cum smearing a perky buttcheek.

When it came time for desert, he ordered the waiter to bend over his table. He fingered his buttered butthole while Ricky jerked himself to a squirming orgasm.

Satisfied by the exemplary service, Luke promised himself to make this stop a regular thing.

FRIDAY NIGHT IN ROOM 69

Jeff Funk

The first man to come into my room wasn't exactly my type, but I let him play with my dick and everything was fine—until he threw a hissy fit because I refused a blow job.

His voice was full of emotion. "I did not pay all this money to come here and *only* jack off." He acted as if I had insulted his honor.

I pulled my towel up from the foot of the bed and covered my cock. "I understand," is all I said. I gave him a hard look. The message was clear: *You ain't sucking it, so get out*. What could I say? If he had sweet-talked me a little, I might've given him what he wanted, but his attitude made me go soft.

He mumbled as he wrapped a towel around his thick waist. Then he shot out of my room and slammed the door.

I calmly opened the door back.

Next.

The hallway was dark. It was a blackout night at the bathhouse. In fact, all of the lights were off on the third floor, even in the bathroom. There was a thick curtain draped over the doorway to the orgy lounge. At the end of the longest hall, before the turn to the inner corridors, was my room: room 69.

The towel boy had smiled when he pulled that key off the board, warning me that it was a lucky room. *Let's hope my luck changes*, I thought.

Now I watched as men walked past my door, observing me stroking my dick. They were faceless in the grainy twilight. I could mostly make out their shoulders, and I saw white towels floating by. Often, their bodies were still wet from showering. There were fully dressed men skulking around the building, too.

Across the hall, a group of college boys in gym shorts gathered in the sling room. The ringleader and his buddies joked and made smutty suggestions to someone named Jason. Their voices were filled with heathen camaraderie. Then two more dark Adonises joined the scene.

I figured some bottom was in for a helluva pounding. The pretty boys were lining up to get that ass.

I was debating if I shouldn't look into getting a turn, when a stranger in jeans slowed down upon spotting me. He approached with tentative strides, gauging whether I was interested. I offered my hand toward his tall, alluring silhouette as if I were reaching for him.

He leaned against the left side of the doorjamb and gazed at me with intense eyes, which were illuminated by the porn playing dimly on the television.

He was a sexy bad-boy type.

He wore a leather bomber. He was scruffy with dark whiskers. His hair looked greasy by nature, and even wetter with the gel he had worked into it and slicked back with a comb.

I got a charge out of being naked while he was still in his street clothes. It reminded me of the funny feeling I've always gotten when I'm barefoot and comfortable, then company comes over, and they're wearing shoes. I fiddled with the engorged head of my dick, rubbing my fingertips over my piss slit. Then I glided my hand over my shaved balls and touched my hole for him.

"Nice," he said.

Just then, a big-chested jock rushed out of the sling room and scared my stranger away. I decided that I would be ready for him when he came back.

I reached into my little black satchel—my "fuck bag"—and pulled out a blindfold.

I sat up in bed and turned off the television, making my room even darker than the hallway. After taking a sip of water, I put the blindfold on and got back into position. I lay with my hands clasped behind my head, and I spread my legs.

Disco music from a satellite radio station played throughout the building. There was moderate foot traffic in the hallway, bare footsteps and flip-flops popping.

Then I sensed someone standing in the doorway to my room. The floor creaked, causing my body to break out with goose bumps. I took a deep breath, hoping to stop my slight trembling, and smelled cologne and poppers. The door was eased shut, and the television crackled back to life. *He wants to see me*, I thought. I heard a baritone growl of approval: "Woof."

Suddenly, there was a mouth on my left nipple, the sensitive one.

"Oh, Jesus," I moaned while the man licked his way around my torso. His hand roved downward, where he teased my cock and balls. Several times, I felt something cold on my skin, which had me puzzled until I realized that it must be his room key dangling from his wrist.

I was curious. I had to see if this was my stranger in jeans or someone else. I brought a couple of curled fingers to my face and pulled the cover from my eyes.

"Hey," said a mustached butch daddy. He was naked with a boner emboldened by a silver cock ring.

I let out a growl of my own.

He stared at my dick, studying it like he needed a moment to make a decision. Then he bent down and gulped it into his mouth. He sucked it *good*. His clean-shaven cheeks caved in with intense suction as he suckled and slurped. He probed my larger than average pisshole with his tongue, giving me the only type of tickle that makes me squirm.

"Could you, like, *slap* my balls?" I asked.

"Huh?"

"Just tap 'em a little."

"Like this?"

"Mmm, that feels good," I said. "You can do it harder." He hesitated then smacked them in a steady rhythm and continued to suck me. "Oh," I hissed with a satisfied exhale. I was about to come from him roughin' up my boys like that.

He then hiked his leg, straddled himself over me on the bed and backed up until his musky butt and nuts were in my face.

I gave each of his balls a good slobbering while he went back to servicing me. He now sucked from a better angle; it could go deeper into his throat. I gasped from the sensation then tongued his taint. I eased his body sideways so I could crane my neck to get at his pecker.

Daddy groaned loudly from what my mouth was doing to him. He reached down, jerked himself and nutted a *huge* fuckin' load all over me. I stroked my spit-slicked meat and added my cum to the mess.

He climbed off the bed and gave himself a casual wipe down with his towel. He patted my balls and said, "Stay out of trouble."

"Thanks, man," I whispered and closed my eyes.

When he left, the door clicked shut. Locked.

I rolled over in bed and felt streams of cum slide from my hairy belly. I snuggled into my pillow and drifted to sleep, listening to the masochist in room 73 getting his ass spanked.

THOSE WHO LISTEN

Jamie Freeman

The apartment is dark and quiet. I click the light switch and hear the refrigerator humming, and then the plinking sound of the fluorescent light flickering slowly to life above my head. There's a lag between the sound of my feet hitting the hardwood floor and the jingle of Woody's tags as he thumps down the stairs. I sort through the mail on the table while Woody rears up, dancing and panting, silently recounting his long day alone in the apartment. I drop into a squat, my knees cracking, and scratch the middle of his round dachshund head, his floppy ears slapping against my hand. He whimpers with pleasure.

I clip Woody's leash to his collar and we pop down to the sidewalk. My old metal Zippo clinks and rasps as I light my cigarette. I take a deep drag, the traffic sounds drowning the sweet crackling of that first puff. Woody waters the steps, sniffs around the wrought iron fence and then tugs at his leash when he's ready to go back upstairs. I take a last drag on my cigarette and crush it against the bricks.

The ding and rusty screech of the elevator doors startle me back to myself. I follow Woody into the elevator, pressing ten and making soothing sounds at the old dog.

Back in the apartment Woody goes nuts at the sound of the ceramic lid banging carelessly against the cookie jar. I hand him a dog biscuit, which he crunches and gulps down, snuffling and padding across the kitchen tile toward the hallway. I glance at the clock: 2:30 a.m. My roommate Billy's probably out somewhere trolling the bars for a late-night fuck.

I'm exhausted from a double shift at my job as an operator for an answering service that specializes in medical practices. I've spent the last sixteen hours listening to callers recounting descriptions of rashes and bruises, aches and pains, lungs that barely fill, and hearts that beat too slowly, each caller trusting a stranger in a midtown cubicle with his innermost secrets. *I may be impotent. I think I have crabs. My wife is cheating. My boyfriend just left me. I think I have cancer.* I listen and imagine their faces, lips moving close to the receiver, or their hands dialing and redialing my number; looking for the doctor; expecting a call back; aching to tell their lonely stories to someone who will listen. And I am that person: the absent husband, the father who never listened, the boyfriend who never should have left. Each night, I stumble home exhausted, climbing the stairs to my loft bedroom, flipping on the television to chase away the echo of the callers' sad laments.

Tonight as I strip off my clothes, Jack and Chrissy are pretending not to dig each other on an ancient episode of "Three's Company." I drift a little, my mind already rambling into the silent river of thoughts that'll lead me to sleep. I struggle out of my socks and underwear and crash naked into the silent warmth of my down comforter, Woody curling protectively beside me.

A sound awakens me from a dead sleep; I sit up and listen intently. I feel around for Woody and find him curled up near the head of the bed, old and asthmatic, no longer interested in keeping watch in the darkness.

I hear the sound again—a whisper, a low laugh.

It must be Billy with this evening's delight.

I grab the remote and mute Jack Tripper. Silence. Then the squeaks of my ancient sofa downstairs, the harsh sounds imbedded in the softer sounds of lips and whispers and stretching cloth.

A stifled laugh fills the air for a moment and Woody looks up, puzzled, sniffing the air and then curling himself back into a ball of wheezing sleep.

The sounds have settled into a pattern of scraping (shoes against the arm of the sofa) and sighing, the wet sounds of lips and tongues and then, after a few moments, the sound of the first shoe hitting the floor.

The sound is followed by three more soft thuds, then the crisp sound of cotton and skin, socks being pulled over bare feet. A soft slurping brings my cock to instant attention. I know Billy's foot fetish is being indulged less than ten yards from where I'm lying naked on my bed. Billy's laughter is high and light, underscored by a deeper rumbling laugh that's cut off in midlaugh, likely stifled by Billy's round heel or blunt, perfect toes.

I grab a bottle of lube and squirt out cool liquid onto my hand, sliding it along the hot length of my throbbing erection. I think for a moment that the cold has made me gasp, but the sound came from the sofa below. I stroke myself slowly, pushing hard against my pubic bone and then sliding back up along the full length of my cock.

Downstairs there's a frenzy of movement: the clattering of belts, the thump of underwear or a T-shirt hitting a lampshade, and then words so distinct they surprise me: "Can I fuck you?" The voice is deep and hurried. Not Billy's voice.

And then, "Yes, fuck me now."

My hand's speeding up; my breath's becoming shallow. My cheeks are radiating heat in waves, my stomach muscles tightening.

"Oh, yeah!" Is it Billy or me?

"Oh, yeah, yeah, yeah…" This litany is syncopated by the sharp slapping of the stranger's pelvis against Billy's tight little ass. Voices mingle in the space below my loft, chanting out the chorus of their mutual pleasure. My fingers begin to fly up and down my cock, tickling the head on the upstroke and then drumming down hard against the base. I reach down and yank on my balls, stretching out my own pleasure as Billy's voice grows louder.

"Oh, yeah, harder, baby."

I listen obediently, my hand pounding harder, my breath growing ragged. The sounds of their bodies in motion fill my ears. The sofa groans under their weight, their bodies slamming together wetly. I feel a tingling behind my balls.

I close my eyes and concentrate on the voices, the groans, the slapping sounds, and I see Billy on his knees, facing away from me, growl rising to a scream as I fuck him from behind, pounding into him and letting the unbridled animal rise through my throat. I pound my cock until I hear Billy's voice cry out like a clarion, a partially articulated cry that drops to a whispered, "Oh, fuck, I'm coming," and I feel the hot come splatter across my stomach, long stringy spurts that fly in a crescendo of sensation. I stroke and stroke until the last droplet of cum lands in the valleys between my abs, and then I lean back, listening to the sounds of Billy and his trick's heavy breathing and sighs; "Oh, babys" punctuating the darkness as the object of my unrelenting affection lies exhausted under the heaving body of a stranger on my old green sofa.

My shoulders collapse and I drift restlessly into disturbed sleep, dreaming of symptoms and sex and sofas and the cool loneliness of those who listen.

FUCKING
HOT DADDY

Jay Rogers

S unlight filtered through the window and reached my eyes. I breathed in deeply and stretched my body, shifting position on the bed. The soreness and slackness of my asshole reminded me of last night's activities. I smiled and stretched again. Smitty had fucked me for over an hour before pulling his cock out of my ass and driving it deep into my throat, just as he unloaded four waves of spunk. I had come without touching myself, shooting my own load all over his back. The smell of our sex was still on the sheets. If that was Friday night fun, I wondered what sort of plans he had for Saturday. When you work opposite shifts and are renovating a house, you have to make the most of your time together.

The day's original agenda included working on our list of renovation projects, including hanging some bead ply. Fixing up a hundred-year-old house that had been a triplex for part of its life took energy and some imagination. The tiny kitchenettes on the second floor were being transformed into much-needed walk-in closets, and bead ply on the ceiling and walls would give them a vintage look. In fact, it sounded as though Smitty was down in the basement, now, getting ready to cut some of the panels. I propped myself up on one elbow to listen. The whine of a circular saw drifted its way upstairs. He was definitely at work.

Throwing the covers back and sliding out of bed, I pulled on a pair of gym shorts and stepped into flip-flops. Making my way down to the basement, I found every work light blazing and Smitty in jeans, gloves and safety glasses. A light sprinkling of sawdust covered his muscular, furry chest. He set down the saw and removed the glasses.

"Hey, sleeping beauty. 'Bout time you got your ass down here," he growled. "But you're not dressed for work."

"Wasn't sure what you had in mind," I replied, cocking my head. I shifted my eyes from my lover's chiseled features to the sheet of wood that lay across the sawhorses in the cramped space. "Help you with that?"

Smitty rubbed his chin with the back of a gloved hand. "You bet. Lay it up against the wall, here."

We lifted the wood panel and leaned it against the brick wall of the old foundation. "What now?" I asked.

"Bend over that sawhorse."

I blinked at the unexpected command.

Smitty gestured at the slender wooden support beside me. "Bend over that sawhorse, baby. Right now. Daddy's gonna nail your ass."

"But it won't be…" I began.

"No butts involved but your own sweet ass, baby," Smitty explained, yanking my shorts down to my ankles. "Now, bend over and hold on." He took hold of my shoulders, turned my body and pushed me down till I was draped over the sawhorse. The smooth wood was hard against my gut, and it took more effort than usual to breathe. I didn't have much time to think about it before I heard the clatter of boards behind me and the comment, "This oughta do the trick." Then, "You like spanking, don't you, boy?"

He knew that I did. The sting of Smitty's big hand on my backside never failed to turn me on. Even now, just the suggestion of a spanking made my cock bob beneath me as blood rushed to fill its length. I could feel a drop of precum oozing from the tip.

"I can see you like it a lot," Smitty said, having noticed. "Well, you bring that sweet ass down to the workroom and I'm gonna work it over for you. Might even give that boy toy some attention, too." I felt his gloved hand grab my cock and squeeze. I groaned. "First, I want that ass."

There was another clatter of wood, and I gripped the legs of the sawhorse tighter just as the stinging blow hit my right asscheek. "Uh!" The sting had been delivered by the flat side of a thin board. I'd never felt anything like it. It was followed by another smack on the left cheek, then each side of my butt received another strike of the wood. Every slap sent a jolt of desire right through me. My ass felt raw and sensitive to everything. I could feel the precum dripping freely, now. "Aw, fuck," I whimpered.

"That's next, baby," came Smitty's rumbling voice. A thumb was probing gently at my pucker, circling around it, teasing. "You want my cock?"

"Shit, yeah," I gasped. I didn't care that my gut was sore from the sawhorse, my breath was coming hard, or even that my ass still felt as though it had been skinned. My whole body was alive to all the sensory input it was getting. I wanted to feel more. "I want your cock in deep."

I heard no reply except for the bark of Smitty's zipper. The blunt end of his hard tool made contact with my well-used hole, and then a bomb went off in my brain when he drove it into me in one brutal thrust that was only the first of many. "Ahh," I screamed as he drove his cock into me over and over again, shredding my ass ring. I didn't know how much more I could take, but I didn't want him to stop, either. It was a good kind of hurt. "Fuck me, Daddy! Don't stop!"

The sawhorse skidded on the concrete from the force of Smitty's driving hips. His balls were swinging hard. Every time he drove his dick home, some air was pushed out of my gut in a grunting moan, and my prostate fired a hot jolt of current through my cock. We were in full rut. The noises and the smell of sex were driving us crazier every second.

"Daddy's gonna come. Oh, god, yeah…yeah…" The warm spunk filled me as Smitty's thrusts slowed and finally came to a stop. With a sudden pop, he pulled out of me, leaving a rope of cum hanging from my hole. I couldn't have moved if I'd wanted to, but Smitty's hand on my back made it clear that I wasn't going anywhere. "Shit, you're a good boy. Lemme take care of you."

Leather wrapped around my throbbing dick again, but this time Smitty's gloved hand stayed put, stroking up and down, yanking hard on the downstroke. I was being milked, and the cream wasn't far behind. My balls crawled up tight and sent liquid pleasure shooting out of me. I couldn't breathe or yell or anything. I could only feel the intensity of release and watch as the white ropes landed in the sawdust, beneath me. The glove let go of my cock and smacked my ass. "Grab a panel and follow me back upstairs, boy. I'm not done with you yet."

I was raw and dripping cum all over. Unfolding my stiff body to stand up, I found that my cock was still stiff as well. It's hard work being Smitty's boy, but he's one fucking hot daddy.

THE XXXMAS GIFT

Michael Bracken

For three consecutive years my roommate hung an extralarge jockstrap from the mantle on Christmas Eve. "Everyone else hangs stockings," Kevin said each time he did it, "but someday Santa's going to fill this for me."

The fourth year I decided to do something about it.

Kevin had been flirting with Delray, one of the weekend bartenders at the Glory Hole, and I was certain the attraction was mutual based on comments I'd heard Delray make when Kevin was out of earshot. When I heard Delray wouldn't be making his annual trip home for the holidays, I approached him with my idea.

Arranging things was more difficult than I anticipated—especially getting Delray into the house in the wee hours of Christmas morning without waking

Kevin—but it was worth the effort, and I cherish my photo of the surprised look on Kevin's face when he stumbled into the living room that morning and found Delray posed next to the fireplace wearing nothing but a Santa hat and the jockstrap Kevin had hung from the mantle the night before.

I couldn't help myself, but the view of Delray's near-naked body had the candy cane in my pocket pointing due north. Delray spent his time away from the bar pumping iron and it showed in his broad shoulders, thick arms, six-pack abs, tight ass and tree-stump thighs. He'd exfoliated the previous day and the twinkling Christmas tree lights reflected off his glistening, lightly oiled bronze skin.

And I wasn't the only one who appreciated the view. Kevin slept in the nude and, because he hadn't tied the sash of his robe tight enough when he'd come out of his room, his red-nosed reindeer was peeking through the gap.

"Don't just stand there with your mouth open," I told my roommate. "Unwrap your gift."

Kevin crossed the room and stopped in front of Delray. He placed one hand on the bartender's thick chest and then let it trail down Delray's abdomen and under the wide elastic waistband of the jockstrap. His eyes widened in surprise when he discovered the long, thick phallus constrained by the pouch.

"I must have been a very good boy," he said huskily.

"I've been waiting all year for this," Delray said. He

grabbed Kevin's head between his two big hands and planted his lips on the lucky man's. My roommate practically melted against his Christmas gift as the kiss grew longer and deeper.

When the kiss ended, Kevin dropped to his knees, drawing the jockstrap down to reveal Delray's turgid erection. He cupped Delray's balls as if judging their weight as he drew the bartender's cock head between his lips.

By then I had settled onto the couch to watch, and as the only one of us fully dressed, I felt the need to loosen my belt and unzip my fly to release the pressure on my own cock.

Kevin took the first inch of Delray's cock into his mouth and then drew back. He took a little more in the next time and a little more the time after that, as his head bobbed forward and back.

Apparently he was moving too slow for Delray. The bartender grabbed the back of Kevin's head and thrust his cock deep into Kevin's mouth. After Kevin accepted it all, Delray drew back until only his swollen cock head remained between my roommate's lips. Then he thrust forward again.

He thrust harder and faster, face-fucking my roommate, his heavy balls bouncing off of Kevin's chin with each thrust.

I couldn't help myself. I reached into my pants and wrapped my fist around my cock shaft. As I watched the two men going at it in front of the fireplace, illuminated by the glowing embers and the twinkling of Christmas tree lights, I stroked up and down, matching my pace to Delray's, going harder and faster as Delray pumped harder and faster.

Delray came before I did, holding Kevin's head still as he unloaded against the back of his throat. My roommate couldn't swallow fast enough. Delray's cum seeped from the corner of Kevin's mouth and dripped to the hardwood floor.

I came then, firing a thick wad of warm spunk all over my fist and the inside of my boxers. As Delray withdrew his still spasming cock from Kevin's mouth, I excused myself and slipped into the bathroom to clean up.

By the time I returned to the living room, Delray had lost the Santa hat and Kevin had shed his robe. The big man had my roommate bent over the back of the couch and was slamming his thick cock into Kevin's ass.

I hadn't bothered to replace my clothes after cleaning myself up, and I was just as naked as the other two men. I stepped up behind Delray and slipped one hand between his thighs and Kevin's to wrap my fist around my roommate's swollen cock, and I jacked him off as Delray continued to pump into his ass.

Kevin came first, spewing cum over the back of the couch. Then Delray came with one last powerful thrust, unloading himself into Kevin.

When Delray's cock finally slipped from my roommate's ass and he turned to face me, he saw that my cock was once again hard. He grabbed my cock and said, "I didn't realize you came as part of a package deal."

"That wasn't the original plan," I told him. "But now that we're all in the Christmas spirit—"

His mouth covered mine and I never finished my sentence.

I'm not certain how many more times and in how many more combinations the three of us fucked that Christmas morning, but I know Kevin and I were exhausted by the time Delray left.

I made hot chocolate for the two of us and served it with a peppermint stick in each cup. Wearing only our robes, Kevin and I relaxed on the couch, sipping our drinks and staring at the unwrapped gifts still piled under the tree.

My roommate finally broke the silence.

"Next year," Kevin said, "I'll put up two jockstraps, so I don't have to share my Christmas gift."

THE COASTER

Stephen Osborne

couldn't possibly get on that thing," Mike told me as he craned his neck. "You know I've got a fear of heights."

It was true. Ladders, even step stools, had an adverse effect on my Mikey. He once refused to get into an elevator at a hotel we were staying at because it had a glass front, so all weekend we had to climb the stairs to get to our room, six floors up.

"I'll be there with you," I assured him. "You'll be safe with me."

Mike watched as a train of cars plummeted down a steep incline above us, its occupants screaming with joy and terror. "Fuck that," he said. "I'll be safe here on the ground." He turned and gave me an apologetic look. "Shawn, I love that you brought me here for my birthday. And I'll treasure this for the rest of my life," he said, hugging the stuffed Scooby-Do I'd won for him at the ring-toss booth, "but I'd piss myself if I got on that thing."

"You love horror movies," I reminded him. "You love being scared."

"This," he said, gazing up again at the structure towering over us, "is different."

"Trust me. You won't be scared. I'll make sure of it."

He laughed nervously. "How? Are you going to knock me out before the thing starts up the first climb?"

I pulled at his hand, almost yanking him into the long line that snaked around the turnstiles. "Trust me!" I yelled. An older couple glared at us as we went by. You could almost hear their thoughts. *Fags. Holding hands in public. What is the world coming to?*

Fuck 'em. We were young and in love, celebrating my Mikey's twentieth birthday. I'd hold his hand if I fucking wanted to. I smiled and flipped the couple off. They quickly moved away, heading toward the bumper cars like they suddenly remembered they had somewhere else to be.

Mike and I got into line and prepared for the long wait. Mike was nearly bouncing with dread and excitement, looking like he was going to bolt at any moment. "You're sure I can do this?" he asked, needing reassurance.

"I'll be right there with you," I told him. "I'll even hold your hand during the ride."

He looked up into my eyes. Reading his face I saw love, anticipation and terror vying for dominance. His eyes were watering, just a little. "I trust you," he told me.

I knew he did.

We drew closer to the front of the line. I led the way, making sure we got into the right spot for the rear of the train. As soon as he realized this, Mikey's eyes went wide with terror.

"Isn't the back of the train supposed to be the worst? Doesn't it feel more like you're lifting off the tracks or something?"

I shook my head. "We want to be in the very last car. The very rear seats."

"Why?" Mike asked. "So no one sees me piss my pants?"

It was finally our turn. We climbed in. I made sure Mike got in first so that he'd be on my left. He flashed me a puzzled glance over this but said nothing. We lowered the bar and the attendant, a pimply faced blond kid, checked to make sure we were secure. The train jerked forward and Mikey let out a tiny yelp.

"I don't think I can do this," he muttered as the train pulled away. He was clutching my hand tightly.

"You can," I told him. I made him release my hand. Then I reached over to his crotch and began to rub. In the year that we'd been together I'd learned just how to manipulate Mike's dick for the desired effect. Before we even started up the first climb he was hard. He was still staring straight ahead, fear oozing out of every pore, but he was stiff as a board as I unzipped his fly. Mikey always went commando so I didn't have to worry about underwear. The train began click-clacking up the hill as I began to stoke his dick. Mikey sighed.

"Told you I'd take your mind off of it," I said, jacking him harder.

We were halfway up the incline and he was panting harder and harder, bucking his hips against the safety bar. For a moment I thought his noise would make the teenagers in the seats in front of us turn around but they didn't.

I knew we only had a few more seconds before we hit the top and began the long fall so I jacked him harder. To clinch the deal I leaned over and nibbled on his neck. Mikey has the most sensitive neck I've ever encountered. With a groan he spilled his juice all over my hand.

Then he screamed as the car jerked into its descent.

I held my hand up and allowed the rush of wind to dry off some of the semen. Mikey was still unzipped, but he wasn't worried about that. He had a death grip on my knee with his right hand and was yelling to wake the dead.

The ride finally ended. Before the train pulled to a stop Mikey managed to zip himself back up and get his breath back, sort of. His voice was an octave higher as he said, "I can't believe that I rode a roller coaster."

There was still some cum on my hand as we came to a stop. I wiped it on the seat. Fuck 'em. I helped a shaking Mikey get out of the car and onto the platform. "It wasn't so bad, was it?"

He looked at me and laughed. "You're a sneaky bastard, Shawn. You know that, don't you?"

I put my arm around him and we followed the crowd out the exit.

You know how these roller coasters often take a picture of you while you're on the ride so that you can buy a print as a memento of your experience? Mikey and I have one, taken at the apex of the first climb. In front of us, the teenagers are open-mouthed and screaming. So am I, for that matter. Mikey, though, has a look of serenity on his face; serenity and love. The camera caught him just as he'd come.

DRAPE IT,
THEN RAPE IT

Robert Glück

Someone gave me a photo of my ex-boyfriend's asshole. I was shocked since I was still obsessed with him. It was a little square image with a peel-off back that his affinity group made to publicize safe sex—you write things like *Slap it, then wrap it* on the photo and stick it up on walls and mirrors in public restrooms. My ex is kneeling on a couch that looks like his couch, the way it catches the light—he pushes his ass out, his lower back arches, the muscles lift on either side of his spine, and I imagined his group standing around, posing my ex under the bright lights, everyone on the planet touching his body. My ex is pulling the halves of his butt apart. Naturally they chose him—every being in the entire cosmos desires him, and I figured my ex had no problem exposing himself because he's an exhibitionist and a slut. I hid the photo from myself—it gave me such a pang of grief to see him, and when I did take the image out I felt an inside out vertigo, my knees and elbows weakened by fear, and I could not believe that a need as strong as mine would not be satisfied. How could he open his ass to everyone but not to me? I wanted to be inside that circular grip at all times. We had continuously pushed ourselves inside each other, cocking our heads as though trying notes till we located the exact nerve and strummed it. I recognized the view, the thick ribbon of skin that connects his scrotum to his perineum, the head of his cock a nodding flower drooping past his balls. I recognized his square hands, the moons of his fingernails, the strong fingers that pull his butt apart, the ample cheeks I outlined in the air with my hands— his hole just the merest blur of shadow and highlight. I continuously tried to find and separate the silky pucker from the loose pattern of benday dots that made the image. I needed to arrive at some kind of silkiness.

So it came as quite a surprise to learn that it wasn't a photo of my ex, just some porn shot they found in a magazine. As soon as I heard his voice on the phone I realized my ex would never spread his cheeks for his affinity group. He told me they searched a long time to find the "ass of pornography." He thanked me for making that mistake. Now I can see that it's heftier than his butt would be in a position that lengthens the muscles, though I still think his cock and balls look the same from behind. Now the image doesn't say much to me except to record the blindness of my love. I use it as a bookmark.

Maybe the moral is that nakedness means asshole. If it's hidden from view by his position or perhaps by his balls or whatever, it makes clothes of them, clothes of his asscheeks. I don't know why—people are often surprised to find shit inside asses. If I desire a man I want to be in his asshole, and I know I'm cooling off if that stops being important. My attitude toward his shit is entirely contingent on the pitch of my desire. And I can guess how he feels toward me by his attitude toward mine. What does the reader think?

An abyss becomes visible but not personal.

TWO MEN
IN A BOAT

M. Christian

The party was distant bass, a steady beat that was more distinct than their view of the house. Alex and Jorge both thought, as they silently paddled out onto the lake—still and quiet as the surface of a silver tea tray—that the sound of the party had lasted longer than their sight of it. They could still hear the *pound, pound, pound* of David's disco (for god's sake!) beat even after the lakeside house had vanished into the late afternoon mist.

Neither of them had spoken—hadn't ever to each other. They didn't even know where they'd come from: maybe this tall, pretty boy had been brought by one of David's artist friends—one of the bohemians with the shaved skulls, the stainless-steel piercings, the stained jeans, the Act-Up Golden Gate T-shirts, the bashed combat boots.

Maybe this swarthy micro-bear, this compact Zorba with the dancing brown eyes had been brought by one of David's leather friends? One of the leathermen with the crew cut, the stainless-steel piercings, the burnished leather chaps, the Spanners T-shirt, the thigh-high leather boots.

Whoever they'd come with they'd both ended up at the railing, watching small ripples undulate across the lake's glassy surface. Maybe it was a magic lake, its spell generated not by bell, book, candle or cum but rather by special silences. The effect on them had certainly been magic: they both knew that speaking would ruin it, break a spell.

They wanted to, sure: Alex wanted desperately to say: "You're polished and fine, something executed with perfect strokes of a brush, the tapping of a chisel."

Jorge ached to say: "You're a feral beast, a wild thing that wants to run, hunt and fuck in the woods."

But they didn't. They remained mute. Alex was at the railing first. Jorge came after, stood next to him. Noticing each other looking, they'd smiled in concert. Then Alex touched Jorge, took his elegant hand in his earthy mitt and led him down to the water, the pier, the boat—

Silently, they moved out onto the lake—the only sound the gentle slipping of the paddles into the water and the distant *thumpa, thumpa, thumpa* of David's endless disco.

Then, the music faded. Silence wrapped around them. There was a moment of uncomfortable fumbling—who should do which?—but that passed as Jorge glanced his silken lips across Alex's. For a moment, the universe ceased for both of them—everything distilling down to just two pairs of lips, two tongues. But then the universe cleared its throat and reminded them of its existence by rocking the boat.

Laughing at almost spilling into the water, Jorge and Alex eased themselves down—Alex on top, Jorge under.

They kissed again, losing themselves in the feeling of lips on lips as their hands started on buttons and belts, T-shirts and shoes, underwear and pants. The boat rocked again, but soon the two men quieted down: lips to lips, a narrow golden hand on a rough, strong cock—a rough, strong hand on a golden cock.

Then with his strong, furry arms, Alex pulled Jorge till Jorge's chest passed by his eager lips. With his firm lips he tasted and teased the narrow man's nipples—coaxing out sweet gasps, moans. Then he was at Jorge's golden cock. Without pause, Jorge was in his mouth, and the taste of him (bitter salt) was ringing on Alex's tongue as he eased him down his throat.

Jorge bucked and whined, sounds exploding past his lips. Alex worked him, teasing, swallowing, gumming and tonguing Alex's cock till the tall boy began to buck his face, pushing and pulling till Alex tasted, down deep, the glory of his come.

Still flushed and steaming, Jorge gently pushed the swarthy Alex back till he was lying on his back, hairy shoulders pressing back onto one of the boat's wooden seats. Reaching down between his legs the pretty boy worked his asshole, opening himself up till he was ready to do what he wanted to do most in the whole wide world: to have Alex's big, fat cock inside him.

Then he was—Alex's cock was big and thick, a brilliantly red dick topped with a fat, and surprisingly soft, head. As he slowly and persistently stuffed himself with it, Jorge had a flash (just a flash) of panic—too big? But it was a magical boat, a special time, and too big or not, Alex fit perfectly into Jorge's asshole.

There, together, they rocked back and forth—Alex's meaty dick easing in and out of Jorge's silken asshole. As he rocked, Jorge wrapped a strong hand around his rock-hard cock, stroking himself as he eased up and down on Alex's dick.

It was a magic time, a magic boat. It was completely unrealistic, completely implausible, but they did it nonetheless: easing in and out of the tight squeeze of Jorge's asshole, Alex felt the come burst out of his balls, rocket out of his sac and into the deep insides of his new lover and, right then, in that instant, Jorge felt his own start the same route—a skyrocket of pleasure that blinded him for a moment to everything but purple and red stars as he squeezed his eyes shut against the bursting joy... and came all over Alex's heavily furred chest.

Time passed, the boat drifted. For a while they both

slept, carried through the mist on gentle dreams. Some-time later (who could say how long) they awoke.

Alex kissed Jorge, a lover's *thank-you* kiss. A special kiss that promised more, offered a special tenderness.

"That was great," Jorge said, shocked; embarrassed that he'd done it—slapping a sudden hand over his mouth.

Alex smiled and kissed him once more—and for a long time, as long as they enjoyed a slow second round, they were silent again.

WRONG

Simon Sheppard

It wasn't supposed to be so crowded that early in the summer, but it was, damn it. The trail to the waterfall was wall-to-wall tourists: obese American parents with their squalling kids, European parents with their rug rats whining in foreign tongues, Asians with their chattering and their big-lensed cameras: the usual, and not another readable gay man to be seen. Mandatory heterosexuality was—quite obviously—the order of the day.

The only thing distinguishing the guy in question was that he was shouting at his—presumably—wife, or at least the browbeaten woman who was, presumably, the mother of the three pale, miserable-looking young children they had in tow. Tattoos, beer belly, Harley T-shirt, bad attitude; it was as if central casting, asked for a redneck, had sent him over to Yellowstone. Oh, and that little ponytail? Priceless.

He might have been just another forgotten unpleasant face in the crowd if he hadn't popped up again later in the day, waiting in line for a National Park Service toilet. It was one of those cinderblock-outhouse-in-the-wilderness jobbies. All day, bathroom lines had been fierce, but here, beside a lesser roadside attraction in late afternoon, the only one already waiting in line was Mr. Harley. He turned his ponytailed head and mouthed a single word, which seemed for the entire world to be "fag." Not promising. Not surprising. But then, rough trade and rednecks had never seemed all that appealing, not as company and, lord knows, not as sex objects.

The metal bathroom door opened and out stepped a shirtless twentysomething hiker whose shorts revealed near-perfect legs. Fuck, now that guy *was* appealing, but he just hurried on his way, no doubt back to a girlfriend whom he did not shout at, but rather cooked vegan dinners for. Over a campfire. Life sure was unfair.

Mr. Harley was, inexplicably, standing in the open outhouse door and looking right at him. What the fuck?

And then the guy jerked his head with an unmistakable *come on in* gesture. Now, ordinarily that would have been out of the question; danger was decidedly not an aphrodisiac for Mark, not like it was for some guys. But this was a national park, damn it, where the buffalo not only roamed, but blocked the road whenever you were trying to get somewhere on time. What bad could happen, really, when a single, alarmed scream would catch the attention of dozens of Middle Americans, some of whom were probably not even homophobic?

The man smiled. He was missing a tooth, and he looked, for one fleeting, startling second, like a naughty little boy.

Sold!

A furtive glance around to make sure no one was watching, a few quick steps, the click of a door lock, and it was done: he was alone in a Yellowstone shitter with wife-abusing redneck scum.

Where had that little boy gone?

"You want to suck my dick, don't you, fag?"

Well, yeah. Shamefully, regrettably yes.

Without waiting, the man with the ludicrous pony-tail whipped out his dick: long, uncut, flaccid.

This was exciting. *Why* was it exciting?

The floor was hard and of dubious cleanliness. The stranger's dick was more than a mouthful, unsnaking readily at the touch of a tongue. Did Mrs. Harley ever do this? Willingly?

At eye level, the biker's hard-on was impressive; the head, fully emerged from foreskin, swollen and glossy red. If this had been edgy gay erotica, there would have been a copious amount of cheese. Luckily, there wasn't. The cock looked, if anything, inviting, a shiny drop of precum already seeping from its slit.

The man was rough. Hand-clamped-on-the-back-of-the-head,   I'm-gonna-shove-this-big-cock-all-the-way-down-your-throat-till-you-sputter-and-choke   rough. And it didn't take him long to come, which was either a good thing or a bad thing...or both. He came in a jiffy. In a wink. There was a moan, a mouthful, a backing away.

But then, just as it was over, the man, all unexpected, reached down and gently stroked Mark's cheek. Just for a second.

There was a knock at the door, then another one, louder.

"Just a fucking minute," Mr. Harley called out. He walked over to the already-open chemical toilet, took his softening cock in his hand, and pissed like the proverbial racehorse.

"Stand over there, out of sight," he said when he was done, dick tucked back inside his grimy denim cutoffs. After his exit, Mark quickly relocked the door.

Someone tried the door handle, twice: too bad. It was time to quickly jack off, standing up above the toilet's chemical maw, suddenly aware of the functionally ugly surroundings, the unpleasant smell, the usual sign over the can urging visitors to aid ventilation by shutting the lid after use, something no one ever did.

Sperm spurted into the mess. Then, in short order, urgent piss.

Cock put away, he hurried out the door. The four men in line all gave him variations on "a very weird look." What were they going to do? Report him to a ranger?

There on the path leading from the outhouse to the parking lot stood Mr. Harley and family, the kids looking like Dust Bowl children from a Dorothea Lange photo.

"...to know where the fuck you were," the man was shouting at the woman. "Is that too fucking much to ask?"

Wrong. It had all been so wrong. And yet...

Birds were singing somewhere.

Mark hurried away.

ARCHIE'S TONGUE

David Holly

Through our senior year, Archie Davis and I had been inseparable to the point that everyone scented the flowering of our relationship. However, this was the Florida Keys, where a gay fling was considered a minor peccadillo (though worthy of rich gossip), even among high school students. Farther north where the Bible Belt buckled, we would have been shunned, battered, investigated and jailed.

In our high school's sailing class, the coach teamed Archie and me up, and on our first voyage together, we beached on uninhabited Tavernier Key, smoked a joint and ended up jerking each other off. Over the next few months, we discovered the pleasures of anal sex, fucking each other with the innocent freedom of the 1960s. We also sucked each other a bit, but nothing we did prepared me for what happened on the night of the Fourth of July.

Archie's father, who owned a boat dealership, had presented Archie with a twenty-five-foot sailing sloop for his birthday. That vessel saw a lot of action during our voyages around the Bay of Florida. We explored little islands, camped out, befriended key deer and developed our sexual intimacy. Then, on the Fourth of July, while fireworks were blossoming off Tavernier Point, Islamorada, and Marathon, Archie Davis placed his lips on my asshole.

We had anchored off an unnamed key, cooked a supper of burgers and baked sweet potatoes over an open fire and eaten naked on the warm coral sand beneath swaying palm fronds. As the sun sank into the Gulf of Mexico and night-blooming jasmine scented the air, we discovered that our cocks had erected themselves. Setting aside his can of Busch beer, Archie fingered the swollen head of my dick. "No need to ask what you're thinking, Dave," he said.

No need, indeed. His cock was as hard as mine. I gripped his thick shaft and began diddling his dick-head.

"Hold off, Dave," Archie said. "I want to try something we haven't tried before."

I could not imagine what that might be.

"Roll over," Archie suggested.

I rolled onto my stomach and pulled up my right leg. However, this was nothing we hadn't tried. Archie had fucked my ass about twenty times by then, and I had fucked his tight butt an equal number. We had been topping each other for months. However, it wasn't his dick that I felt against my asshole; it was his mouth. Archie pushed his face between my buttocks. His long red hair brushed my buttcheeks as he drove his nose and mouth into my crack. His tongue darted out and touched my anal sphincter.

An explosion of joy filled me. Only kings, potentates, emperors, commanders, caliphs and werowances could have felt what I felt then. As Archie licked around my asshole, my cock nearly exploded. I was in raptures. I had a sense of power, deep erotic power, and the power mingled with a sense of adulation. Archie idolized me. He adored me. He worshipped my ass.

I sighed with euphoric contentment as Archie rimmed around my hole. He licked up my crack until his tongue bathed the small of my back. Then he licked downward until he reached my ball sac. As he bathed my buttcrack, he became more urgent. His lust to drive his tongue into my secret place grew upon him. I felt his exalted need, and for a moment, I thought that our consciousnesses had merged. I was Dave, jubilating from Archie's oral ministrations, but I also felt what Archie felt. Somehow, I tasted the enchantment of kissing another boy's asshole, though I had not done it myself.

Archie continued ravishing my anal cleft while his enchantment grew. He rimmed my hole for a long time while my body tilted on the verge of rhapsody.

"Oh, yes, Archie," I gasped, and he sensed my hedonistic soul's desire. With aching transport, he opened my anal sphincter with his tongue and pushed inside. Nothing I had ever experienced, including the joy of having his cock and his expended semen inside of me, prepared me for the gay beatification. I was Dave the Blessed, bewitched, enraptured, and borne to paradise. Titillating, thrilling, intoxicating tickles transported me.

"Archie!" I yowled, sounding more like a wild thing in heat than a human being. Words fail me now: overused metaphors such as "banquet of the soul" or "cockles of my heart" could not describe the ecstasy that was so much more than the purely physical. *Archie's mouth was on my asshole—his tongue was up my ass*—such profane terms to describe a sacred action.

The contractions and dilations of my asshole as I passed through shuddering orgasm, a sexual punch that grew from the delectable scent of violets into the prankish joy of throwing a rock through a windowpane, met Archie's firm tongue like a game of truth or dare. Archie drove his tongue deeper and held it in place while my orgasm grew and heavy spasms shook my groin. My cock flung my semen upon the warm sand. As my orgasm stilled, a cloud sailed across the face of the moon and a tropical bird warbled from the mangroves.

Afterward, Archie slipped his cock into my ass. He humped me, and I met his motions gleefully. But even as I received his wild dick ride, I knew I could never give back the gift he had given to me.

Since then, hundreds of men have touched their mouths to my asshole before they drove in their cocks. Most of the time, I feel a shadowy echo of the ancient thrill, but only an echo. When Archie licked me, he was doing it because he genuinely loved my asshole and made love to it with his tongue. Thus, when men kiss my ass before fucking me, my mind harkens back to that strange Fourth of July, that final night of innocence, when Archie Davis placed his mouth in my anal cleft and I discovered that I was born to command that men worship my asshole before I granted them the pleasure of filling my booty.

BROAD STROKES

William Holden

He stood on a paint can in front of the glass door to my office. I wasn't expecting to see anyone, especially him. A brutal snowstorm had blanketed the city with several feet of snow. I was anticipating a quiet day by myself. Luckily, I was wrong.

I didn't know his name but had enjoyed seeing him around over the past few months as he worked to repaint the common areas of our building. His light olive complexion and buzzed black hair inspired an immediate attraction. The small dimples that dotted his cheeks whenever he smiled didn't hurt either.

I sat behind my desk and watched as he raised himself on his toes, reaching toward the ceiling with paintbrush in hand. His pale red sweatshirt and white undershirt pulled up out of his pants. The first glimpse of his stomach came into view. A thick line of black hair ran above his waistline to his navel. The rest of his stomach was as smooth and hairless as his face. His balance wavered on the paint can. The movement caused his pants to fall lower on his hips, exposing his blue and black plaid boxers. He stepped off the paint can and caught my eye. He smiled and nodded his usual greeting.

I kept my eyes hovering over the monitor while I waited for him to step back up on the paint can before taking another look. It was then that I noticed his hands gripping the bottom of his sweatshirt. I felt my cock expand as I watched him pull the sweatshirt up and over his head. Most of the thin, white tank top came up with it. His nipples were large and erect. A few strands of dark hair covered each. He raised his arms to pull his hands out of the sleeves, exposing the thick mass of dark hair that covered his deep armpits. He looked at me out of the corner of his eye. I saw a brief smile curl his lips. He climbed back up on his makeshift ladder.

My cock stiffened further in my slacks as I watched the muscles of his arms and chest flex with his movement. I slipped my hand in my pants and adjusted myself, making room for my growing cock. I lowered my eyes from his nipples that were pressing against the thin undershirt and noticed a heavy shape swaying between his legs. A spasm raced through my cock as I realized he was getting aroused. I watched his cock lengthen behind the light brown khakis, patting and thumping against the cotton material. I couldn't take it any longer. I stood up and walked around in front of my desk. His hand fell from above and adjusted himself. I walked to the door. I could see the outline of the head of his cock pressing against his pants. I opened the door and came within inches of his crotch.

The scent of his body surrounded me. It was heavy and masculine. I looked up his body. He was looking down at me with a smile. The door hit me from behind. It pushed me into him. My face inched closer to the growing bulge in his pants. I grabbed his large, firm legs for support.

I looked away with a nervous smile and slipped around his body. My hand grazed over his erection as I walked into the bathroom. I looked into the mirror as I washed my hands. The door opened, and he walked in. We looked at each other through the mirror as he passed. He walked to the urinal next to the sink. I heard him lower his zipper. The sound sent a shiver through my groin. He sighed before a thick stream of piss splashed into the bowl. I hesitated, wanting him but knowing it was neither the time nor the place. He peered around the wall of the urinal. The look in his eyes drew me in. I walked up behind him.

He took my hand and guided it to his cock. I held it as he continued to piss. It was thick, meaty and warm to the touch. I took my free hand and unbuttoned his pants, which fell around his ankles. I let go of his cock and knelt behind him, pulling his boxers down his thick muscled legs.

The scent of his crotch, damp with sweat, wrapped its muskiness around me. I spread his asscheeks. He groaned and leaned against the urinal as he continued to piss. I licked the fine, dark hair that spread along the edge of his asshole. The muscles contracted as the tip of my tongue glided over the tight puckered skin. I licked deeper, tasting his musk and inhaling his ass sweat.

His balls were large and heavy. I massaged them, pulling and tugging the loose, hairless skin. I felt his ass muscles contract against my tongue as he squeezed out the last drops of urine. I turned him around and slipped the head of his cock into my mouth. I ran my tongue under his foreskin, licking the remaining drops of piss from the folds. His cock grew in my mouth, swelling until I gagged from its length. He pulled out and slapped my face with it. His warm precome smeared across my cheek.

He grabbed the back of my head, gripped his cock and guided it into my open mouth. He held my head firmly in place as he began to fuck my face. He reached above me and held on to the wall with his free hand, giving him more leverage and force. Spit and precome filled my mouth. I swallowed what I could; the rest leaked out of the corners of my mouth and dribbled down my neck.

He began to grunt and moan with every thrust of his hips. I could feel his balls tightening in my hand. His thrusts became more pronounced. He gripped my head with both hands now and shoved his cock down my throat one final time. He held my face tight against his crotch. His tight, curly pubic hair pricked my face. His increasingly sweat-dampened crotch filled my nose with its pungent smell. I felt his cock pulse as his orgasm shot through his shaft and exploded into my mouth. He held his hips and crotch steady as wave after wave of his hot come rushed into my mouth. It ran down my throat in thick rivers of bitter saltiness.

He pulled his cock out of my mouth and cupped his hands under my armpits, pulling me up to face him. His breath was both stale and inviting as he kissed me. My mouth opened up to him and gave him a sample of his own warm come that was still pooled in my mouth. He broke the kiss and smiled at me before pulling up his pants and leaving. I stood alone in the bathroom with the taste of him lingering on my tongue.

MAKING
THE GRADE

Brian Centrone

Drew was not the brightest college student. He had ability, but lacked motivation. I encouraged him whenever he did his work, though that wasn't often. The days he came to class, he would sit quietly in the back, muscles flexed, lips pursed, eyes heavy from smoking up. I would sneak glances at him, hoping no one would notice. At the end of class he would stand up and stretch, his shirt riding up to reveal a flat stomach, perfect *V* cut and treasure trail. It was all I could do not to see where it led. I always wondered if Drew suspected I was hot for him. He never let on, and I tried my best to seem unbothered by his sexiness. It was undeniable though. Drew was a stud. Young, hard and built to fuck. He liked to wear thin sweatpants that showed he was packing major, major meat.

By the end of the semester, Drew was failing and I was blue-balled. On the last day of class I called him over and waited until all the other students had filed out before speaking to him. I asked if he knew he was failing. He nodded, looking right into my eyes. His stare was intense and I stirred. My dick began to swell. I hadn't planned on it, but I couldn't help what I was about to do.

"Is there anything you can do to pass?" I asked, looking him over with my eyes pausing just long enough on the bulge under his sweats.

He moved his full lips to speak, but said nothing. Instead, he inched closer to me and grabbed his crotch. "I can give you this," he said slowly, "if it will help me pass." He released himself.

My heart started to beat faster as an overwhelming feeling took over my body. Could this really happen? I felt the strain of my now fully hard dick pressing against the fabric of my trousers. I swallowed hard and looked up from his crotch.

"I see you looking at me," he went on. "Checking me out," he grinned.

So he knew.

"You hungry for cock, Professor?" he asked, rubbing himself. "I'll feed it to you for a passing grade."

My eyes were fixed on Drew handling his meat for me. I knew it was wrong, but I had to have it. I had desired it for months. I was more than hungry for this young guy's cock—I was starving for it.

I nodded my head yes. Drew smiled.

"We should go someplace," I finally managed to say. "Not here." I checked the door to make sure no one was pressed up against it, peering in.

"My car's in the back lot. You know which one it is," he winked.

I nodded and proceeded to gather up my books and papers as he left. Somehow I got everything in order, fumbling hands and all, and carefully placed my brief-case in front of my raging hard-on so no one would notice as I walked out of the building.

Drew was waiting in his car when I reached the back lot. He had parked all the way in the far corner. His seat was fully reclined and his legs were spread wide. He was still clothed and had just finished smoking a joint.

"Get in," he ordered. I did as I was told. I tossed my briefcase into the back and took my place in the passenger seat. He looked over at me, then down at his hard-on.

"Suck it, Bitch."

I obliged. I leaned over and mouthed my student's cock right through his sweats. The hardness of his cock felt good against my lips. I mouthed down the shaft and found his balls. I kissed and licked them through the thin fabric, loving every moment of it, but my hunger for flesh overtook me and I lifted my mouth off his meat just long enough to pull down his sweats and release my prize. His cock was mesmerizing, thick and veiny with a bulbous head. He was hairy, which I liked. His balls were big, heavy low hangers, and as I took them in my mouth, I knew I wanted the juice building up inside of them.

Drew moaned. "I can never get my girl to eat my balls. I might have to come back for more," he said, rubbing my head.

I indicated I'd be happy to feed on them anytime he wanted.

Drew pulled my head up by my hair. He reached for his cock with his free hand and slapped it against my face.

"You want it?" he asked between slaps.

"Yes."

"Of course you do. You've wanted it for a long time." He teased my lips with the head of his cock. "You should have asked for it the first day of class. I wouldn't have had to come so much." He slipped the head in my mouth then took it right back out. I was busting. The boy knew control. "Maybe I won't give it to you after all." Drew pulled my head up far enough so I could look at him. He had a sneer on his face that almost made me shoot my load.

"Say 'please.'"

"Please," I said gently and began to rub myself. The pressure building inside my pants was getting too much.

"I can't hear you. Say 'please.'"

"Please." This time I said it louder.

"That's more like it, Professor Faggot. Now choke

on it." Drew forced my head down and rammed his cock into my mouth. The girth of it alone was hard to contain, but he kept holding my head down while arching himself up so his cock would go deep down my throat. I gagged a bit at first, which he seemed to get off on, but my willingness to please him took over any gag reflex that existed. I sucked on his cock with everything I had. All those weeks of desire, and now I was finally slurping on the meat I had dreamed about.

Drew moaned heavily as I deep-throated that fucker, and pretty soon he released his hold on my head, letting me go at it on my own. I could feel his balls tighten against my chin and I knew Drew was about to offer me dessert. I gave his shaft one last deep-throating before rising up to suckle on the fat head. He let out a loud grunt as his cum began to flow. As soon as I tasted his juice I dove back down and took all of his cock, down to his balls, letting Drew's cum empty into my stomach. It was enough to make me shoot my own load in my pants.

When he was empty, I cleaned his cock for him and then sat upright in my seat. He looked over at me with those heavy eyes and that cocky smile. "So what'd I get?" he asked.

I looked at the cock I had just drained. It really was huge. "Oh, I think that was a C-plus," I said casually. He looked at me funny. "But I can tell you what you can do for an A."

PRETTY BOYS SUCK

Derrick Della Giorgia

He was tall, with a shaven head and blue eyes, white as a ghost and super defined, browsing three movies down, toward *Fist Time* and *Bareback Roulette*. He kept fixing his sunglasses over his head as he crouched to check the titles on the bottom shelf. He was wearing a white tight tank top, light jeans and flip-flops. Every time he reached for a DVD, his arm inflated around his deltoid and more of his sculpted chest was visible from the side of the tank top. Also his boxers, with the movement, went down a bit and a thin line of skin appeared right below the hem of the tank top. I couldn't keep up with my breathing and my tight black bathing suit was already growing, but I wouldn't move. I was in a dead end corridor; to leave I would have had to walk by him. Instead, I kept playing with *Pretty Boys Suck,* pretending I was reading the description and using the DVD to study the hot guy's reflection in the cover. He knew I was looking at him and every now and then he looked over to my side to check me out too. He was older than me, probably in his twenties. I had just gotten out of college. We were the only two people in the store and the owner was watching a little TV by the front door, a good room and a couple of corridors away from us. It felt like I had two hearts galloping inside of me, one in my chest and another one farther down, in between my belly button and my asshole.

When I could almost recite even the names of the actors on the DVD I was holding, he finally made a move. He turned his head to my side, looking down and staring at my crotch and my smooth legs escaping from the wet shorts. I stared back and he lifted his tank top up to his chest, introducing me to his marble abs. His skin was the color of milk and the only imperfection I could spot were the grooves that divided his six pack and the transverse lines on his flanks that ran down into his boxers. He caressed his lower abdomen and went down, finally encountering the top of his nicely trimmed black pubes. He passed his hand over his bulge and suggested his shape and size, squeezing between his thumb and the rest of his fingers. I still held the DVD and didn't even try to hide my erection that had started to push on my left thigh. He came closer to me and looked around. Once he had made sure there was nobody watching us, he hung his sunglasses on the shelf and cupped his hand under my balls, attempting to grab as much cock as he could. He smiled and that made his sexy massage even sweeter. But he didn't speak a word. He had perfect white teeth and a big nose. I could smell his cologne and the mint of his gum on his breath. With both hands, he pulled down my shorts and took my cock out. It banged against the DVDs in front of us, but he promptly grabbed it and held it in the position that excited me the most, parallel to my stomach. He pulled my balls and started spitting saliva on his right hand to lubricate the sliding of my foreskin over my cock head. I was paralysed with pleasure, and he had to take my hand and put it on his abs to break the spell. His skin was warm and smooth like a statue. Under my palm, I felt the hardness of his muscles, their shape, their contractions of desire. He licked his lips and kept jerking my meat, despite the arches I was already making with my back and the sweat that started on my chest and forehead in the poorly ventilated corner where we hid.

When his expert hands made me sigh, he looked around and went on his knees, swallowing my cock down to the root, until I felt his lips brushing my pubes and the beginning of my scrotum. Then he pulled it out of his mouth and dug his tongue into my foreskin, bringing me more than once to the point of orgasm. He concentrated with his tongue on the tip of my cock and with his thumb stimulated the area of my cock that kept my foreskin attached to my cock head. Seeing that I couldn't take it anymore, he stood up and went behind me, pressing his erection against my ass without taking his clothes off, just pressing as hard as we could handle. I thought I was about to shoot off the ground and make a hole in the shelves of DVDs, propelled by his arrogant tool. I turned around and laid both hands on his chest, under the cotton of the tank top, then slid them down to his abs again, scratching him a little bit, desirous of breaking that iron barrier. Then I undid his pants enough to take his cock out and I slapped my face with it, making sure I got it on my cheeks, on my wet lips, on my eyes and next to my nose to smell all the man scent his boxers preserved.

"Suck on it!" Those were the only three words he told me, the only command erupting from deep down his throat, the wave of sex impulse he couldn't stop. I licked the base of his cock head with the tip of my tongue, where the circumcision wound made it a little uneven, and teased him with my lower lip. He was suffering and grabbed my head with both hands and penetrated my mouth as if it was an ass, without respecting my respiration pauses or my need to swallow—simply riding my throat as I was forced to admire the movements of his abdominal muscles. In and out of my mouth he went, his balls tight against the shaft I was sucking on. The rhythm increased and then his whole body petrified: his legs, his arms, his ass contracted to expulse the white-hot juice into my throat. I felt it smashing against my palate, my tongue and my teeth, dripping down by my tonsils, obliging me to swallow to get air. It was sweet and thick.

He lifted me and turned me around, my back leaned on his body. He pulled my shorts down to my knees and from behind started playing with me. I wanted him inside of me. I wanted to be had. But as I thought of that I was invaded by the orgasm and I came all over *Pretty Boys Suck* and a couple more DVDs, mixing my balls' secretion with that of the actors. He waited for me to release the last drops of pleasure, and then he pinched my ass and left me standing there, feeling the pleasure of release in my cock and between my legs.

JUSTIN
FROM 360

Jonathan Asche

His ass gleamed in the sunlight, his high, round buttocks several shades lighter than the rest of him. Brian's hands glided over those globes of flesh in easy, circular motions. He pried the buttcheeks apart and allowed a hand to slide down that furry channel. He played with the man's hole, making him gasp. With his other hand Brian beckoned me.

I didn't move right away. I still couldn't process the turn of events; how an afternoon in the complex pool could end up with our relationship taken to the brink—but to the brink of what?

It was the middle of the week, Wednesday; Brian and I had the pool to ourselves, and we took full advantage of the privacy. We were in the water, my arms around his body, my hands moving down his back. I pushed my hands past the elastic waistband of his suit, cupping his ass. My cock stirred as Brian ground his crotch into mine. I could feel his dick swell. One of my fingers slipped into the deep divide of his buttocks. Brian's mouth moved to the nape of my neck.

Then *he* showed up: Justin from apartment 360.

I tried to ignore him; ignore the sun glistening on his golden skin, highlighting the taut muscles bulging on his lean frame. I tried to ignore the way his light blue swim trunks clung tightly to his narrow hips, his cock and balls, his shapely ass. I tried to ignore him as he strutted past, looking down at us in the pool. His eyes were hidden behind sunglasses, but I was sure I detected a slight smile, a smile I recognized.

Brian pulled away, saw my eyes following Justin as he walked to the opposite end of the pool, spread a towel out on one of the chaise lounges and lay face down.

"You told me he moved," Brian said.

"I thought he had."

"Guess he's just visiting, then."

"Stop it."

"What are you, six?" Brian's laughter had an edge to it.

"Fuck you!"

He pulled away, kicking toward the pool's edge.

Brian climbed out of the pool, shook the water from his dark hair and strode over to the deck chairs where we'd deposited our towels and other accoutrements. He grabbed a bottle of sunblock and started walking. I was puzzled at first and then horrified as I watched Brian approach Justin and strike up a conversation. I heard voices but not what was said. Brian smiled a lot, shifting his weight from one muscular leg to the other, casually letting a hand run down his abdomen, and just as casually adjusting himself in his black-and-white box-cut. He looked over at me in the pool and his smile broadened.

He knelt beside Justin and squirted some sunblock on his back, leaning closer to whisper into Justin's ear as he rubbed the lotion into his smooth skin. Justin chuckled and squirmed, his body twisting provocatively beneath Brian's caress.

I remained in the pool, my face burning. This game was going too far.

Still, Brian took it further. He stood up, grinned in my direction and stepped out of his suit. Justin rolled on his side, looking up admiringly. Brian was thirty-six, had thickened a little over the years, but still cut an impressive figure. He nonchalantly stroked his cock, at half-mast and rising.

Justin rolled back onto his stomach. Brian eased himself onto Justin's back, his cock pointed toward Justin's ass. Justin and the chaise groaned.

Brian continued massaging Justin's back, his hands moving lower and lower, until they reached the waistband of the light blue trunks. Then the trunks began to move lower and lower, until they were waved in the air like a victory flag before being dropped onto the deck.

When Brian motioned for me to join him I knew I

should've swum the other way, gone back to our apartment instead of participating in this proverbial train wreck.

Instead I lay down on the track, finding myself standing on the deck, dripping at Justin's feet, my eyes going from his perfect ass to Brian. He was rock hard.

Brian pried Justin's asscheeks apart, showing off the pink hole. "Look familiar?"

"Don't."

"You're overdressed."

"Stop this."

Brian insisted, and I gave in. He told me to kneel between Justin's legs and I did so, using my wet trunks as cushion for my knees. Brian gently brushed his fingertips over Justin's asshole then raised those same fingers to my lips, pushing them roughly into my mouth. When Brian withdrew his fingers they were dripping with my spit.

Those dripping wet fingers disappeared into Justin's hole, eliciting a loud moan. Brian pumped Justin's ass, using his fingers as if they were his dick, a malicious smile on his lips the whole time. His cock was oozing.

"He's got a tight ass," Brian said. "But you knew that."

"I told you it was over," I whimpered.

"Not yet, it isn't."

Brian withdrew his fingers from Justin's ass and brought them to his dick, gingerly rubbing his cock head, swabbing up his precum. Brian returned the fingers to

Justin's pulsing asshole, glazing the puckered lips with his juices.

"Bet it tastes better now," he said.

Then he ordered me to eat Justin's ass. When I refused Brian grabbed my arm, pulling me forward. *"Eat it!"*

I lowered my face between those succulent hills of flesh, my nose filled with the twin scents of sunblock and natural musk. My tongue prodded the rubbery knot of muscle around his hole, gently lapping. Brian chided me, telling me I was doing it like one of those gay-for-pay porn stars. "Eat it like you love it," he barked. "Like you've done it before."

I pushed my tongue past Justin's ass ring, into his hot chute. His body twitched, and I heard Brian say, "Yeah, that's it." Even though tears streamed down my face I could feel my cock stiffening, thinking of the stolen afternoons in apartment 360, when Brian was at work. My tongue burrowed into Justin's hole, like it had so many times before, and his body trembled like before. I stabbed that hole repeatedly; licked the engorged asslips; gnawed the hard ring.

Brian jacked off, and between heavy breaths he said I was a shitty boyfriend but a great fuck, that he knew I could eat ass for hours, that Justin was a lucky man. "But his ass has never tasted as sweet as it does…right… *now*!"

Brian's load rained down on Justin's butt in hot, heavy splats. Cum trickled down into the channel of Justin's asscrack, over his winking rosebud. Without being told I lowered my lips to that cum-frosted orifice, slurping loudly as I licked Justin's asshole clean. Brian was right: it had never tasted sweeter.

I met Brian's eyes: his gaze was hard but not unforgiving. He grabbed me by the hair and pulled me toward him. We kissed, Brian's tongue pushing into my mouth violently, tasting Justin's ass, tasting his own cum.

I stroked my cock, sobbing loudly as I fired my load.

"Now it's over," Brian whispered.

IN MEDIAS RES

Penboy 7

Looking for company?"

You don't respond; just remain face down on the cot, the odor of the men who came before fueling your urgency. The stranger evaluates your body from the doorway. Beyond him are the whisper of bare feet and the percussive slap of flip-flops circling your room. Through the thin wall you hear the intimacies of the men next door: a metronomic pounding of a meaty butt, the throaty grunt of a man on the verge.

The door closes.

The cot creaks under his added weight. A heavy hand brushes the small of your back with surprising tenderness, then slides down your spine to the cleft of your ass, which you raise to meet his touch. You are already lubed up and his finger slips in easily, then a duet, a trio.

"Oh, yeah." His rough fingers explore your depths and graze your prostate; your body bucks instinctively. His right hand parts your legs to dig deeper, calluses on his palms. You wonder idly if he is a builder or farmer but know it doesn't matter who he is outside of this room. The stranger withdraws his thick fingers and you wait for him to refill the void.

"Quiet, ain't you?"

His breath is heavier than when he entered a minute before, his muscles tiger tense. It excites you that you have had such a pronounced effect on him.

"What's your name?"

"Doesn't matter."

"That's cool."

He carefully drapes his towel across the foot of the bed and you look back to make sure he puts on a condom; you don't allow yourself to look above his waist. He wets his cock with his own spit, rolls latex over his erection, then slicks himself up with glistening lube. The man squats between your outstretched legs, then lies on top of you, clumsily shepherding his limbs into position. The heat of his dick swells against your asshole and you bite your lip anticipating it. The man's hand dives between your legs to guide himself in. He pokes too high, then too low, before hitting the sweet spot. He gasps when he enters, his breath scented with mints masking a meatier odor.

The head of his cock pops into you in one push; your muscles tense and then relax. The man sinks until all of him is inside. You separate your buttcheeks with your hands to accommodate another half inch.

"You okay?"

"Yes."

The man pumps his hips and you reposition your smaller frame to accommodate his bulk. He lifts his pelvis and plunges in, rises and falls, leaving you empty in the upstroke, crammed full on the down. He varies the tempo, rides you with breathtaking patience before pounding like a jackhammer. You grit your teeth and receive him, imagining another above you instead of the man who is there. You almost speak his name, but the word is eclipsed by a groan.

His lips whisper against your ear, a background purr in his throat, dialogue ripped from a porn movie you've probably seen and jerked off to. He grunts, his body grows rigid, and you fear he is going to come too soon. You freeze. He pants, his hot breath feathering your hair. After a minute he starts the cycle over, building the pace from exploratory strokes to a teeth-rattling drive. The man pulls you up on all fours and pounds your ass without mercy. You watch your cock bounce between your legs, the pulse of the man's hairy thighs behind you. You understand that you are exactly where you need to be, an intersection of sweltering limbs.

He buries himself, grunts long and low. "Coming." His dead weight collapses the transitory structure of your bodies. Sweat glues your skin together. He holds you in his arms as his breath slows, then quiets. He kisses the back of your neck and you breathe in your combined odors merging with the other scents from the mattress.

"That was hot."

You nod noncommittally. He senses your postcoital detachment and swings his legs over the side of the cot. The stranger peels off the condom, knots it and drops it to the floor. He stands and cleans himself with the hand-towel left on the table next to the cot. You watch him, fascinated at how differently he washes than you would have.

He picks up his own towel, knots it around his waist and opens the door.

"You want to keep this open?"

"Yes."

"Okay." The man's legs vanish into the hallway. Murky light floods onto your skin and bathes you in red shadows. You drop your head to the mattress and sniff out the lingering smells, detecting your own woody scent from the legion. You listen to the flip-flops and bare feet circling your room; hold your breath when a man stops at the door; close your eyes as you try not to imagine what he looks like. You shut your mind and try not to think about *him*. The man steps into the room, the cubicle warming with his presence. You exhale.

"Are you...?"

THIS BOY

Xan West

This boy pulls my focus. I look at him and see his need. The predator in me can see his eagerness for my attention, his aching to be touched, his yearning for something he hopes I might have for him: some safety enmeshed in cruelty, some darkness wrapped in pleasure. This boy sits at my feet, his hands in mine, and his hungry eyes hold mine as he babbles earnestly about life after college and trying to figure out what to do next. He is basking in the intensity of my full focus, preening, rolling onto his back and showing me his belly, unaware of what he is asking for or what it would mean.

This boy is teasing me with his eagerness. This boy does not know what he is offering. I sit and watch, my muscles tensing as I stop myself from reaching for him. I breathe in, slowly, feeling my hunger grow, as my sadism rears its head, a beast on the prowl.

I want to stalk this boy around the room, until I've cornered my prey against a wall. I want to watch the pulse in his throat speed up. I want to savor the scent of his fear, build it up as I menace him with my size and ferocity. I want to speak to him softly, about sadism, about the beast that roams in my skin. I want to detail all of the ways he has been teasing it, describe exactly the promises he has made and how he has been asking for it. I want this boy to realize what he's been doing and be afraid. And then I want to take his breath, and watch him struggle with a smile on my face. I want him to know what it is to be at my mercy and to see exactly how merciless the beast inside me can be.

I want to sink my teeth into this boy. I want to ravage him with claws and fear and relentless pain. I want to strip him down to his boots and jock with my knife, watch his eyes as he hears his clothes shred, and pull him down to the floor by his hair. I want to ram my boot into his cock, watch him writhe on the ground on his back as I grind the heel into him. And then I want to kick him, rain blows into his flesh, stomp him to bits on the floor.

And then I want to pull this boy onto his hands and knees and claim him for mine, ram my cock into his ass in one hard thrust, grip him by the hair and jack him back onto my cock as I drive my teeth into his neck. I want to mark every inch of this boy as my territory, scratching furrows into his skin with my nails, thrusting into him so deep he can taste it. I want to be thorough and ruthless and fuck him into oblivion, growling my triumph in his ear as he trembles on my cock. I want him raw and scared and mine.

And then I want to pull out of his ass and make this boy clean himself off my cock with his mouth, while I'm telling him exactly what he is: my hole to fuck. I want to slam so deep into his throat and his mind that he is full of me; until all he breathes is me; until he is relentlessly focused on me; until his breath is gone and he is gasping and choking and pouring tribute out his eyes, just for me.

I want to teach this boy exactly what he is asking for.

ROOM
FOR CREAM

Natty Soltesz

M ark and I were working at the coffee shop. Lee had left for the evening, so it was just us. Outside it was rainy and dreary, and business was suffering. We hadn't had but three customers in the past two hours.

"Fuck, I need random hot girls to have sex with," Mark said. He was horny and frustrated and being very vocal about it.

"Well, if you want I'll suck you off in the back," I said, figuring I could pass it off as a joke if needed. But Mark got this look in his eye.

"Seriously?" he said.

"Yeah, sure."

"All right, let's go." Mark walked into the back kitchen and I followed him. It was warm; it smelled like fresh-baked banana bread.

"What if a customer comes?" I wondered.

"Fuck 'em. Nobody's coming in, anyway," Mark said, unbuckling his pants. I got down on my knees in front of him as he pulled his pants down. His cock was getting hard under his boxer shorts. I'd figured something like this might be possible with Mark since we'd started working together, but hadn't been sure until now. I reached inside the fly of his boxers and brought out his cock. It was warm and hot, and it grew more and more as I held it in my hand. I put my lips around it; it was smallish but it fit in my mouth perfectly.

Mark moaned. I could imagine what he was feeling— that first heavenly instant of a warm, wet mouth swallowing your hard cock, sliding down it. As I bobbed my head up and down his boner I reached underneath his cock and pulled his balls out of his shorts, holding and rolling them in my hand. I leaned down farther and started licking his balls.

"Fuck that feels good," Mark said. He was looking past me. I noticed the bottle of honey we use for tea sitting on the counter by his head.

"Give me that honey." He reached over and handed it to me. I held his erection up and poured the honey onto the head. It coated his cock, trickling slowly down his shaft. I licked it off. The sticky sweet taste was delightful. I went down on him, hard-core, and he was really enjoying it. He held my head still and thrust into me, fucking my mouth. It seemed like he might be getting close.

"Can I eat your ass?" I said.

"Seriously?"

"Yeah, totally."

"Won't that be gross?"

"Well, I'll use the honey," I said, holding up the bottle. Mark was standing there, boner sticking out of his shorts, throbbing. He thought about it for a second.

"Just lean over the table there," I said.

"This is weird, but I'll give it a try," he said, putting his elbows on the table. I pulled his boxers down and lifted his shirt up. He had a big ass; it looked so hot. I pulled his cheeks apart. His hole was pink and clean. I poured a little honey down his crack and it drizzled over his hole. I got my face in there and started eating the honey, running my tongue all over his slick butthole. It instantly relaxed and I pushed more of my tongue into it. Mark was laboring to catch his breath; he leaned farther onto the table and pushed his ass into my face, really getting into having his ass eaten out.

"Does that feel good?" I asked.

"Yeah, keep doing it." I kept doing it. I could have done it all night. His ass was so big, it was a fucking feast. I wanted to have him sit on my face. I wanted to grab anything I could—whipped cream, mocha syrup, whatever—and eat it off of his ass.

Mark began jerking himself off.

"I want to come like this," he said. I kept my face buried in his ass. It would have been nice to eat his cum, I was thinking, but if this was how he wanted it...

It only took him a few seconds of jerking his cock before his cum started spurting all over the floor under the table. His butthole clenched, but I kept digging my tongue into it as hard as I could. I could hear his cum splattering the floor under the table. Then I heard a voice coming from the front.

"Yoo-hoo!" it said. "Anybody back there?"

"Fuck, shit!" Mark said. "Customer!" He turned around, face flushed. His cock was still hard and dripping cum.

"Let me clean you off," I said, and I slurped the cum off of his dick, savoring the taste. Mark moaned. I stood up and wiped my mouth. Mark pulled up his pants while I went to attend to business.

"Sorry about that," I said to an overweight, annoyed-looking lady with three little kids in tow. "What can I get for you?"

TIME DISAPPEARS

Eric K. Anderson

We're on our way to meet the in-laws for an obligatory Easter Sunday meal. At the train station Susan struggles with our young son Sylvan who has been hyperactive and whiny since he sneakily found his chocolate this morning and ate it all. "I'm going to the loo," I say and rush off feeling guilty for leaving her to it. I need some time to myself. Today I have a dry roast and awkward conversation with Susan's old man to look forward to. Also, I'm certain they'll lecture me for being late because I forgot to set my watch forward when the clocks changed. The next train up north was canceled and now we're waiting for a replacement service. I'm horny and peeved.

London Liverpool Street Station is teeming with people. I zigzag through the crowd. Everyone is carrying

bunches of flowers or boxes containing oversized chocolate eggs. Handsome men wear tight suits normally used
only on weekdays. They've ironed them, especially for
the holiday. I find the stairs leading down to the toilets.
The fumes of disinfectant and piss rise up to greet me
as I make my descent. I dig out twenty pence from my
pocket to go through the row of metal turnstiles at the
entrance. There is a line of urinals off to my left. I stand
up against one and unzip my trousers. Wondering if I
have enough time to get a paper before boarding our
train, I look at my watch and notice that it's still an
hour behind. I feel a relaxing release as a stream of piss
splashes onto the blue urinal cake in front of me. A man
a few urinals down clears his throat. When I look up I
see his head is half-turned toward me and he's staring
directly at my dick while I urinate. His arm is moving
back and forth. An electric shock travels down my
spine. I have that male instinctual reaction signaling that
something sexual is happening. I turn and look around
nervously. I see at another line of urinals there are two
men standing next to each other, their arms crossed.

My throat goes dry and I simply stare down at my
limp dick. I shake it dry and get that involuntary post-
piss shiver. The sounds of the urinals flushing in unison,
rushing water from the sinks and hot air dryers echo
hollowly throughout the room. The man slyly eyeing my
cock looks similar to me: late twenties, dirty-blond hair,
wide jaw and neatly pressed suit. I tilt my head to the
side as if stretching my neck so I can get a look at what

he's clutching in his hand. His heavy cock rests in his palm surrounded by a few wiry pubic hairs. It's maybe half erect with veins already straining at the sides. He pushes the loose foreskin back and forth so the plump pink head is alternately revealed and hidden. I have an urge to flee, but something holds me in place. My heart beats rapidly. I swallow hard feeling his look, feeling his desire and tension from waiting for my response.

A backpacker wearing a bright red baseball cap comes in and steps up to the other line of urinals. The men stroking each other zip up and scatter like pigeons disturbed by someone jogging by. They wash their hands quickly and then stand at the hand dryers rubbing their hands together over and over. I see this out of the corner of my eye while staring at the wall, staring down at my exposed cock and then staring back at the wall.

One of the men at the hand driers tilts his head toward the stalls at the back. While the backpacker washes his hands, this man walks casually to the back of the room. The urinals automatically flush again and I stare back down at my cock. The man who was looking at me earlier raises his head to the ceiling and quietly whistles. The backpacker walks back through the turnstiles and the other man at the hand dryers goes to the stalls.

Sweat prickles the back of my neck, dampening the inside of my shirt collar. The normally toxic odors of urine and bleach create a tingling sensation in my gut. The man tucks himself in, steps up beside me and pulls his cock out again along with his bulbous pink testicles. He now stares openly and half turns to me, stroking himself with his mouth slightly open. His nearness combined with the feeling of danger and the rush of smells causes my cock to stiffen. He tilts his head motioning toward the stalls, zips himself up again and walks to the back.

It's crunch time. Susan must be wondering what has happened to me. It feels like I've only been down here a few moments, but when I look at my watch I see fifteen minutes have passed. Other men come in and piss near me. Memories of drunkenly fumbling in my teenage bedroom with my mate Turner and getting sucked off in the gym showers once flood through my mind. The pulse-quickening excitement of pure bestial sex and a need to get off take over and suddenly I don't care about continuing with the dreary day ahead of me. A couple more stolen moments in the toilets can hardly matter.

One stall door is half-open and I see the dirty-blond man facing the wall. Quickly I slip in beside him and lock the stall door. He leans forward to kiss me and I lean my head back in disgust. Instead, his mouth goes to my ear and his hot damp breath fills it. My eyes are shut and I feel his hard dick out in the open pressing against my arm. I unleash my own cock. My trousers puddle around my ankles. He slides down my body, and I skin back the foreskin of my dick. Precum has seeped out of the tip so the head is damp and full of sensation. I feed it to him and his eager sucking noises fill the stall. A big fistful of his dirty-blond hair is in my hand. I slam myself into his face, humping his mouth with urgency. My muscles tighten and I have to stop myself from moaning loudly at the intensity of this. His hands caress my thighs and grip my ass. I tighten my cheeks together to stop his fingers from worming their way into my hole. Nearing that climatic tingling I try to pull out, but his hands hold me insistently and his warm wet mouth is clamped around my dick. Pleasure floods through my body and I have an iron-tight grip on his head as I explode down his throat.

Swiftly I pull up my trousers and when I bend down I get a glimpse of pearly cum dripping from the corner of his mouth. There is also a damp cloudy puddle on the floor beneath his still-stiff cock. I can't look at his face as I hurry out of the stall. The atmosphere of the room seems charged with electricity as I rush through. I'm shook up and embarrassed walking unsteadily back up the stairs past waiting men whose eyes all seem trained on me now. The last dregs of sperm are slowly seeping out of my softening cock and making my underwear stick to my front.

My heartbeat slows back to a normal pace. Everything readjusts around me and looks calmly ordinary again as I walk back to the platform. In the waiting room Susan is on her mobile phone. From the way she is nodding her head and digging her heels into the floor I know she's speaking to her parents. Sylvan is crouched on the floor below her, hopping along slowly like a frog.

I grab him and lift him into the air, calling him my funny little frog.

"I'm not a frog! I'm the Easter Bunny!" he objects.

I sit down holding my son protectively on my lap.

Susan gets off the phone and asks what took me so long. Luckily, the loud voice overhead announces that we may now board our train for Norwich so we have to scramble to collect Sylvan and our things and there is no time to answer. We get on the train and walk down the aisle looking for empty seats that aren't reserved. By the time we find some, the train is already moving. I unconsciously glance at my watch and do a double take realizing I still haven't moved it forward an hour. I pull out the little dial on the side and hand the watch to Sylvan. He twists it around and around making the minute hand spin wildly. People walk down the aisle looking for seats together because it's quite crowded. A family walks past us: first two young girls, then a woman and then the suited man from the toilet stall. He's carrying a baby in his arms and says to the woman that maybe there are seats with a table in the next carriage. Suddenly, our lives are laid out brutally before us. I suppose we're all just perverts after all. He moves along and doesn't notice me, as I'm not real to him anymore.

AIN'T
ENOUGH TIME

Diesel King

I got to bust this nut. Spray this cum. Milk this bull. I spent the entire night in a hot, sweaty room with a large hand that has proven over and over again to be an unsatisfying lover.

It is near the brink of darkness, no longer night and not quite near daybreak. I am scouring the bushes of the park across the street to find something decent— purely ridiculous. I am too rich and too handsome to be on the prowl like this. I am too old and slightly graying to be doing this anymore. And yet I am too full of a youthful sex drive not to. I know exactly where to look. I know exactly where to cruise. I know that if there was a police sweep earlier, there is nothing out now but the second-rate prostitutes earning bail money for their first-rate friends. If not, I can have my pick of the litter, free of any monetary charges.

I cannot hit the bars because of the damn city ordi-
nance drastically rolling back the club hours. I cannot
hit the baths because they are frequently raided now by
undercover officers. I cannot phone someone to come
over—ain't enough time. I have an important meeting in
the morning, which means I cannot have my usual free-
for-all without the smell of condom or ass whiffing from
my dick hours later.

There is no moonlight, just a streetlight from the far
distance. I cannot see. It has been a very long time since I
have done this, too damn long. I make my way through
the maze based on the pure carefree memories of yester-
years. Once I know I am in a safe space, listening to the
subtle rumblings of wet mouths against moist skin and
pounding flesh pounding into more flesh, I unzip my
pants and let my swollen dick swing through.

The old parade route, I remember, peeling back my
shirt behind my head to show off my home-gym body.

A hand reaches out, followed by several more as I
pass through, a touch here and a touch there. One hand
is too hard, too rough, too calloused and too manly.
Another is too soft, too gentle, too smooth and too
girlie. Even if I find my right fit right off the bat, I cannot
immediately pull over to make inquiries. The point of
the strut is to get as many interested men out of hiding
to check me out, having the boldest of the bold pursue
my dangling participle. As the dust settles, I come across
some of the most beautiful of fucks; a number of them

too beautiful to be hiding in the darkness and shrubs. Others are so grotesque that they should never have left the zoo—much less the wild. As I mature into a salted goatee, I know that some of the best headhunters in the world are men who should never see the light of day.

So I do not flinch when this skinny eighteen-year-old with bad skin and buck teeth crosses my path. He reaches over to caress my piece, touching it like it is the first time he is touching another dick, no technique whatsoever. Again, this is not where I am looking for technique. I am very patient with him, although he proves to be trying. My final straw comes when he tries to press his cracked lips against mine. He is a guileless newbie looking for love in trade. For his benefit, I boorishly blow him off for this short, attractive bulldog-built guy.

He wastes no time in stroking my meat. He does not even fall to his knees. He just bends down to give it a quick tongue swab, turning around and bending over to expose his fine-looking light-skinned ass. He wants some dick; bareback or safe, he doesn't give a shit.

Any other day, man, any other day, I think, shaking my head. I would take it over behind the bushes and mark it as my territory before the glorious sunrise.

I don't have time to explain. I move on.

My many prospects from before dwindle into nothing. I am left with a hard dick, dubbed by the peepers as being too choosey.

As the seconds morph into a multitude of minutes, finding someone to suck my dick becomes increasingly hard. Deep throats and mouths for some reason have gone on strike, and asses have become their new union scabs. Never in my life have so many bastards wanted to come off their asses rather than their orals.

Time is running out.

I need to shoot some cream. Empty the trash. Haul some ashes. Get over that mountain. Paste the glue. Spew a load and jizz on a dream.

I am pulling at my dick as if it is a war cry. It is soon heard by this stunning guy with a phenomenal paunch that looks becoming. He will go down on me then and there, but I cajole him over behind the bushes just in case. His mouth is like a wet dream. He needs no extra coaching about working the head or inside the piss slit or thoroughly tongue-bathing the balls properly. He knows what he is doing. I just need to lean back against a tree and enjoy the ride. He receives even more encouragement when I put my hand on the top of his head.

"Damn, I want to fuck the shit out of you." The words slip through my lips.

"I don't get fucked," he announces, sorrowing.

"I didn't mean it. I can't have any ass on me."

He sucks me for a short while, then suggests, "Getting it between my thighs isn't getting ass."

I take his words into consideration. After some tender fondling I have him posted up against some old tree, humping away between his clamped thighs. The only thing that is stopping me is this small bit of hanging ass on the other side that I proudly blast my wad against.

I am satisfied. He seems satisfied because I am satisfied, but I want to make sure that he is satisfied by tugging on his dick. He tells me that he is all right—because there ain't enough time.

AFTERNOON DELIGHT

L. D. Madison

After glancing at the clock on the far wall, Jack looked around the university chemistry lab and began to put away his work. Even though he still had an hour left on his shift, the work in queue would require overnight observation and that was for the night shift to do.

Reaching into the specimen refrigerator, Jack pulled out a strawberry Popsicle from the box he kept hidden there. He knew that Dr. Harding frowned when he put food in there, but with the Miami heat melting everything in sight, there was no way he was going to live without his afternoon treat.

Licking the Popsicle as he skimmed one of the racing magazines, he kept an eye on the clock. He'd barely gotten started on his icy treat when his boyfriend, Scott, came into the lab looking hot and sweaty.

"You look like a five-year-old," Scott said, snickering as Jack kept licking his Popsicle. Putting away the chemicals he'd picked up during his errand run, the tall Hispanic came over and kissed him. "What am I thinking," he snorted, "you are a five-year-old."

Looking down at his treat, Jack narrowed his eyes. Every day, Scott would tease him about his choice of treats—and he was tired of it. Now he cast about for some way to shut his boyfriend up or at least make him think twice before he teased him again.

When the idea occurred to him, Jack had to bite his lip to prevent a chuckle from escaping. *He couldn't. No, really... But...it would definitely shut Scott up for good.*

Finishing his Popsicle, Jack reached into the minifridge and pulled out another, leaving this one unwrapped. Getting his small bottle of lube from the desk drawer, Jack put both items in his lab coat pocket and approached his boyfriend.

"Scott." Jack's voice was deceptively soft, and that should have scared his boyfriend.

"Yeah," Scott replied absently, going over the invoice and checking off the materials as he stored them.

"Remember the bet you lost yesterday, when you gambled on the Dolphins?"

"Yeah," Scott said, barely paying attention to him.

"I'm ready for my payment." It took all of Jack's willpower to stop from rubbing his palms together while he cackled in glee.

Whipping his head around, Scott looked at Jack. "What? Now?"

Raising an eyebrow wickedly, Jack nodded his head.

Noticing the evil expression on Jack's face, Scott swallowed hard. That particular look never boded well for him. He'd done some of the stupidest things in his life because of that look. "What do you want?"

"Come with me," he said, turning away and walking toward the overflowing supply closet. When he reached the door, he noticed that Scott was taking baby steps behind him. "Hurry up, you wuss."

Once inside the small, cramped room, Jack locked the door and turned to Scott. "Lean over the table and brace yourself."

"Not at work." Horrified, Scott gaped at Jack. "You wouldn't dare."

"Oh, but I would," Jack drawled, his voice heavy with power and authority. "If you welch on this, you'll owe me something even more substantial…like your scuba gear."

Jack and Scott had always been competitive and becoming boyfriends had not changed that one bit.

Scott was right to be afraid of Jack; the last time Jack had claimed his scuba gear, it had taken him a month of slave labor to earn it back. Despite his fear of getting caught having sex in the lab, nothing could be worse than losing his gear for a month.

Turning around, he bent over the table and placed his hands on the surface, all the while muttering curses in Spanish.

Quickly, Jack stepped in behind him and opened Scott's pants, lowering them to midthigh, leaving his boyfriend bare-assed in the cool, creepy room. Wrapping his fingers around Scott's cock, Jack stroked him expertly, doing everything he knew his boyfriend liked.

Scott bit his lip to stop a moan from escaping. Something told him that this little punishment was going to be fantastic; maybe it was just what he needed.

"Scott, you know how much you like to tease me about my afternoon Popsicle?" Jack asked softly, not ready to betray his nefarious intentions.

"Yeah. Popsicle," Scott moaned, loving the way his boyfriend was teasing his slit with every stroke.

"I'd really like you to stop that," Jack said, giving his boyfriend a chance to redeem himself.

"God, yes," Scott hissed. "You look so funny when… you suck…on it."

"Is that right?" Jack asked, unwrapping the Popsicle one-handed and using his teeth. With his warm hand, he parted Scott's buttocks, rubbing his entrance, watching as his boyfriend clenched and unclenched his entrance. Applying pressure on Scott's neck, Jack forced his boyfriend to bend over even farther over the table.

Laughing silently, Jack rubbed the tip of the Popsicle over Scott's hole.

"Jack, what the hell are you doing?" Scott yelled.

When he tried to straighten up, Jack held him down easily, putting his weight behind the hold. "Yes?" Jack asked innocently.

"Stop that!" Scott shouted. Again, he tried to move his hips away but Jack was relentless.

"Will you relax, it's only a Popsicle," Jack said, snorting. "We've done worse at home."

"Ohhh," Scott cried out, as he felt the Popsicle enter him little by little. Jerking his hips, Scott shivered at the feel of the ice cooling him from the inside. Closing his eyes, he threw his head back and moaned. They'd played around with other things before, but this was different. Reaching down, he stroked himself, surrendering to the thorough fucking Jack was giving him with the icy treat.

He was going to kill Jack...as soon as he recovered from this...

Tightening all of his muscles, Scott clenched around the melting Popsicle as he came all over his hand. Slumping forward against the table, Scott panted, unable to move a muscle.

He felt Jack clean him up as rivulets of cold, melted Popsicle trickled down his legs. Minutes later, his boyfriend had him tucked in and zipped up. Turning around, Scott leaned back against the table, shivering from the cold inside and out. "When I get my hands on you," he said, his voice raspy from all the shouting he'd done, "You're dead." He would have sounded more threatening if he'd been less sleepy or relaxed.

Jack laughed as he kissed his boyfriend languidly. "You can try, but I always win our bets."

Scott stayed behind for a few minutes to recover. By

the time he walked back into the lab, Jack was sitting at his desk, licking another Popsicle. He almost opened his mouth to say something, but he remembered what had happened the last time.

Quietly, he walked to his workstation, fidgeting as if he could still feel the icy treat in his ass. Without a single word, he got back to work.

Grinning, Jack looked around the lab and wondered what else he could use to torture his boyfriend at work.

SPURNED

Simon Sheppard

I guess it all started when I spotted your shoes: those handmade Prada loafers, ruby red as Dorothy's slippers, as the bleeding Sacred Heart of Jesus. I mean, I'll admit I'm a foot fetishist, but who *wouldn't* be attracted to a man with a fashion sense like yours? So I looked at you, you looked back at me, I felt my cock getting hard, and—presto—it was True Love. And within a few cum-drenched weeks, there I was, whisked from sitting beside my backpack on the Spanish Steps to being ensconced in a spiffy villa on the Amalfi Coast.

Yes, those Positano sunsets were enchanting enough, but those nights, ah, those nights. We fucked, we ate ripe strawberries—red as your shoes, red as the shiny, half-revealed head of your prick—drenched in clotted cream, the juices running down over our bodies, down to erect dicks, and then we fucked again. I was, dare I say it, in Heaven.

Moonlit nakedness with you was endless, sacred joy. I gobbled down your sweet, salty sperm like it was the Savior's blood. And you fucked me. You fucked me so good. You could perform miracles with that hard, throbbing thing of yours. I'd always thought of myself as nothing but a top, but when you speared me with your swelling scepter, I was hooked. Sometimes you'd even let me wear your fanciest outfits; try on those lovely shoes, like a small boy doing mommy drag. And I knew, knew then for certain, that I would stake my salvation on you. You were my very own guardian angel, my saint. Like the old Calvin Klein cologne ads said: "Eternity...The smell of it!"

And if we had to keep our affair on the down low, well, I understood. You had your job to protect, a job that kept previously impecunious me in tiramisu and Valpolicella.

Okay, I suppose I was a fool; a fool to ever believe in eternal love. But still, the fall from grace, when it came, was hard and swift. You got your new job, rose in the ranks, and I was left behind.

You could have just quietly dropped me. Instead, you went public. You began to talk about how people like me are a threat to peace, how I was helping to destroy the family, even that my kind was to blame for global warming. Protesting, as the saying goes, too much. I knew, of course, that all that was ridiculous, that you just were forced into saying those absurd and hateful things because of your job, because someone in your position could never be suspected of keeping a stud like me in a villa by the sea.

And, romantic fool that I am, I couldn't help but want you still. You could disuse me, refuse me, verbally abuse me. But in a funny way, that only made me love you more. I continued to believe that my only hope of salvation was through you. You and your divine dick.

Old story, right? Old as Adam and Steve. Perhaps— no almost certainly—I should have moved on, found someone else. But instead I mooned around, lit candles to you, even started stalking you. I'd try to bribe your advisors to get an audience with you. At first they said that they'd ask you, but after a while they, like you, refused to even talk to me. So I began showing up at your personal appearances. When, on Sunday mornings at St. Peter's Square, you strode masterfully onto the balcony, there was always one guy—one lonely, longing, and though perhaps I shouldn't mention it, excessively well-hung young man—standing in the near distance carrying a placard that read, I LOVE YOU, DARLING. PLEASE COME BACK. Remember? That was me. See, even then I had faith in your innate goodness. Call me "objectively disordered" all you like, but I knew that if only you could hear the truth…

Only the attacks didn't cease. If anything, they grew worse. And when you denounced gay men as "gravely immoral," I knew you were talking about me in particular, as though insults could erase the memories of those nights spent fucking between your 1500-thread-count sheets.

But the heart is a lonely, even stupid, hunter, and none of that made, in the final analysis, any difference. You know that gay cowboy movie, how one of them said to the other, "I wish I could quit you but I can't," or something like that? Well, I knew how he felt. I sought help from a group of queer Catholics, thinking they could wean me from your spell. But they, despite everything, were, like me, strangely besotted by you. "He'd be infallible," they moaned, "except for that...one... little...thing."

And that's when I came up with my plan. I would make one last brave attempt to tell you how I felt. And so on Christmas Eve I made my way to St. Peter's; to where I knew you were going to be. I positioned myself at the barricades, staring up at the dome designed by the divine, divinely gay Michelangelo, and I prayed for guidance.

And that's when I heard God's basso voice thundering, "DO it!" and then a choir of angels sang and when you and your entourage approached, you crowned in glory, wearing your lovely red shoes, I said one more Ave Maria and launched myself over the barricade and up into the cool night air and it was as if I were flying, ascending to my love. Soaring, soaring, my dick surprisingly, shockingly erect. But when I landed on you, flesh to flesh, I could only blurt out, "I adore..." before I was tackled and roughly pinned to the ground.

Later they said I was trying to harm you—a lie—as if anything I could do to you could match the hurt you'd inflicted on me, in any case. And some tried to say I was mad, though we both know that hearing the voice of God makes you holy, not insane.

So now here I sit in my jail cell, alone with my hard-dick dreams of you. I think of you after lights out and jack off. I lick my sperm from my hand, bittersweet as my memories of you. Sometimes, like Tosca, I want to throw myself to my death, but they make prison bars stronger these days. Most of the time, though, I'm quite content to pray and meditate on your glory. I know whatever evil comes from your mouth is the speech of the devil, not you. And I still remember what an amazing fuck you were.

No, my love, no one will ever understand my undying devotion. And that's okay. I live for art. I live for love.

I live for you, in dignity.

Because the world knows you as Benedict, but you'll always be Joey Ratz to me.

JEFF AND SAM: BIG COUNTRY BREAKFAST

Jeff Mann

I set the Styrofoam cups on the dresser before double-locking the door. Sam's naked, lying on his back, a black leather blindfold strapped over his eyes. He's snoring softly, tangled in the sheets. Opening the window drapes a bit, I look out on gray clouds sifting February snow, a creek winding over stones, waterside sycamore trees.

I sit on the bed's edge and study Sam. Pretty soon this concert tour will be over. I'll be back to my lone-wolf existence and he to his pretty wife and his three cute daughters. They'll have me over for dinner some-times. Sam's specialty is spaghetti and meatballs; Hope's is roast turkey with cornbread stuffing. It'll hurt a little, watching them together. I'll be careful not to drink too much, so I can maintain self-control, keep my hands off him. He and I will manage a few trysts in hotel rooms like this one, once or twice a month. We'll see each other at the studio—there's a new CD to record. Otherwise, he'll live his life; I'll live mine. That's fine. It's all worked for ten years. I believe him when he says he loves us both. Hell, I love her too.

Sam rolls over on his belly, starts up snoring again. I run my hand along his muscled back, the pale curves of his fur-dusted ass. Such soft skin atop such dense strength. The boy works out constantly. Country-music sex symbols have to. Me, I'm the guitar player, just another member of his band, the gray-bearded, leather-vested bear in the back, diddling those Martin strings while Big Star Sam gyrates before me, wiggling and shaking that perfect marvel of a butt as the horny audience howls.

I finger the hair between Sam's asscheeks: thick and tasty. All the times I've been up inside him—makes me believe in God.

Sam sighs. "Morning." He arches his rear a little, reaches back and spreads his buttocks: sweet tacit invitation. I bend, run my tongue up his crack, probe his hole.

"What time's it?" His mumble is muffled by pillow.

"About ten," I say between tastes. His cleft-hair tickles my nose. "Fetched us some coffee from the lobby. Ain't too bad. You hungry?"

"Yeah. But my head hurts. Too much damn Bud Light last night." Sam pulls his cheeks wider. I work my tongue deeper. We're silent for a while, except for my soft happy growls and his soft happy sighs.

"I finally found that damn lube. I really need to fuck

you, Sam." I tug off my cowboy boots, unzip my jeans, haul out my hard-on. Beneath a pillow, I fetch soft black leather straps. Gently I cross his wrists behind him and knot them together.

"Can't, man. I'm still too sore from last night." Sam chuckles. "You're real big, I'm real tight, you just used spit, took my ass too fast. Then you let me drink too much. Now I'm hurting at both ends. No butt-fucking for you, buddy. Price you pay for ruthlessly raping me backstage."

With a second strap I bind his ankles. "I was over-eager. Sorry. You just...all that hot sweat, and the smell of you." I kiss a buttock. "I just had to get up your ass, and with no lube and little time...You said you wanted it. I'm really, really sorry."

"I did want it. Wanted it bad. No big deal, Jeffy."

"Don't call me Jeffy!" I give the same asscheek a little slap. I'm sounding stern, but we both know his silly nicknames make me melt with thanks.

"Jeffy, how about I blow you instead? How about you give me a big country breakfast?"

I need no further coaxing. I position us on our sides. Sam takes my cock head in his mouth, nibbles it, then gulps my length down his throat. He bobs and sucks, drool coursing down his bearded chin, down my taut flesh.

"Umm MM mmm mm MMmmm mm MMM!" The boy loves to speak with my dick crammed in his mouth. Half the time I can even figure out the garble.

I hand-cup the back of his head, pull him onto me, hold him there till he's choking, then let him surface for air. "What was that?"

"I said, I always love me some steak and eggs in the morning."

"Shut up and suck." I tousle his hair, then roughly push his head back down onto me. I fuck the sweet tight sheath of Sam's lips, slow and deep, fondling the faint gray featherings in his beard, tugging his stiff nipples. What is it about beauty aging that makes it more precious, more endearing?

Sam slobbers and groans; I thrust and sigh. No rush today; we can take our time. When I do come, after a long, luxurious ride, Sam clamps his mouth around my cock-base, greedily gulping every drop.

I let my dick grow soft before pulling out. "Your turn." Retrieving his white briefs from the floor, I stuff them in his mouth. "Woof!" Sam grunts. I slide down his body, suck his tits till his hurt's a tenor keening. Sliding farther, I swallow his cock; start a deep and steady rhythm. Sam hammers my mouth as hard and mercilessly as I hammered his ass last night. I caress his crack-fuzz; I stroke his hole, nudge in a mouth-moistened fingertip, very carefully, so as not to hurt him further. In a few minutes, his body goes taut, his lean hips are bucking wildly against my face, he's shouting into his mouthful of cloth, and I'm the lucky one gulping down a load.

For a few minutes we lie there, drained. I pull out his

makeshift gag, remove his bonds, and spoon him from behind.

"God, that was hot. I love this," Sam sighs, snuggling into my embrace. "I love you."

"Tour's over in a few weeks," I say.

"Yep." There's all the stoicism of Southern history in that sound.

"Head still hurting?"

"A little, yeah."

"We got all day. Don't need to leave till tomorrow. I told the boys you needed some alone-time bad. There's a Cracker Barrel down the road. How about you stay here and snooze a little more and I fetch us some vittles? We could spend the rest of the day in bed, cuddling and watching shitty TV. What would you like to eat?"

Sam takes my hand in his, squeezing it. "You know what I like, Daddy."

"Yep, sure do." I slip the blindfold back over his eyes. Rising, I zip up; pull on my boots, my jacket and my baseball cap.

"I'll take care of you, Sam. I'll always take real good care of you."

Sam doesn't hear me. He's already snoring, hugging a pillow, exhausted from weeks on the road. Very gently I kiss his forehead and tuck him in. I close the door behind me, as softly as possible, so as not to wake him. Around the doorknob I hang the DO NOT DISTURB sign before heading out into the fine fall of snow to fetch my beautiful boy breakfast.

COCKSUCKER
IN JAIL

Bearmuffin

How I got put in jail is not important but what happened to me there is. It was my first offense so the judge had to see me within twenty-four hours or let me go. My adventure took place in the infamous Glass House in downtown Los Angeles.

The guards put me in the "queens' tank" which is where they put gays, drag queens and anybody else they think is a freak. The guards laughingly referred to us as "ladies." They seemed to get a kick out of calling us that. The butch studs were kept in cells on the second floor so they couldn't mix with us. The guards always referred to them as "gentlemen."

The guards took away my glasses for safety's sake probably thinking that I might commit suicide with the lenses. But they were made of plastic, which shows you how much they know.

I remember the little banter the guards had between themselves when I handed them my specs. "So what does he need his glasses for?" asked one guard, to which his smartass buddy replied, "To better see the cock dangling in front of him." I felt like saying, "I'll bet I wouldn't need glasses to see your big cock, would I, officer?" But I thought better of it. Of course if I had it might have resulted in a hot session with two or maybe even three of them, but that's not the way it happened so there it is.

I had been warned that the queen's tank would be safer for me. Otherwise I ran the risk of being raped by the other inmates who were mostly Latin and black men. The prospect of fucking these men was tempting. But since I'm not into rape I agreed to be put into the queen's tank. As it turned out I had just as much fun there as anywhere else. I fucked a young Texas drifter, a black dude and a robber.

The Texas drifter (I'll call him Don) was a boyishly handsome nineteen-year-old with long blond hair, friendly blue eyes and a mischievous smile. Don spoke with a sexy Texas drawl. He didn't say why he was in jail. He just said that he pretended to be gay so he could fuck. "I love to fuck gay boys!" And Don fucked me royally! He laid me on my side, pumped me hard until my eyeballs almost fell out of their sockets and then shot his sweet Texas wad into my asshole. Then Don hopped off my cot and went on to the next trick.

I'll call the black dude Leroy. I woke up the next morning with Leroy's big cock in my mouth. He was standing by my cot, feeding me his cock, humping his hips back and forth. It didn't take Leroy very long to cum either. I guess he was either horny or just wanted to get it over with before the guards caught him. Leroy's cum-wad was so big that it flooded my mouth and stained the bed. I even had to wipe my shirt off. After that Leroy hurried back to the far end of the queen's tank where his cot was.

Just then there was an uproar in the queen's tank. One of the Hispanic drag queens accused a guard of forcing her to have sex. Supposedly this incident took place the night before. She was bragging about it and said that the guard's cum was "hotter than the water from the pipes." She made a big stink. So the guards and prison officials came around to question anybody who would back up her story. About an hour later she was dragged off kicking and screaming. I never saw her again.

Around 8:00 a.m. I was taken downstairs to be transferred to the bus that was supposed to take me to court. I was handcuffed to three big Mexican-Americans. One of them was dressed in a blue suit and had a gold tooth. He was the one who started talking to me. I'll call him Miguel. I told Miguel that I was freaking out. I was scared because I'd never been in jail before. He grinned and said that he would take care of me. Miguel said the three of them were in jail for robbery. He was handsome in a rugged and macho way but not obnoxious or homophobic. He seemed to have taken a liking to me and treated me with respect.

Since I was chained to them I assumed we were being taken to the same court. We were placed in the back of the bus. Miguel told his buddies to sit in front of us. We were linked together with a thick chain but they managed to do it so the guards couldn't see Miguel and me.

Miguel waited until the bus started moving and then pulled out his cock. He told me to suck it. His cock was fat, brown and crisscrossed with thick, blue veins. Miguel was uncut so I pulled back the foreskin to lick the fat cock head, which was as wide as a doorknob. Miguel didn't seem nervous. He laid his hands on my head as I sucked him, taking his cock all the way down my throat while I squeezed his big, fat balls. Just before we got to court, he came in my mouth. The cum just kept on spurting out of his cock. But I managed to swallow all his cum since it was so tasty.

Everybody was hustled into the receiving room. And that's where I was separated from Miguel and his buddies and put into a separate room. While I waited to be called up in front of the judge I wondered if I'd ever see Miguel again. I could still taste his sweet, tangy cum in my mouth and the odor of his pubes was still in my nose. Just thinking about blowing that con got me hard again, but I managed to control myself before the bailiff called me into court.

I was released with no probation. A few months later, I happened to be in that same court to pay a parking ticket and that's when I saw Miguel again. He said he was surprised to see me, and I said I thought he had been put in prison. He said, "No, I got a good attorney." "You still my girl?" he asked me. I said sure. He was rubbing his crotch and smiling. Miguel told me to go into the men's restroom with him.

I thought he was crazy but I wanted to suck his cock again so I went in with him. I sat down in one of the stalls and he pulled down his zipper and out popped his cock good and hard and ripe for sucking. I pulled back the foreskin and licked the head. Then I sucked on his cock for a while until he was moaning and groaning. Then I sucked on his balls while he jacked off. He jacked off until he finally shot a heavy cum-wad that splattered all over my face.

I wondered what would have happened if Miguel and I had wound up in the same cell in prison. He was a nice guy actually and we probably would have had a great time. But I never saw him again, and I probably never will. I've stayed on the right side of the law ever since.

A GAME OF SHIRTS VERSUS SKINS

Gregory L. Norris

Fresh sweat tumbled down Aaron's unshaved chin. The warmth of the first decent day that Spring gusted over him, carrying the smell of the burgeoning green around the basketball court along with the scent of athletic male bodies, pumped up and perspiring—his sweat; Lindsey's, too.

Focusing, Aaron moved in closer, shadowing the dark-haired man's moves intimately, skin against skin, sweat and scent colliding, mixing into a narcotic, magnificent haze. Aaron blocked the shot, recovered, pivoted, fired. The ball sailed through Lindsey's groping hands, bounced off the backboard, took a spin around the rim and dropped through.

"Fuck, yeah," Aaron said.

"Fuck *you*," Lindsey chuckled. He grabbed the ball and dribbled.

"Later, if you insist." Aaron strutted over to his water bottle, aware of the swell of his balls with the steps, the *sweat* of them. A warm breeze whispered over the glistening flesh of his bare arms and hairy legs. He reached down, scratched his nuts through the fabric of his camouflage cutoffs and damp boxer-briefs. Aaron's meaty twins felt as big as the basketball, its hollow *clang* off the time-blanched blacktop carrying through the afternoon air with a reassuring cadence. He gulped a sip of water, pulled the bottom of his T-shirt up to mop at his face, and when he looked again, two dudes in baseball caps and shorts, sneakers, no socks, were standing on the court, shooting dirty looks.

Thing One was tall, with puppy-dog eyes and a trim, tanned physique, smooth on the patch of chest visible around his black wife-beater, his legs dark with pelt. Thing Two balanced a basketball reverse-scoop, like some arrogant French waiter might hold a serving tray. He didn't look much brighter than his counterpart; young, early twenties maybe. Their scowls, meant to intimidate, brought a smile to Aaron's face. He tipped his chin in that universal greeting among males, the one that normally makes instant bros and buddies of strangers on a baseball diamond, a football field or a hoops court. In this case, however, the gesture failed.

"You gonna hog the place much longer?" Thing One didn't so much ask as demand.

Lindsey ceased dribbling and strutted over. "That depends, I guess."

"On what?" This from Thing Two.

"On whether you're willing to suck my hog, dude."

Aaron snorted a chuckle. The look of insult at the assumed disrespect followed by macho roostering restored his smile. The two dudes postured. Thing Two dropped the ball. They started over, their expressions hardened into typical tough-guy game faces—so like the young grunts Staff Sergeant Aaron Bullen routinely broke, reshaped and fine-tuned into real men and true soldiers.

He stepped between Lindsey and the charging young tigers and held up his hands, creating a barrier between opponents. Both sides dug in their heels. "Hold on, now. This is just some friendly hoops court banter. Guy talk. No reason to go to war over it. There's enough of the real thing out there in the world as it is."

Thing One shifted from his right foot to his left. "You think we're gonna take that kind of shit from him?"

"Yeah, and you dudes have been out here *manipulating* the net," Thing Two added.

"That's *monopolizing*, you ignorant sac of low-hanging nuts," Lindsey corrected.

Thing Two puffed up his chest and tested Aaron's barricade. "I'm ignorant? What? *What*?"

Aaron straightened. At six-one, his body a lean mass of ropey muscles that was not to be fucked with, both Things retreated, though only so far.

"My buddy and I have as much right to use the net as you," Aaron said. "But if you're so hot to show us your stuff, why don't you turn our game of one-on-one into some two-on-two? Prove you've got the biggest sets of balls out here, at this very moment."

"And if we beat your geriatric hillbilly asses," Thing Two said, bookending the statement with a laugh delivered on a sigh meant to belittle, "what then? We get to kick you to the curb?"

Aaron shrugged. "Sounds fair, but just for the record, technically he's the only hillbilly here." He tipped his chin at Lindsey. "I grew up here, just up the road in La Jolla. And my boy Lindsey here's on the front side of thirty, so he won't be getting the senior discount for a few decades."

Thing One ran an eye up and down Aaron's body, from his silvering jarhead haircut to his big feet in his well-worn sneakers. "How long until they let you into the movies on the cheap, grandpa?"

"Son," Aaron snickered, "your balls are gonna shrivel up long before mine do."

Aaron shook his junk for effect. Lindsey was waiting for the low-five he delivered with the same set of fingers once they released their choke hold.

"Fuck off," said Thing One.

Thing Two said, "Fine, you're on. We win, we get the court and bragging rights. Not that it's going to happen, but what do you two want in the off chance you beat us? Someone to push your wheelchairs home?"

Aaron said, "I think my buddy here already summed it up decently: we humiliate you, which is the only scenario that's going to play out in this matchup, and you and your pal wrap your pouty, pretty lips around our dicks and hum."

Aaron smiled. All arrogance washed out of their adversaries' faces, leaving only young male anger, righteous and blind.

Lindsey moved closer, and Aaron caught the other man's scent, male and magnificent, on his next sip of breath. "I know it's early, but I'm claiming that one." He indicated Thing Two with his thumb.

"Good, because I like the other one. Real *purdy*. Of course, that's assuming that they actually man up and don't forget to follow through. I wouldn't blame them if they ran. You and me, we're a couple of studs, real forces of nature." Aaron slapped the taut six-pack of Lindsey's abdomen.

Thing One retrieved their basketball from the ground. Thing Two protested.

"Come on," Thing One countered.

"But Michael, *dude!*"

"The day anyone disrespects us like that and we let them get away with it, we deserve to lose. And that ain't gonna happen."

Aaron exchanged a silent look with Lindsey before peeling off his shirt, exposing the T-pattern of coarse hair that cut him across his pecs and down the middle, pausing only to make a circle around his naval. The situation taking place beside him was equally spectacular; Lindsey wasn't as hairy, but no less ripped.

Their dog tags jingled and glinted.

"This is going to be fun," Lindsey said.

Aaron only grinned in response. He wiped his face on his sweaty shirt and tossed it. The air smelled of his sweat and Lindsey's, and something else less tangible. Fear, he realized. And maybe just the barest trace of excitement on the part of their opponents.

"Let's get this sausage-fest started," Lindsey chuckled.

Aaron assumed the position close to Thing One, who bounced the ball, his back turned. The cute, tall fucker attempted to pass to his good buddy, Thing Two, but deft maneuvers by Aaron soon landed him the basketball. He faked it to Lindsey, broke free, bounced, and shot: two points.

Twenty points later, the game was effectively over, and Aaron stood in the bushes, unzipping his pants. A warm breath spilled over his ripe, loose nuts. Thing One's fingers extricated his thickness from his underwear.

"Pucker up, son," he sighed.

Aaron half closed his eyes and savored the spoils of that day's victory.

SWITCH

Daniel W. K. Lee

Yeah, my hefty cock was bitchin' to be fed after seeing Alex, the new inmate, lather every jagged inch of his brown body in the showers. Through the blurring steam, I could still see all the clean cuts that defined the massive slabs of his pecs and the indentations of his torso, which tapered down to the V-shaped muscle plate leading to his cock. But his cock, his midthigh-length, thick serpent, made me bite hard on my lip. Seeing how his gourmet ass flexed, I knew that past the hardness of the cheeks, past the gloved grip of his untampered-with hole, was soft fuck-flesh like the inside of a honeydew.

Sweat. Steam. Men. Every shower made my eight inches rage, ooze, beg for a piece like Alex. I walked toward his humming body from behind. A quetzal tattoo, tiny loop earrings, black hair with a serviceman cut and the cleaved ripples of his upper back came into view. My tense shaft bobbed like a drooling cobra, leading a jolting tackle that pinned him: one hand restraining his neck, forehead against the wall, ass clenched—as if it mattered—breathing like each hard gulp would be his last. My other hand grabbed a fistful of ass then kneaded it slightly between my fingers. Oh, yeah, his ass was ripe.

I dismissively kicked his legs apart; snarled in his ear, "Scream if you want. No one cares even if they hear you." For a moment, I could smell his natural musk no soap could wash away. He smelled like cumin, guajillo chilies and sex. Looking down briefly to route my cock between his coy crack, suddenly my chin hit the tile floor with my arm jammed behind my back.

"Good!" he spat. He moved above me and crouched. His villainous rod reached beyond the length of my cleft and spanked the top of my smooth globes, leaving a thick thread of precum on the slight slope to the small of my back.

"So you wanna fuck me? How about I fuck you?" With that, he raw-rammed his damp agitated tool so deep into my surprised ass it knocked my voice out of its box. He ground his pelvis to make more room in me for him, then tore back out and pounded back in. My jaw dropped, my eyes rolled back, and little stuttered sounds escaped my throat as if it too felt the crashing force in my interior. He began moving in and out in short thrusts, pulling out and pushing back in a little farther each time. I felt his warhead pushing against my prostate, and slowly the pain bled into pleasure.

I was panting, gasping, desperately trying to swallow the trembles knifing through my belly at this drilling obelisk of fuck rhythms. Just when I tried to relax my body to steal more pleasure, Alex yanked me up by the hair, bent me over in the shape of a gun and held on still pumping inside me like a greasy piston.

Harder and harder he thudded against my burning bottom. Louder and louder his moans and curses got. "Oh, yeah! Oh, yeah! Oh, FUCK yeah!" he grunted. Oily bullets of sweat flung off him and rolled down my back. Faster and faster he slammed, then slowly, slowly... gyrating, thumping, banging...bucking...banging.

"You love it..." he growled, again withdrawing completely then plunging back in. I said nothing.

"You love it! Say it!" he shouted and trounced me as before.

"SAY IT!" he yelled and then cursed and barraged my asshole with jackhammer power mixed in with loud breathing and another "Oh, fuck yeah!"

"SAY IT!" he roared, letting go of my twisted arm and hair and placing his hands firmly on my waist to steady me.

"Fuck you! Ride me you piece of shit!" I ripped back. He rushed in me like an avalanche, like a needy army, his cock a welcomed invasion. Every line and curve of his savage dick I knew through his desire-swelling force fitting. The rougher he tried, the more defiant I got, saying, "Is that all you can do, pussy boy?"

Alex replaced his hands on my shoulders and dug his thumbs into my back. I leaned forward while he pulled back, and deliberately collided with his pelvis. Again and again I hammered back against his straining legs. My back arched into a wide shallow bowl. Every atom in my body shook as the clap of my fevered rounds met his upper thighs. I could see in backward glances how the blocks of ab muscles tightened and released, how the veins in his neck fattened when his head leaned back as though drowning in my fucking.

Yes, *my* fucking.

I thought of his smugly curled lip and imagined his mouth swallowing my tool like an eager child with a Popsicle in the middle of July. Sucking, licking, slurping so not a drop would be lost; Alex's mouth would blow me just as reverently—on his Catholic knees, awaiting a new host. I grabbed my tense prick and made long, slow, tight strokes from base to tip. I hastened, twisted my nipples with my free hand, and the pleasure became more maddening. As I was clamping down on Alex's anaconda with my ass muscles, from his mouth came the faint stuttered sounds my own throat had leaked before. "Oh, god! Oh, god! Oh, god!" he hollered as the sounds and heat of our bodies became a frantic drumming of flesh against flesh, beat against beat, fuck against fuck.

Alex's thighs began to stiffen, his breath shuddered and he shoved me off his cock as I too was about to cum.

As I turned up from the floor to face him, waves of ecstasy crested in our sacs until relentless gushes of fiery, milky cum detonated in intoxicating unison all over my heaving chest.

Alex fell to his knees between mine and looked at me with half-closed eyes; no smile, no grin. His assaulted body left sheets of sweat and his musk rose into the steam: cumin and cum.

"Lick me clean!" I commanded, my cock starting to engorge again. Hungry, he finally came to feast.

WHAT
SPRINGS UP

Michael Bracken

Every spring the community garden in my neigh-borhood brings together green thumbs and brown thumbs, all intent on growing our own produce within blocks of our townhouses. I enjoy the fresh air and the opportunity to interact with my neighbors, but what I enjoy most is watching Nicolas Carter.

He's broad shouldered and thick chested, with a trim waist and six-pack abs that he's earned through several years of spring gardening and winter workouts at the gym. He wears his sandy hair in a short brush cut and his pale blue eyes are always sparkling with amusement. When he's in the garden, he wears cargo shorts and work boots, and more often than not his T-shirt is slung over the fence or lying in a heap on the ground at the end of his plot. His chest and back are quite smooth and

I suspect that's more a matter of personal grooming than genetics. Often the first in the community garden on Saturdays and Sundays, he's always available to assist the other gardeners.

I'm not much of a gardener and my little plot, despite my best efforts, is often among the least productive. I usually tend my plot Saturday mornings, but one Saturday this past May I was called into the office and didn't reach the community garden until late in the evening. The sun was already setting by the time I retrieved my gloves and hand tools from the shed where we all kept our gardening supplies in assigned cubbyholes, but soon I was on my knees in the dirt.

I thought I was alone in the garden and had weeded half of one row of scraggly tomato plants when a pair of boots appeared in front of me. Startled, I looked up to see Nicolas standing before me, wearing only his boots and cargo shorts, his T-shirt hanging half out of one pocket. I straightened up, but remained on my knees, my face mere inches from the bulge at the crotch of the taller man.

"You look like you could use some help," he said.

The bulge in his shorts seemed to be enlarging, and I wet my lips before answering. "Do you have the right tool?"

He smiled. "There's only one way to find out."

We were obviously thinking the same thing. I removed my gloves and reached for his zipper.

"Not out here," Nicolas said. He took my hand and

helped me to my feet. "The toolshed."

He led me into the shed and closed the door behind us, leaving us in near darkness. The only light filtered in through the gap around the door, but it was enough for what we were about to do.

"I've been watching you all Spring," Nicolas said, "and I know you've been watching me."

He pulled me into his muscular arms and covered my mouth with his. He smelled earthy and musky, and his kiss was deep and penetrating. I felt his cock growing against me through our clothing.

When our kiss ended, I dropped to my knees on the shed's dirt floor, unfastened his cargo shorts and let them drop to his ankles. Nicolas had gone commando under the shorts and his tumescent cock slapped my cheek. I wrapped one hand around the thick stem to hold it steady and took the swollen purple blossom into my mouth. I watered it with spit and then slowly took every inch of his dick into my mouth until his soft crotch hair tickled my nose.

When I felt Nicolas begin to tense, I grabbed his asscheeks and pulled his crotch tight to my face. With his cock head pressed against the back of my throat he came hard, and I swallowed every drop of his hot cum.

Nicolas wasn't done with me, though. When his cock stopped spasming in my mouth, he pulled me to my feet and spun me around. After I unfastened my pants, dropped them to the dirt floor and stepped out of them, he bent me over a wheelbarrow, grabbed a bottle of hand lotion one of the older women kept in her cubby-hole next to her sunbonnet and squirted it on his hands. Then he ran his slick fingers up and down the furrow of my asscrack, repeatedly teasing my bunghole. Finally, he slipped a finger in, and then a second, preparing me for the garden tool to come.

He slathered more lotion on his rejuvenated cock and pressed its head against my ass pucker. When I pressed back against him, letting him know I was ready, he planted his cock deep inside me. Then he held on to my hips and plowed into my ass hard, fast and deep. Before long the wheelbarrow rolled out from beneath me. I thought I would fall, but Nicolas wouldn't let that happen. He just gripped me tighter and continued plowing into me.

My cock had grown hard and needed attention. I wrapped my fist around it and stroked hard and fast, never quite in rhythm to the gardener behind me.

Nicolas came first, plowing into my ass one last time. He held me tight against him as he fired a thick stream of hot cum into me.

And then I came, spewing cum over the wheelbarrow that was now just out of arm's reach.

We stood together in the darkness of the toolshed until Nicolas's cock finally stopped spasming. Then he pulled away and I turned to face him.

When we had caught our breath, Nicolas said, "You ready to get to those weeds?"

We dressed, finished weeding my little plot and then

went our separate ways. I didn't see him all that week.

When I arrived at the community garden the following Saturday morning, half-a-dozen people had already surrounded Nicolas, asking his advice on compost and fertilizer and other gardening topics.

He nodded to me as I walked past, and when I returned from the shed with my gloves and my hand tools, he interrupted his conversation to ask if I needed any help.

"Maybe later," I told him with a wink. "I have something in my garden that keeps coming up."

SLEEPER LOVE

R. Talent

The chat lines are full of them: white boys hungry for *Mandingo* dick. What? Never heard it put so blunt? Let's just call it what it is. Bubby the Big Black Burly Truck Driver doesn't mind. He knows firsthand that driving cross-country throughout the lower forty-eight states all alone can leave a man dripping with pure testosterone awfully horny. He is blessed to be hung like a work mule. He knows what he's got and he knows how to fucking use it! He isn't in the business to be anybody's black man fantasy, so much as he's always looking to get his dick milked by some tight hole he can stretch well beyond oblivion. If it happens to be one in the same, so be it. As long as he gets his middle leg well taken care of, who gives a shit? He can't be mad. Like them, he's got preferences of his own too. But the black boys and the brown boys are harder to come by on the line. There are even fewer than that nearby whenever he needs one to grab ahold of their ankles. Fewer than that can sneak away without being missed, those fortunate enough to be mobile and without baby momma drama. So he doesn't player hate or discriminate.

It isn't even insulting or uncommon when he hears a corny white boy say, "I've never been with a black man before."

Bubby the Big Black Burly Truck Driver doesn't care one bit. He knows that it is just part of the M.O., just like when he says he is big and black, it must be backed up by a dick worthy of its own freak show to be savored and remembered for years to come: blue black and uncut; beer-can thick and ruler long with a flared mush-room head bolted to the tip and big low-hanging balls that sag like an old pair of crumpled titties.

It is a part of the grand old dance. That is unless they admit to being a bona fide black-cum whore right out the gate. It isn't like it matters either way. It isn't like this is about preferences or want. It is purely about need, the need to get his load off. The white boys flood the line and know their way to the truck stop. They are hungry for dick—the bigger the better—down the throat and up the poop chute. They are turned on by the taboo of black skin. To be with a black man is exotic and new, sometimes daring and risky, given the awful stuff of violence and rape seen in the news.

"That would be hot," a baited white boy says, giving

a detailed account of his deepest, darkest desires. "I want you to slap the shit out of me if I can't take it like a good pussy bitch!"

"Right across the face, sweetheart," Bubby grins, groping himself, "just come through with those panties on like you said."

Bubby gives him the locale where he parks his eighteen-wheeler and specific instructions as to exactly where they are to meet.

The white boy shows up ten minutes early. Bubby knows who he is right off the bat. Even without the description, Bubby sees that his eyes are on the prowl and his mouth a drooling mess anxious for the first black man to cross his path.

As the white boy peeks around the corner scoping out another black man who happens to be there, Bubby is right behind him, covering his sweet mouth and body with his large mitts and pressing his hard denim-encased dick alongside his back.

Bubby tells the boy to be quiet. He is just going to take him over to the side of his truck to look him over. The boy obliges nodding, clearly flushed with excitement and fear.

The white boy looks to be a freshman still in dick-riding school, eager to start his career in the dick-riding rodeo. After some confirmation, Bubby discovers he has twenty years over the boy.

He is legal, but still. He's just a babe.

Bubby was a full-grown man, thirty-nine years old,

about to lead this fresh-faced skater punk to slaughter.

He was playing on the line. A man got needs. The punk got to learn some time.

Bubby looks down at the pink lace sticking out of the top of his pants.

He's definitely freaked. At least he isn't a virgin.

Bubby gets a feel of where his head is at by dry-humping the boy against the side of his sleeper. He listens to everything, his breathing and his tone, casually whispering in his ear. He takes it a step further by reaching under his shirt and copping a tweak at his nipples.

This boy is hot and popping like a firecracker!

Bubby pulls off, tossing him like a rag doll to the side. He climbs up into his truck and undoes his pants. He wants to give the boy fair warning of what he is signing up for. The boy gulps and gasps and thanks the starry skies above for coming prelubed.

"Open up, bitch," Bubby tells him, sitting on the edge of his sleeper bed.

The boy coyly opens his mouth and swallows eagerly, displaying his very talented skills. Up and down, in and out, Bubby is gripping the side of his face and pushing him down on his lap. The boy isn't anywhere near gagging on his big dick, turning Bubby on tenfold.

"Oh, damn, a sweet pretty mouth!" Bubby groans, ready to shoot.

"Don't shoot in my mouth, please!"

"You're right. Flip that bitch-ass on over!"

Bubby positions him on all fours, facing the wall.

His dick is glistening with spit, as he's pulling down the thong just below the boy's cheeks, teasing the elusive crack with his big pipe. He parts it open, eyeballing the juicy pink center, teasing it even further.

The white boy moans earnestly, warning him to go slow. He never had someone so big before. He has never done it with a trucker or in a truck before, so he doesn't know how thick the walls are to muffle his screams. Bubby loves being the first on so many fronts, knowing that as the white boy's first black man, every man hereafter would have to be compared to him in the unusual confines of his cramped sleeper.

Bubby guides his dick into the hole with these thoughts, feeling the slimy ass muscles spasm around him. Bubby grabs at the boy's waist, pushing in and pulling out, probing his tender prostate at the same time.

The boy wails and moans as the thrusting becomes harder and longer, faster and violent.

"Let me dig up in this bitch," Bubby pants, slapping him hard on his sweat-slick ass.

His excitement grows painfully relentless. Bubby needs this, and the boy knows he is only meant to be used. He is gripping him from all over, holding him steadfast to the hilt as he grows bigger inside of him.

"Oh, shit," Bubby screams, with his balls nestled against his ass kicking out warm white milk into a warm white ass.

ALEA
LACTA EST

Karl von Uhl

He hated himself, but it didn't matter. What mattered was getting dick, and dick could be found here, in the second-floor Macy's men's restroom at Sun Valley Mall in suburban Concord, California. Everybody did it. If you didn't suck, you got sucked. Every man liked good head from a skilled cocksucker, and if you liked good head, you'd do anything to get your cock sucked. This much he knew, and he repeated it to himself every time he came here. Sometimes he'd write it on the wall: *If you like good head, be here* and a date. He could go to the City, if he wanted to, go to San Francisco—which everyone called the City; you could hear it capitalized— but he never did. He couldn't bring himself to act like those others. That wasn't him. No matter how stylish they considered themselves, style wasn't his style. He

was sick. Even though the APA had recently said otherwise, he knew better. He had been sick in high school, he
had been sick in 'Nam. He knew he was sick, but there
wasn't anything he could do about it, other than hate
himself and still want dick. That's why it didn't matter.

He sat in his stall and waited. There was a tiled wall
on one side, and a particle-board partition that separated
his stall from the next. There was a hole in the partition,
at a good height, not too big but serviceable enough. Big
enough for dick. Some said the Sears tearoom had better
action, with more suburban working-class dad types,
the sort who would buy a son a baseball mitt and call it
love. But he preferred Macy's; the action was primarily
married men contending with their shopping wives. All
that feminine consternation took its toll. He especially
liked the married men; they were straight.

Twos and threes of men had come in, but only to
piss. He kept his stall door closed, but caught quick,
slender glimpses of them through the gaps in the lami-
nated particle-board walls.

The quarter hour passed like a sleepwalker, then a
lone man came in. He was somewhat tall, with sandy
hair and a slightly ruddy face, Lee jeans and a tan velour
shirt, untucked. Reminiscent of Glen Campbell or Jon
Voight. A real man, as evidenced by the gold ring he
wore and the green vinyl handbag he held; a married
man as well, enduring the ultimate test of married life:
being held captive to a purse. The man went to a urinal,
tried testily to find a place to set his wife's bag. The man

balanced it precariously on the plumbing at the top of the urinal.

He peered through the cracks in his stall. That man was taking an awfully long time to piss, he thought. Noiselessly, he opened the stall door, his hands inside his pants, fumbling at his boxers, hoping his impatience wouldn't scare his quarry away, and that this approach, far riskier because it involved eye contact, would work.

The handbag slid off its perch and crashed on the floor. Mascara, a faux-alligator billfold, wads of used Kleenex, a tortoiseshell compact, lipstick, pillbox, Tic-Tacs and tampons skittered about the tiles. The pissing man cussed and saw the door to the stall open.

This time it wasn't a dick pushed through a rough-hewn hole. This was the moment he lived for, the reason he sat for so long, if only eye contact wouldn't ruin it. This was the moment when he knew he could suck that man's dick, if only that man would let him, if he could will that man to let him. But identity would ruin everything. His face was affectless as he groped himself, a small movement, a trifling so subtle you'd think he'd perhaps yawned in some new and casually different way if you didn't know it meant *I'm a cocksucker*. The man at the urinal walked over, his dick hanging out of his fly, a few droplets of piss glistening on the tip. He stepped into the stall and closed the door behind him.

The man on the toilet took the dick into his mouth, tonguing the circumcision scar. He liked men who were cut. They were clean. He blinked a few times, then closed his eyes, the image of the man's short, ragged fingernails lingering in his head. He ran his tongue along the underside of the glans and brought his mouth down around the shaft. The cock hardened quickly in his mouth. He could taste the man's piss, and his own cock throbbed.

He closed his eyes and took the man's cock into his throat, reaching up to stroke the man's balls. The man started thrusting, slowly but steadily, his cock quietly parting the soft wet lips of the one eagerly sucking him, and the man on the toilet sucked him good.

This was the cock he wanted, this was the cock, this very cock sliding into this throat, along his tongue, lubricated by spit and lust. This is what some men must do, he thought, discreetly jacking his own cock in time to the man's thrusts. Already there was a telltale taste of salt in his mouth. The man was getting close. He wanted them to shoot together.

Abruptly, the man rammed his cock into the back of his throat and held it there. It throbbed once, twice and oozed its load. The man on the toilet sat stock-still, swallowing. A few more seconds and the married man was done. He stepped back, withdrew his dick from the man's mouth. He looked at the man, looked at the detritus on the floor. "Shit," he said.

He left the stall. With his dick still hanging out of his fly, he stooped over and started picking up his wife's effects. A large drop of jizz grew at the tip of his cock; unthinking, he wiped himself with a wad of used Kleenex he had just picked up. Realizing what he'd done, he tossed it back in the purse, exasperated and resigned. He stuffed his dick back in his briefs, zipped his fly and gathered what remained on the floor. He left without looking around.

The man on the toilet closed the door to his stall. He stayed for another man with another dick. He left the restroom still wanting dick shortly after the seventeenth man of the afternoon entered. He could always come back, he thought. Two were sufficient for now, but sometimes he just needed cock after cock after cock. Everybody did it.

SHOW DOG

Dominic Santi

Clint should have been a show dog. Not only is he an exhibitionist, he's drop-dead gorgeous, and he can lick his own dick. He tips back onto his shoulders, until his knees touch the bed on either side of his neck. He lifts his head, grips his deliciously long cock and pulls it forward. He strokes until his foreskin is all the way back and his glistening, plum-shaped knob is all the way exposed. Then he sticks out his tongue and goes to town.

His slurping makes my cock drool—almost as much as his does. The first time I saw him lick precum from his piss slit, I came in my pants. He'd taken me to his room at his frat house. I knelt next to him, kneading my crotch and moaning as he lapped up the clear pearls oozing from the thin dark slit. He licked his lips in satisfaction, then pointed his tongue and dug in for more.

If I hadn't just emptied my balls, I would have shot again.

I was more than a little bit embarrassed at my lack of control. Clint just grinned and asked me to climb up next to him on the bed.

"Shit, man," I said, sitting next to him in my seriously sticky jeans. "Why do you even bother having sex with other people?"

Limber as he is, it turns out Clint is seriously into cuddling. He's also really picky about who he dates.

"So many guys only want to watch and beat off—them together, you know? I'm just the entertainment, not part of the action. I'm getting really tired of it."

At the ripe old age of twenty-two, Clint was tired of being the entertainment. He wanted a boyfriend. Somebody like—me?

Grinning like a fool, I stripped and snuggled up next to him, rubbing his shoulders and kissing up the side of his butt. His crack was so open, his asshole was fully exposed. When I blew on it, it winked. Clint moaned.

"You like that?" I smiled, doing it again. The shiver that went with the wink was definitely appreciation.

"Oh, yeah!" He moaned as I bent closer. His hole was dusky pink, the edges covered with a dusting of soft, dark hair. He smelled like soap and horny man. I leaned forward and licked.

Clint cried out, shaking.

"Oh, god, yes!" His asshole fluttered as his tongue

licked frantically over his cock head. "Do it again!" His hand squeezed his shaft, like he was trying to get enough movement as he pulled his cock head even closer to his lips.

I licked again, slowly. He shuddered and moaned. I washed the edges. The tip of my tongue swept into the center. With each stroke, his whole body trembled.

"Please," he whispered, slowing his licks to match the strokes of my tongue. "I love having my ass eaten."

"Like this?" I pressed my tongue deeper.

He groaned and arched up. "Yes!"

I pointed my tongue, drilling in deep as he pleaded for more. His tongue skipped erratically over his now-drooling cock head.

My dick didn't care that I'd already come. I knelt back, spit dripping down my chin, letting him watch as I stroked myself. My cock wasn't real thick, but it was long and it was pointing almost straight up my belly. We had enough mutual friends that I figured my talents in the fucking department had preceded me. Clint lowered his legs, stretching his back and shoulders.

"Condoms in the nightstand," he panted, his hand working his foreskin over his knob again.

I grinned and shook my head. "First I want to watch you lick your dick—while I eat your ass." I wiggled my tongue like a snake. "Can you come that way?"

Ooh, my cutie pie was blushing.

"Yeah," he laughed unsteadily. "It's hard to do, though. My back gets tired." The blush on his cheeks was fucking gorgeous! But my sweetie knew what he wanted. "If you eat my ass, I'll come faster."

"As long as your tongue stays on your dick, my tongue stays in your ass." I grabbed a leg and lifted. "Deal?"

"Oh, yeah!" Clint grinned as he tipped back onto his shoulders. His cock was slick with clear, glistening juices. He stroked until his shaft stood up stiff and strong again. Then he lifted his head and stuck out his tongue. He pulled his dick forward, groaning as his mouth connected.

"Fuck, you are hot!"

Grinning like a fool, I put one hand on each of his buttcheeks, pulling them farther apart. He was squeezing his shaft in short, hard pulls, once more washing the precum from his dick head. I stuck out my tongue and leaned down, matching him stroke for stroke as his moans echoed in my ears.

It didn't take him long at all. I alternated between fucking my tongue deep into his hole and sucking the edge of his ass where it met his perineum. I felt the tremors start against my upper lip.

"In," he begged, his tongue moving frantically over the bared head of his cock. "In—d-deep!"

I happily obliged, pressing my fingers firmly where my upper lip had been.

Clint yelled and shot into his mouth. Streams of spurting white cream jetted onto his tongue, running over his lips and down his chin. His whole body jerked as he pumped his dick, his asshole twitching against me.

The condom was on the bed by my knee; I tore open the wrapper and slipped it on. Then I pressed my dick to his still quivering hole. His legs were shaking, so I pressed my other hand to the back of his thigh, massaging him, spreading his ass as I guided myself in. In all my life, I'd never felt a hole more ready to be fucked. I slid in like a knife into hot butter, groaning as his still-twitching rectal walls wrapped tightly around me.

His eyes were closed, his sweat-soaked body glistening as he smiled with each delicious squeeze. It didn't matter that I'd already come. I fucked him fast and deep and hard, yelling as I shot a second huge load up his ass.

I spent the rest of the night with him, talking and laughing and fucking him once more as the sun came up. We did it again the next weekend, and the weekend after that. Four months later, we graduated and moved in together. We've been together ever since.

Clint's still an exhibitionist—more so now that I'm watching his back, and his backside. He knows that regardless of what anybody else does while he's licking his dick for an audience, when we get home, I'm going to dig my tongue in his hole and eat his ass until he comes in his mouth. I'm going to fuck him until we both see stars. And in the morning, I'll still be cuddled up beside him. Showtime or in private, he's always part of my action.

THE HIGHEST BIDDER

Gavin Atlas

"The final item up for bid is the opportunity to fuck Jason Tate's ass," said Elliot, the auctioneer. The audience of horny men cheered and howled like coyotes. "Listen, folks. With the other boys, you were merely bidding for time with them, but as always, Jason guarantees you'll plow him. Right, Jason?"

"Yes, sir," I said. I positioned myself on all fours facing away from everyone and arched my naked rump.

"Oh, god," Elliot muttered. I looked over my shoulder to see if he'd said that merely to encourage the crowd, but from his stare his reaction was sincere.

"We'll open at five hundred dollars."

"One thousand!"

"Two!"

"Three thousand!"

Holy shit, that was fast. Last year was a record. A doctor bought me for five thousand. The lodge gave the auction's proceeds to a children's hospital, so I felt justified in being this much of a whore.

"Three thousand for the best bottom in porn. Do I hear four?"

"Five!" That was the doctor's voice. I smiled, knowing he wanted a repeat.

"Twenty-five thousand."

My eyes widened. That voice sounded familiar, too. Who was that? Fuck! It was Jim! What was he doing here? There was no way I was letting him have my ass!

"No, Elliot," I whispered to the auctioneer. "Don't take bids from him. He broke my heart."

Elliot didn't hear me. "Twenty-five thousand going once...going twice...sold to the gentleman in the brown leather jacket. Jason's ass is yours for the fucking."

Goddammit.

The audience whooped and applauded as Jim came up to claim me. Sure, Jim was gorgeous. He was about six inches taller than me—maybe six-two. He had the thick frame of a wrestler or firefighter, and spiky strawberry-blond hair on top of a boyish, mischievous face. He shot me a gleaming smile I didn't return as I rose to face him.

"Why are you here?" I demanded.

He grabbed me and threw me over his shoulder. The crowd applauded louder. "Because I want you."

I bounced as he carried me out into the frigid night,

wishing I'd brought clothes. "I told you I never wanted to see you again. Why do you think I don't take your calls?"

"That's why I bought your hole. So you'd have no choice, boy." By the time we reached Jim's cabin I was freezing. He tossed me on the king-size bed and ran his hands over my crotch and ass. My dick stiffened in his hand, and I began to moan. I felt heated humiliation. Why was I always helpless to stop cruel men from reaming my ass? And why did I love it?

"You shouldn't get to fuck me," I protested weakly. "That's not fair."

He spread my legs and fingered me. "Sounds like you want things to be unfair." I moaned again.

I shook my head as I lifted my legs and let Jim lube me up. I remembered one night when he fucked me four times. Afterward, if Jim just blew air on my hole, I nearly cried because I was that sore. I whimpered in bed for two days. It was sublime.

But he dumped me, and I'd never gotten over it.

"I quit school because of you," I said. "I ended up getting fucked for a living because you said I was stupid and had no future."

Jim had already slid on a condom and was aiming his dick at my hole.

"I'm sorry," he said. "I was mad because you let everyone hit it, and I wanted you for myself. I've changed."

He punched in deep, and I yelped in surprise. Even

being a porno bottom, my ass wasn't stretched enough for his huge girth. I gritted my teeth and breathed deeply in and out, concentrating on relaxing my muscles.

"That's it, Jason," Jim said. "You always were such a good bottom."

The transition from pain to pleasure began, and I felt strings of ecstasy in my gut being plucked with every stroke. But I wanted to stay mad. "Yeah, I'm a good bottom. You said that was the only thing I was good at."

Jim growled and bit my earlobe. "Hush," he whispered. "Let me fuck your ass, and I'll explain."

Now that I could take his dick, I rolled back farther, and Jim rumbled with appreciation. His thrusting sped up, and it began to hurt again. But it hurt wonderfully. With each stroke, a bolt of hot pain and lust shot up from my prostate to my teeth and forehead. In a frenzy he flipped me on my side and fucked me more. I couldn't help but moan and thrash. Then he flipped me onto all fours and fucked my ass doggie-style like a madman. My own dick was so hard it hit my stomach with each push inside.

As he stuffed me again and again, I had to grimace and bite a pillow, constantly grunting. Getting my ass fucked by Jim was better than ever, and all the reasons I had wanted him came flooding back.

The fucking went on and on. I was about to scream that I couldn't take any more when his pounding intensified, and he came with a primal roar. His orgasm ignited mine, and I shot all over my stomach and his sheets. My knees buckled, and I collapsed on the mattress in my own cum. Jim was still lodged in me and thrusting reflexively.

"Oh, my god, that was good," Jim said, shaking his head. "I've never had better."

Neither had I. The adrenaline rush from coming made me light-headed with pleasure.

Jim handed me a towel while he wiped himself off. "Considering I paid twenty-five grand, I'm going to fuck you again. Maybe a few times."

Hell, yes. "If I have to."

"Look, Jason. I was jealous. I wanted you for myself and thought you were shallow when you didn't want monogamy."

"I still don't want it."

"Then don't do it. It's okay. But it's not just that. I read the article in *Frontiers*. You're doing charity work. Always volunteering." He smirked as he caressed my rump. "And always offering up that ass for a cause. I've seen your heart now, and it's a good one."

My anger subsided. "It is?"

"Absolutely." Jim stroked my stomach and kissed my throat. A rapturous whimper escaped my lips. "The article said you dreamed of starting a foundation for gay seniors," he said. "Now you will."

"What?" *Was it possible I could get Jim's incredible dick and his respect, too?*

"I'm putting you through college, young man, so you

can have that dream. Did you think you'd be a porn star forever?"

"I...don't know." Now he fingered my ass again.

"You don't have to be monogamous for this deal," Jim whispered, "but I get to fuck you a lot. And kiss you. And caress you. And take you to dinner." Now he knelt above me. He began lubing me up again. "Do we have a bargain?"

Stunned, I could only manage one word. "Yes." An incredible offer from the man I loved and the best top ever. I moaned and lifted my legs. "Jim. Thank god you were the highest bidder."

THE WAVE
POOL

Zeke Mangold

It wasn't quite 10:00 a.m. and the temperature had yet to climb above sixty degrees, but it was sunny and it was March, which could only mean one thing: pale tourists from colder climates, despite the nippy Las Vegas weather, were sunbathing on the pool deck and bodysurfing in the wave pool. And it meant that Dell was back at work, lifeguarding his best summers away in exchange for an insignificant paycheck. If only these tourists were remotely attractive, he thought, then the eye candy might justify the extreme boredom.

To Dell, the weather felt freezing. He'd likely wear his sweatshirt all day. But when it's sunny, he had noted, there will always be people in a pool, especially in the one at Baja Palace Gambling Hall & Oasis. The hotel-casino, despite being located off-Strip and on a stretch of hillbilly infested trailer park–strewn real estate known as Boulder Highway, boasted an honest-to-god wave pool. Even cynical Dell, just twenty-two and already too old for this job and completely exhausted by life's consistent lack of surprises, had to admit the pool was pretty rad. Indeed, it could be counted on to provide a flash of spontaneity in an otherwise carefully controlled corporate landscape.

For example, just this morning, the first demonstration since the badly needed hydraulic overhaul created much mirth for Dell and his coworkers. All of the executives had come out to watch, standing there in their suits, sunglassed to protect their Botoxed eyes from the sun's wrinkling power. The first wave the pool engineer sent cresting in their direction was so massive that it ran way up the ersatz beach, soaked everyone and sucked most of the lounge furniture and a fair amount of sand back into the pool.

"Um," said the engineering director to his underling. "Can we turn it down some?"

Dell had been pretending to unstack and clean some lounge chairs when he saw the executives nearly drown in the mini-tsunami, and he laughed so hard he began to choke a little. Given his experience and years with the company, he was part of a winter skeleton crew and often worked as a training manager. One of the first things he taught newly hired employees was to be wary of the pool's first few waves, as the computer always needed a few minutes to recalibrate after being idle for twelve hours. If any of the execs had bothered to take his class, they wouldn't have gotten so thoroughly drenched.

Without needing to be prompted, Dell abandoned the chairs and went in search of towels, grabbing a still-warm-from-the-commercial-dryer pile from the cabana rental stand. Trying to disguise the hilarity roiling in his brain, he offered a soft, embroidered Baja cotton beach towel to a rather good-looking Hugo Boss–sporting stud, who had flipped his shades (men's Gucci stainless-steel aviators) on top of his head. He and Dell locked eyes for a moment, and then the exec awkwardly dabbed moisture from his suit.

"Had planned on watching some March Madness at the bar after the wave demo," said the suit, roughly in his late thirties. "But I guess I'll have to drive to the cleaners instead."

"Actually, you're not as soaked as everyone else," said Dell. "There's a big industrial blow-dryer in the back. Betcha we can get those pants ready in, like, ten minutes."

"Sure, but what the hell am I going to wear in the meantime?"

"There's a nice Baja Spa bathrobe back there. C'mon. Name's Dell, by the way."

The exec reached out to shake the lifeguard's hand. "Jason."

Together they walked over to an area behind the hydraulic station, where there were no cameras snooping on them. The odor of chlorine was fierce but not entirely unpleasant. A blow-dryer hung by its tangled cord from a wall-mounted surfboard Brad Pitt had used while filming an unused scene in *The Mexican*. Dell often borrowed the board to ride the first waves of the day. He licked his lips. His gay spider sense was tingling like crazy. He didn't want to be fired for coming on to a VP, but life was too short to be worried about things like that. Jason's wedding ring, for whatever reason, made Dell hornier.

"Let me have those," said Dell, indicating the older man's jacket and pants. He started to unravel the dryer from the wall.

Strangely, Jason pulled his shades back down, covering his eyes, and said, "No, not yet."

Jason commanded Dell to get down on his knees and suck his uncircumcised, corporate cock. Dell did as he was told and began to unzip the exec's pants and undo his belt, pulling out a hard, very large, pink cock. Dell took it all into his mouth, wrapping his lips around it, and began to suck. The older man helped him by grabbing the back of Dell's head and pulling it toward his groin. Jason's cock, wet with Dell's spit, glistened in the soft morning light. The exec began to moan, eyes no doubt rolling back in his head, even though Dell couldn't see past the shades, as Jason experienced an intense orgasm.

Dell pulled his mouth away from Jason's pulsing cock, just as a stream of hot white cum shot out from the tip, splattering the younger man's face and mouth.

Dell licked at the stuff hungrily, using his fingers to shove thick semen from his cheeks onto his tongue.

"Now bend over," said Jason, and Dell obliged.

Jason tossed Dell's salad, pushing his mouth between the younger man's asscheeks and running his tongue across the prostate. With an erection like an iron bar, Dell emitted a whimper as Jason massaged the spot between his balls and bung with one hand.

"Your ass tastes like candy," said Jason. He reached around with his other hand to tug on Dell's engorged shaft.

Dell closed his eyes, bit his lower lip, and resigned himself to a blindingly good orgasm.

"Yes," he muttered, like a guilty prayer.

"All right then," said Jason. "Just relax. When you're ready to come, shoot your load right into my mouth."

Dell did just that, turning around in time to grab Jason's head and shove his cock against the older man's surprisingly soft tongue. He could feel his cum pumping, filling the exec's gorgeous mouth with a heavy wad. The older man swallowed every last drop and then, with the back of his hand, wiped his lips.

"That was nice," he said, shades still on his face. "Forget the suit. Got another one in my office. What was your name again?"

"Dell."

"Well, Dell, if you ever get tired of this job, call me. I have a great position for you lined up in online marketing."

"What is that? Like using Facebook or something?"

"That's part of it. I could use a guy like you to help me maintain Baja's Twitter feed. Here's my card."

Dell's heart did a somersault. He took the card and, later that night, slept with it under his pillow. The wave pool and its risky preopening ritual had brought him good luck after all. Finally, he began to experience something akin to joy.

Now if he could just get through today's boring shift without murdering an ugly tourist.

HE'LL SUCK
YOU IF
I SAY SO

Jeff Funk

I don't know, man. I'm kind of nervous," Richard said as he drove his dad's weekend SUV down Sallee Street.

"What's to be nervous about? It's just good head. You like good head, don't you?" dark-haired Jim asked from the passenger seat. He stopped texting and nodded at Richard with encouragement, then gave a look as if to say, *You're not backin' out, are you?*

Their eyes met briefly before Richard turned his attention back to the road. The muscle near his right ear tightened from his clenched jaw.

He didn't tell Jim that he had only gotten a blow job once before in his life, and that was from an old guy he'd met last semester in the fourth-floor restroom of the college library. Now that he was back at home over summer break, his nightly routine was to go to the gym because it was a good excuse to leave the house without being questioned much by his parents. Tonight he'd told his mom he would be out late with friends after his workout. *She'd shit if she knew what I was really up to,* he thought. "So what does he look like?"

"He's twenty-five, six-foot-five—uh, a *cocksucker*. Come on, man. Listen, he wants to blow me every night, only sometimes I like to pass him around—you know, share him with a buddy? So if I tell him he's gotta service you in order to have my dick, he will do it. He'll suck you if I say so."

The cell phone chimed, alerting them to a new text message.

"What's he saying?"

Jim's dark eyebrows frowned as he read. The glow of the screen revealed a mild sheen of sweat and oil on his handsome face. "He wants to wait a few more minutes until it's darker. He can't host either, and I hate those dirty fuckin' motel rooms. I'd rather get blown outside where it's peaceful." After sending a reply, he shoved the phone into his pocket. "Okay, at the next light make a left."

Richard followed Jim's directions through town and into the back parking lot of Our Lady of Good Hope, where he turned off the headlights and killed the engine. Fifteen minutes later, a black pickup truck arrived and parked next to them. No introductions were made once they were out of their vehicles. The three men walked in silence into a meadow with tall weeds, then climbed uphill until they were able to enter the back of the Lloyd Chalmers golf course.

"Where do you want to do it?" the tall stranger asked.

"Here's good," Jim said. He yanked his shorts down to his ankles and sat down on the green.

Leaving his shirt on, Richard did the same. Once they were side by side in the grass, he couldn't keep his eyes off of one thing.

Jim's dick.

Richard had seen it before in the locker room, but it was always soft during those brief glimpses.

Holding a fistful of blond curly hair, Jim fed his hard-on to the suck boy. "Here you go," he said. He used the man's mouth for a long length of time, then grabbed his head with both hands and shoved it onto Richard's crotch. However, the sucker didn't take that tool inside his mouth; he licked it instead.

Richard gasped when the soft tongue reached his scrotum.

"Oh, he likes that," Jim said to the man, then he tapped Richard on the shoulder. "Why don't you go down on my friend a while?"

Upon hearing this, the tall man peeled off his shorts, lay on his back and spread his long legs. Richard crawled between them and licked the precum leaking from the guy's cock, which was thicker than Jim's but not as long. Then he swallowed the whole thing and sucked it hard.

Jim watched with an ornery smile on his face. "Keep goin' until he busts a nut."

Richard bobbed on the erect cock, working his lips over a length of shaft that he could safely manage without choking himself or scraping the head of the dick with his teeth. The stranger's cum blasted into the back of his throat. He gulped it down and also lapped up the few drops that had spilled into the man's light-colored pubes.

The big guy brought a farm-strong hand down to his spent boner and milked out a final drop of cum.

Richard sipped that, too.

"Your turn," Jim said. He pushed Richard onto his back and kissed him.

Richard noticed that Jim's plump lips tasted like fruity gum. His tongue then found the gum itself. While they made out, the third man's warm mouth engulfed his prick—*now* he knew what good head felt like. "Tell him to suck my balls," Richard said.

"Yo, man. Suck his balls!" Jim ordered, then started jacking him off.

Richard felt a surge building. He panted heavy breaths and shot several skyward-arching streams of youthful spunk, the first hitting his cheek. Other splashes of cum were spread across the chest and one shoulder of his gray T-shirt.

"Good one," Jim said, giving Richard a pat on the arm. "You," he said to the mystery man, "get over here and open wide." He grabbed the guy's head and face-fucked him aggressively. His athletic body was graceful at ramming cock. "Aw dude, here it comes," Jim said, in a throaty baritone.

Richard crouched close to the ground in time to see his buddy's dick in silhouette against the night sky as he gushed a load. The stranger moaned from the taste of cum. Jim's nut sac was so shriveled that it looked like he had been skinny-dipping in a cold lake.

"All right, let's get out of here," Jim said. The men quickly pulled up their shorts and looked around the empty golf course. On the walk back he said, "If anyone asks, we were looking for my cell phone."

At the church, Jim gave his anonymous friend a handshake and a half hug. "Call you later."

As the two younger men climbed into their vehicle, the dome light showed that both of their faces were flushed at the cheeks. Jim winked at his pal when he buckled his seat belt.

Ahead of them, the black pickup rolled out of the parking lot and went east. Richard turned the other direction, back toward downtown.

"It was good head, right?"

"Yeah, it was good," Richard said.

Jim scooted closer and spoke softly into his ear. "That was hot watching you take my bud's load. You licked up the whole fuckin' mess." He grabbed the bulge in Richard's shiny black gym shorts and squeezed playfully until stiffness pressed against his palm. "Maybe next time, you'll swallow mine."

The SUV coasted down Calhoun Street several blocks before Richard responded, "I'll be your cocksucker."

CLOWN

Sleepy Acosta

A y, remember your friend, he brings the dog? You
bring him over here," your aunt points emphati-
cally at the late newscast, and her bird-voice cracks
beneath the weight of inadequate English and old soda.
This talk would have splintered you on most days,
would have put an egg in your throat and made you
wish yourself back to Houston, if not for the homeboy
staring out from the television screen. In his mug shot,
you recognize his dick-sucking lips. A crack in the jaw is
a half smile; eyes like dog eyes, huge and slanted, reach
from the pixilated fuzz of the screen, and you can feel
the eyelids on your throat, his jaw, stubbly, crushing
itself into your thigh.

"Shhh," you hush her. You want to hear the tale
behind the mug shot, but you can't; that part has passed.

All you get is a charge—aggravated assault—scrolling beneath his torso, a phone number to call to claim a cash reward once you've turned the vato in.

"You remember? You know him," she urges over the clank of forks and plates in the belly of the sink, the splash of faucet drool not washing her voice away.

You're in the shower, soon after that, and your dick is hard and drooling. Water hits your throat.

And you do remember him.

You remember him kneeling, your cock fat and slobbery in his mouth.

You remember his throat, the back of it wrapping like a fist about your dick head and shaft, squeezing. And him going, "Mmm," and collecting short breaths quickly each time you pulled your dick out then slapped it down onto his tongue.

You remember unloading over his nose and his scalp, the cum sticking to the stipple of his temple, to the barbell in his eyebrow in a wad of white; another gob of it drooling down his cheek to his chinstrap.

You remember his nipples like bottle caps, beer-glass hued and stiff, how his fucked-up tats looked all whack and back-alley against your deer blanket, against the whiteness of his skin, against your knuckles and his laughter.

You remember he says "cuero" instead of foreskin, dick-hood or uncut when he compliments your "big Mexican dick" and how much he loves sucking on it.

You remember he's not Mexican.

In the morning you'll see that mug shot again on the news. The anchorwoman speaks clearly, "...considered dangerous. Crime Stoppers...advised to contact the authorities..." but you mute her ass and just stare at his smirk.

The fronts of his teeth glint in the shot, which is how you remember him, smiling, always half-smiling, and he's wearing a white muscle T-shirt, his ex's name splayed in black cursive across his neck bone, the silver herringbone chain you gave him that Christmas you drove over to his pad where he stayed with his sister and her five fucked-up kids and his dog, a thick-ass pit mix he calls Diamond...

They feed you tamales made of deer, the oily husks staining your hands, his sister chattering away uncontrollably and yelling at her kids, and when you can't stand it any longer, you drive him to a park under a mesquite tree where he unzips your pants and jacks you off with his mouth.

"Talk to me dirty, pa," he says and licks at the name on your knuckles. His lips wrap around your shaft tightly, the pricks of his goatee tickling your nut sac and making you feel like he might belong. He sucks on your dick real good and stares at your grays, the maze of black lines that sleeve your arms, malleable underneath his fingers and tongue. The sky is gray like your arms. It is about to rain, and it's cold. The Cowboys are playing, you think. "Tell me you like this," he says.

"Chupamelo," is all you can muster up, because he's

got you good, your hands clamp on his skull, and you're about to bust your nut. "Suck that dick, guey. Cometelo." Eat it, you say, your cock head hitting the walls of his throat, and he obeys.

That night, he shows up at your pad after your tia has already taken her pills. You sit in the sala, the flicker of the Christmas tree and the late shows glowing electronically, and this root inside of him growing toward you. On the sofa, he lays his head by your dick and breathes warm and moist over your bulge. When you fuck him, you use spit, and he says it hurts, but he takes it and asks for "More, harder, fuck yeah, papa." You're fucking him, your balls slapping at the lost part of meat stuck between the culo and the trunk of his dick, and you tell him, "Shut the fuck up, guey," in your loudest whisper, because he's loud and your aunt is sleeping in the other room.

You fuck him on his stomach first, then on his back. You can't look at his face, so you stare at his teeth and at the silver chain. You put his knees by your mouth, and you kiss at his ankles, gnaw at his calves, and this way, you get your entire dick inside his hole. He says, "Ay, guey. Ay." And when you're ready to come, when you've fucked enough for your heart to push up against the pulp of your lungs, you put teeth on his neck, at the place where he wears another vato's namesake, and you suck. You come hard, four or five jet streams, causing you to collapse on his back, your heart beating hard against him, into him, and you don't move. You can feel yourself oozing out of his hole. Your dick is still hard, his neck is crimson raw, and he tells you, "Again, pa. Fuck me again."

Now, your aunt continues to pry about the vato who committed this crime, the guy from the TV, the one she's convinced you knew and brought over a few times.

You deny it.

You don't dream shit about him, but you mention his name when you pray.

Sotero.

It was an old name, not a name you'd want, not a name you'd give your kid.

He don't even like that name. Calls himself Clown instead, because he's "always smiling," he explains as he leans against the door of your Regal, and the Thunderbird flocking out of his mouth appeals to you that way.

You see him on the beach, one of the last times you ever hooked up. He tells you too much about his life: his mom's locked up, his uncles, his ex, his dreams. The taste from his lips is crisp and cheap, and he smells of Eternity, which he borrowed from you. The sky has fallen behind the sun. The bottle empties. You sit on the hood of your ride and watch him, shirtless and burned, scratching your name and his, *Por Vida C/S*, with a bottleneck into the firmest part of the sand. The waves crash into themselves and into the shore with a fury that reminds you of Clown.

OUT OF THE SHADOWS

Landon Dixon

He took a look over his shoulder then ducked into a doorway.

He might've spotted me. I wasn't sure.

I'd been following the guy around all day, a shadow job at the moneyed behest of a jealous wife who thought hubby was seeing another woman. Patrick Sedor hadn't been showing his wife, Elaine, any affection during the last three months and counting, and Elaine wanted to know why. By "any affection," she meant he hadn't fucked her in over three months. Those were her words, dripping with venom.

I jogged up the sidewalk and peered into the doorway. A red metal door with black letters spelled out PRIVATE CLUB. There was no one up the sidewalk, just the shop fronts, lit up for the night. My man had gone into the club. I went in after him.

A dark hallway greeted me, a man-mountain at the end of it. I didn't have a membership or guest pass, but fifty dollars got me through the brown-padded portal that led inside. The hot, funky atmosphere of sex hit me like a punch in the gut, as soon as I stepped into the wonderland.

There were men everywhere—naked men kissing, Frenching, fondling, teasing, spanking, sucking, fucking. There were guys on top of each other on couches, pressing against each other, against walls, thrusting into mouths and asses on large, futonlike mattresses. There were pairs, threesomes, trains, chains and every other combination of raw man-sex you could feverishly imagine.

I took a step back, into another man.

He was as naked as the forty or so other guys in the dimly lit room. He was of medium height and weight, with brown, wavy hair; warm, brown eyes; and a long, hard cock. He slid his hands along my chest and squeezed, grinding that impressive cock of his into my tight-jeaned ass.

"New to the club?" he breathed in my ear.

I nodded, glancing around the room for *my* man, not seeing him in the roiling sea of glistening flesh.

A flight of stairs led up to a second floor. I considered taking them, but by then a young blond had dropped down in between my legs. He had my semi-erect cock out and warming up in his mouth before I could make a move.

"I'm Darren," the guy behind me said. "And he's Clay."

I grunted, "Robert," swelling up full length in Clay's wet, hot mouth. I had time, and I could keep the stairs and door covered from my position of advantage.

Darren's hands roamed inside my shirt and grasped my bare pecs. Clay cupped my balls and sucked on my cock, his green eyes gleaming up at me.

Another man approached, hips swishing and cock bobbing. He planted a wet kiss on my parted lips. His tongue made brief contact with mine. And then he was gone, ass bouncing as he checked on another pile of men. Moans and groans and cries of joy filled the stuffy room, along with the brisk, rhythmic splashing of flesh into flesh.

Not ten feet away, a tall, thin redhead was hammering his cock into the rock-hard ass of a glowing muscleman. The muscleman was bent over and holding on to a chair, the redhead bent over and holding on to the guy's waist, pumping his hips like a madman. I could almost feel the impact of that flashing cock pounding into that gripping ass.

What I could really feel was Clay mouthing my balls. He had my whole nut sac in his velvety mouth, juggling my balls with his tongue, pumping my slicked cock with his hand.

My jeans and underwear were down around my ankles now, Darren getting serious with his hard-on. He whacked my cheeks with it. They shivered under the heavy blows. Then he was pressing his cap in between, his cock and my crack already oiled for action. His hood barged through my ring, and his shaft sank into my anus.

I groaned around a third guy's fingers. He'd stuck them into my mouth to suck on, as he sucked on my nipples, while Clay dropped my bag and excitedly licked up and down my cock like he'd just been gifted with the world's yummiest lollypop. All the while Darren's oiled dong moved back and forth in my chute.

I closed my eyes, floating on the wicked sensations, shimmering with heat. I reopened my eyes and spotted Patrick Sedor coming down the stairs, as casually nude as everyone else. He spotted me—getting rocked up the ass by Darren, blown by Clay, nippled by the third man—and he smiled and came over our way.

"Find what you were looking for?" he asked me.

He was a good-looking guy, ruggedly built, with short black hair and clear blue eyes, a dimpled chin and a thick, erect cock. I could see entirely why Elaine was feeling so frustrated. I nodded at him, and he eased Clay and the nipple-teaser aside, setting up shop himself right in front of me, ass positioned and spread.

Darren slowed his pumping, greased my cock. I pressed my hood into Patrick's manhole, popped his pucker and plowed deep into his chute, the both of us groaning.

We got a rhythm going, Darren stroking slow and sure in my ass, me pumping Patrick at the same pace. The guy's anus was oven hot and tight as a drum. I drilled into him from behind, as cock-hungry Clay sucked him up in front.

The room spun. I was sweating, gasping, burning, thrusting, getting fucked up the ass and fucking up the ass. Darren clutched my pecs and hammered my hole. I gripped Patrick's shoulders, plowing his butt. Guys were blowing loads all around us, in mouths and asses, on faces and cocks. I knew we were next.

Darren torqued it up another level, cleaving my cheeks, sawing my chute. I reciprocated with Patrick, rocking him in Clay's mouth. Our bodies smacked together as one, a well-oiled sex machine.

Then Darren suddenly sank his teeth into my neck, and his body jerked against mine. Semen seared my bowels in powerful bursts. I wildly pumped Patrick, out of control.

"Fuck!" I gritted, blowing the guy wide open.

I jerked like Darren, blasting up Patrick's sucking ass. He shuddered in my arms, Clay milking the cum out of his shooting cock.

"Your husband isn't seeing another woman," I truthfully reported back to Elaine the next day.

But I kept up the tail job on my man all the same, heading back to the club night after night after night.

OPPORTUNISTIC

Fox Lee

Katashi arrived at the concert shortly before it started. It had been a long week. Two of his coworkers quit while another was on vacation, leaving the café with only the manager and Katashi to keep things running. Katashi had been up to his balls in double shifts ever since. In return the manager, who knew his taste in music, gave him the weekend off and a concert ticket to a show at a nearby club. Katashi wasn't even sure who was playing, except that it would be fast and loud. He planned to get up front and lose himself in the mosh pit. A couple of hours of frantic energy and sweat would make him a new man.

Inside the club, Katashi wound his way into the swarm of people around the stage. The constant shifting body contact gave him a rush. It intensified as the band got onstage and the throb of a bass guitar began to shake the speakers. The other electric guitars soon joined in and Katashi was squeezed on all sides, as a wave of fans surged to the opening chords of a song he'd never heard before. It was good, and he quickly lost himself in the bone-rattling lyrics being snarled by a skinny man in shredded, leather pants onstage. By the end of the first song, Katashi could feel sweat trickling down his temple. His heart was pumping fast, and his skin radiated heat.

The crowd ebbed, slightly, as the lead shouted the usual routine into the microphone. For the first time, Katashi took a second to notice the people around him. One caught his eye: a slender man with dark eyes and a lion's mane of black hair that ended just below his jawline. As if aware of being observed, he turned his head and locked eyes with Katashi. The younger man gave him a brief *Do I know you?* expression and turned away. Katashi felt his cock stiffen. No longer interested in the concert, he managed to migrate to a spot behind the new object of his attention.

A quick scan of the club confirmed that everyone else's eyes were firmly on the stage. Katashi smiled and aligned his hips with the denim-clad ass in front of him. The band launched into a second song, and the crowd again surged forward. Katashi hit his target dead on. He rubbed lightly at first and groaned at the sensations it created along his shaft. The dark-haired man startled, but made no attempt to dissuade the action. There wasn't room to move away: Katashi was more concerned with the guy twisting around and punching him.

Feeling optimistic, he increased the friction and snaked a hand into the man's right side pocket. There wasn't anything inside; no cell phone or keys, which made Katashi's job easy. With lightning speed, he turned the pocket inside out, tore open the seam and thrust both the ruined pocket and his hand back the way they came. He felt his way across a pair of cotton briefs, and slid his fingers though the slit in the front. The man gasped as Katashi gripped his already half-hard cock. The sounds from the stage drowned out any noise, but Katashi felt the sharp intake of breath as he slipped his free hand under the front of the man's T-shirt.

Katashi stroked the growing erection until he felt precum weeping from the tip. He wiggled closer and darted his tongue against the man's neck. It elicited a squirm, so Katashi did it again, this time followed by a quick bite. The man's skin was salty, and his hairs tickled the bridge of Katashi's nose.

"I'm going to make you come," Katashi whispered into the man's ear.

He knew the man couldn't hear him, but the sensation of Katashi's breath must have been effective enough. The man's cock throbbed, hot and needy, in Katashi's hand. Katashi used his thumb to caress the tip, his own aching erection disregarded.

"I can feel how bad you want to come for me," he said.

Katashi's hand slipped lower to cup the man's testicles. He rolled them gently, while he stroked the man's stomach muscles. Both balls and muscles tensed. Meanwhile, the chaotic jumble of human bodies continued to heave around them. Katashi rode the frantic tide and used its momentum to his advantage. His hand returned to the man's cock and began to stroke it to the beat of the music. Katashi took a nipple between his fingers and pinched hard. The man's face contorted in what looked like a scream and come spurted over Katashi's fingers. Katashi released the man's nipple and gripped his waist so that he wouldn't stumble. More come spilled onto his hand, as the man's cock continued to pulse.

Katashi held on to his prize, until it began to soften. He released it then, and pulled his hand free of the pocket. Most of the come wiped off in the process; Katashi wiped the remainder off on the side of his pants. The man tried to turn around, but the crush of bodies was too dense. Katashi was still hard, and the concert wasn't nearly over. He had a while to decide how he wanted the man in front of him to return the favor.

AFTER HOURS
AT THE GYM

Jim Howard

It was my job to close up the gym after the front desk attendants left for the evening and they and the trainers drove back to their apartments in Silverlake. I was supposed to clean, but mostly I watched TV and ran on the treadmill.

That's what I was doing when somebody pounded on the front doors. I switched off the treadmill and went to the door, panting from my run. Two jocks stood outside in workout clothes and UCLA track jackets. They were about the same height, and both had short black hair and sandy tans. The one on the right had a thick neck and tight shoulders. He was wearing red terry sweatpants with a college coat of arms on the thigh. His buddy had the bulging forearms of a squash player and I could see how his bulge peaked in the soft fold of his thick cotton sweatpants. "The gym's closed."

"But we saw you working out," the one on the left said, the parking lot lights glinting in his dark eyes. The glass muffled his voice.

"I can't let you in."

"Please, man," said the thicker one, scratching his belly under the hem of his T-shirt. "You've only been closed for a half hour."

"Forty-five minutes," I said.

The guy on the left sighed and stuffed his hands in his jacket pockets. Then his friend started pleading. "Come on. We got held up, and we gotta lift. I promise we'll be good." I twisted the lock and opened the door to get a better look at them and realized that the two of them together could fuck me up. The one in the red was solid enough to take me alone.

"What if we did something for you," he said, cracking a sweet smile. The corners of his half-moon eyes crinkled up and he slipped his hands underneath his waistband. "We got held up because we were getting filmed, fucking." He stood there, rocking back and forth on his feet, with his palms flat against his stomach. He dropped his pants, flashing a look at his big cut cock curving in toward his thigh.

His friend looked down at his feet and stifled a nervous laugh. I stepped back into the gym and let them in. I locked the door behind us and led them to the mats. "What did you have in mind, then?"

The skinnier one was still fidgeting with his waistband, trying to look sexy, I guess. The one in the red finally looked up at me. He talked low, in almost a mumble.

"Why don't you start by sucking our cocks, and we'll see where we go from there?" He moved toward me and reached out and grabbed me by the arm. I gave in and sank to my knees.

The skinnier guy stripped off his shirt and started rubbing his cock head through his sweatpants. He put his hand on the back of my head and pressed my face toward him. His skin smelled musky, like the other guy had marked him. I pressed my cheek against his sweatpants and felt his dick getting hot.

I reached toward the other guy, the one who had taken charge at the door. He squared off his feet in front of me and pulled down his pants, letting them tangle at his knees. He had smooth thighs, all the way from the tan line above the knee up to the sharp white edge of his boxer-briefs. I put my hand flat over his Y-front and felt his cock twitch.

I moved my head in, but he stopped me. "Suck him first. You ever had Vietnamese cock before?" The skinnier guy's cock head was fat and round. I swirled my mouth around him, licking it down the shaft. The little jock moaned as I let him thrust a couple of times while I trailed my fingers around his asscrack, underneath his tight ball sac.

Then I turned my attention to the heavier-set guy, the one who'd started it. He'd gotten hard, and the tip of his meat was pointing out the waistband of his boxer-briefs, squeezed against the hard slab of his stomach. I reached out and tugged down the stretchy white material, and his dick fell down toward my wet and warm lips.

I kissed the head and took his foreskin in between my lips and pulled gently. His dick was the opposite of his buddy's, thick and hairy at the base but tapering to a foreskin-covered stub. I reached around the base—it was a real handful—and jiggled the weight of his thick dick against my lips. Out of the corner of my eye, I saw the skinnier jock pumping his dick so fast all I could see was his round pink cock head slipping in and out of his fist in a blur. I took the top of the other dick into my mouth and tasted the residue of his last cum, the cum that he had shot for their movie. I pictured him leveling his cock at his buddy's ass and easing it in, all the way up to the thick base. I swallowed more of him, getting my nose and face closer to his hairless stomach, and reached over and underneath the skinner guy's balls. He let his dick fall from his fist. With one hand, he started smacking it into his palm, and with the other, he ran his fingers through my hair and shoved my head onto his buddy. I took a careful breath through my nose to stop myself from gagging and let the big guy slide into my throat neat.

I let go of his balls so I could reach toward his ass again. He spread his legs and I felt his smooth warm cheeks disappear toward his jock hole. He was rubbing his big round cock head against my furry forearm, leaving streaks of his precum mixed with my spit. The bigger guy stopped thrusting and eased his cock out of my mouth.

"Suck him," he said, and shoved my head toward the skinnier guy. I swallowed his golden-brown cock and felt it tight in the back of my throat. I wiggled my fingers against his ass, rubbing the flat of my forefinger in a circle on his hole. "Oh, yeah," said the big guy, grunting. "I'm going to come all over your face." I turned back toward him and half closed my eyes as a rope of cum shot over me, covering me from cheekbone to chin. He let out another grunted, "Yeah," and spurted again.

The other guy whispered, "I'm coming," like he'd lost his voice, and I opened my mouth and reached down to pull myself off. As he shot in my mouth, filling me up with cum that tasted sweet and sharp, different from his buddy's, my own cock exploded, sending a shower of cum across the gym mats.

"Thanks for opening up for us," said the bigger guy, smirking.

RUSH

D. Fostalove

He came suddenly and laid claim to me like an item from lost and found.

"Keep on playing hard to get...I will have you."

I turned and glanced up into his dark eyes. I did not recognize them or the angry face they were set in. Before I could ask what he meant, he'd climbed onto a forklift and driven toward the other side of the warehouse.

I marched into the bathroom with urgency, but slowed my pace when I saw him standing near the sinks. He glanced in my direction as I bypassed the urinals and moved along the narrow space behind him. In the mirror, his eyes followed me as I entered the last stall and closed the door. Unzipping my fly, I relieved myself, flushed and had turned to leave when I saw the steel-toe boots underneath the stall.

Reluctantly I pulled the door open to see him waiting. He barged inside as I retreated toward the toilet. Closing the door behind him, he took a moment to look me over.

"Hector told me 'bout you," he growled.

"You must have me mistaken with someone else."

"Nah, it's you," he said. "Tight body short dude. Graham cracker brown wit' a gold tooth."

I reached around him and fingered the door handle. "I have to go before the floor supervisor notices I'm gone."

As I pulled the door open, a massive arm sprung from his side and coiled along my waist and around my back, bringing me into him. Caught off guard, I yanked away but his hold was strong. As we stood motionless, pressed chest to chest, I could feel his muscular torso flexing beneath his coveralls, his ragged breath on my neck.

"You smell so fucking good."

I remained frozen as he palmed my ass.

"Touch *it*."

I didn't have to. I knew from initial contact he was completely naked underneath the coveralls. Now I could feel his dick throbbing between us as he held me tighter.

"I ain't going to hurt you."

The restroom door swung open, followed by the distinctive *click-clack* of dress shoes invading the room. The supervisor roared, "Dennison, are you in here?"

With ease, the man lifted me onto the toilet to hide the extra pair of feet in case the supervisor knelt down to search for me. "Nah, he ain't here."

"Quincy?"

"Yeah?"

The supervisor sighed loudly before storming out, the door clanging behind him. I immediately jumped down and brushed past Quincy. He stepped away from the door to allow my exit but grabbed my wrist before I stepped out.

"Meet me here at three thirty."

"All right."

I reentered the bathroom with a bucket of cleaning materials and a mop. Quincy paced back and forth near the urinals. Placing the CLOSED FOR CLEANING sign on the door, I closed and locked it. Quincy watched as I approached. I pointed toward the first stall. He entered. I followed. He turned to face me.

"What did Hector tell you?"

"Busting nuts wit' you is like sniffing coke."

"Take off your clothes and sit."

He unbuttoned his coveralls and let them slide down his body into a crumpled heap atop his black boots. Standing completely naked, tattoos covering both arms and toned chest, he lowered himself onto the commode. I pulled a pair of handcuffs from the bucket and restrained him.

"You know what I want?"

"Yes."

"You do other stuff?"

"Depends."

I dropped to my knees, pushed both of his muscular thighs apart and scooted between them. Grabbing the flaccid flesh dangling dangerously close to the water, I stroked it until it awakened from its slumber.

"I want to see dat booty."

Without hesitation, I stood and disrobed. I could hear the handcuffs jingling against the toilet pipes behind his back. He wanted to touch me so badly. I turned slowly, allowing him to survey my body from the front and back before I returned to the spot between his legs.

His dick was standing intimidatingly tall, like an angry scarecrow with an old war helmet draped atop its dome, stabbed into a field of overgrown vegetation. It throbbed as if a violent gust whizzed by. Undaunted by the battle ahead, I fisted his dick like an ice-cream cone and licked the head. I imagined it was the biggest scoop of double chocolate ice cream I'd seen instead of the weapon of mass destruction it could be if I indulged it anally.

I ran my tongue over the tip and glanced up to see if he was watching. He was. I winked and sucked the head into my mouth unexpectedly. He fidgeted before relaxing as I eased my teasing. While I licked up and down the shaft, I cupped his balls, rotating them like a pair of oversized dice. Instead of blowing on them for luck before tossing them, I brought them to lips and inhaled one. Rolling it around on my tongue, I stroked his shaft with one hand while my other hand crept up his chest.

"Deep-throat my shit."

I stopped stroking his dick and released the ball. I licked my lips before opening my mouth like a serpent dislodging its jaws and consumed him, inch by inch, as he slid along my tongue to the back of my mouth and down my throat.

"Damn, yo."

I accommodated him—his length and girth—like an old friend offering his most comfortable piece of furniture. Removing him, I devoured his dick a second time. As I ran him back and forth over my tongue, slowly at first before speeding up my movements, he groaned lowly. I could tell he was impressed with my skills, as he squirmed beneath me and uttered nearly inaudible curses.

As his dick slipped past my lips and funneled down my throat with each violent thrust of his hips, one of my hands inched up his stomach followed by the other until they reached their respective destinations on both sides of his neck. At first I squeezed lightly while still sucking his dick, but as his breathing became more labored, I tightened my grip around his carotid arteries. His eyes bulged. His tongue slithered from between his lips to wet them, before disappearing. I quickened my pace as the handcuffs clinked loudly.

"I'm about to come, yo," Quincy wheezed.

I clutched his neck even tighter and continued bobbing in his lap, allowing him to slide deeper down my throat as he forced himself upward, each thrust more uncoordinated than the last.

"Fuck!" Quincy stammered barely above a whisper.

I could feel his release shooting down my throat. I kept both hands pressed against his neck as he jerked involuntarily beneath me. I released his throat when his twitching subsided, pulled away and wiped my mouth with the back of my hand. His dick slapped against his thigh and slid down between his legs. Quincy, slumped on the toilet, looked up sluggishly and nodded his approval.

"You suck dick meaner than a muthafucka."

Standing, I leaned over, our faces inches from each other, and reached behind him to release his wrists from the cuffs. As I unfastened him, I whispered, "I know."

PRIMARY
INTERACTION

Christopher Pierce

The Master had been looking for a slave for a long time. The Master was handsome, rugged and muscular, in his early forties. He had his pick of boys, tricks, one-night stands, boyfriends and lovers, guys who wanted to get married and grow old together.

But the Master didn't want any of those things.

He wanted a slave, in every sense of the word, but primarily in the sexual sense. He hated the word *versatile*. He even disliked the terms *top* and *bottom,* finding them weak and tepid in their meaning.

The Master finally found a slave through a local trainer that he discovered online. The Trainer, who shared the Master's view of the way a Master/slave relationship should be, already owned a slave of his own. In his spare time he trained other young men who wanted to be true slaves. When one had completed his training, the Trainer would place him with a local Master that he respected.

The slave that was given to the Master was young—midtwenties—slender, cute in a boyish way but very serious about being a slave. The Trainer gave the slave to the Master and the Master took him home with him. When they got home the Master took the slave into the bathroom, which had a bathtub.

"Strip," said the Master.

"Yes, Sir," the slave said, and removed all of his clothing and folded it neatly in a pile on the floor. Then he knelt in front of his Master.

"I'm going to bathe you now," the Master said. "Get in the tub." The slave obeyed and crawled into the tub and remained on all fours inside it.

The Master reached over to the faucet and turned both the hot and cold dials. Testing the water with one hand, he adjusted it until it reached a warm temperature. From the floor he produced a large oval sponge and a dispenser of liquid soap.

The water in the tub had reached the slave's elbows by the time his Master turned it off. Then the Master pumped some soap on the sponge.

"I'm going to wash away everything you no longer need," said the Master. "Your ego, your pride, your preconceptions, your fears; I'm going to wash away everything that stands in the way of your complete and total submission to me."

"Yes, Sir."

The Master washed the slave then, running the sponge over the young man's back, his arms, his chest, under his arms and anywhere he wanted the sponge to go. He rubbed the slave's flat belly with it, then scrubbed down his abdomen between his legs. The slave closed his eyes as the Master gently lathered up his cock and balls.

Then the Master stroked from the base of the slave's ball sac up between his cheeks, finally settling on the young man's asshole. The Master dipped his hand down into the water, rubbed a little soap on his fingers and returned them to the slave's hole. With precision and care, he gently coaxed the ring of muscle to open just enough for him to slide one finger inside. The slave made a small sound, like a whispered sigh, when he was penetrated.

Watching the slave carefully, the Master put a second finger to the young man's hole, which had clamped back down on the first invading digit. With more soap and gentle pressure, the slave's hole accepted a second finger. The Master continued the encouragement until he had all four fingers of his hand in the slave's butthole.

"Do you know why I'm doing this?" the Master asked.

"Sir?" said the slave in a voice that was beginning to ache with need.

"I'm getting you ready," the Master said. "Are you ready?"

"Yes, Sir."

"Then let's get you out of there and dried off."

After they had rinsed the slave clean, the last of the soapy water flowed down the drain. Dripping, the slave crawled out of the tub back onto the carpet. The Master knelt down next to the slave and dried him with a large white towel. When he was dry, the Master laid the towel under the slave and stood up.

"It's time I fucked my new property," he said. The Master took off his clothes but left his boots on. His dripping cock jutted out from between his legs. "Get on your hands and knees."

The slave obeyed.

The Master spat into his hand, then took his dick with the same hand and mixed his spit with the precum leaking out of his cock's piss slit. The Master descended on the slave from behind, dropping to his knees and mounting the young man.

The Master wrapped one arm around the slave's waist to hold him in place and used the other hand to guide his cock between the slave's asscheeks. The boy's hole was still flexible from the finger-fucking it had received, but his Master's cock was more formidable than his mere fingers had been. The Master pushed his cut, flaring cock head into the slave.

A small noise escaped the slave's lips.

The Master put both hands on the small of the slave's back. "Just relax..." he said.

The slave obeyed, calming himself into stillness and quiet.

"Concentrate on me being inside you," the Master said. "My cock in your ass...that's your whole world right now. I'm a Master and you're my slave. This is our primary interaction: my cock in your ass. You'll come to love it, treasure it, crave it and need it, every bit as much as you need food and air. This interaction will never be reversed. I fuck and you get fucked. You will never fuck me. I penetrate and you get penetrated. I am dominant and you are submissive. This interaction is primal. It is sacred. It is the foundation and purest expression of our relationship. Do you understand?"

"Yes, Sir," said the slave softly.

The Master leaned over so his chest was on top of the slave's back.

"I'm going to fuck you now," said the Master, and thrust himself deep inside the slave. He rode the young man hard, pushing himself into him farther and farther each time. The Master put his whole weight on the slave but the slave's back and arms were sturdy and strong and held them both up. The slave made no further cries or noises of protest during what was undoubtedly a harsh assault.

When the Master was ready to come, he used one hand to jerk off the young man's cock so they would climax together. The Master shot his load into the slave, and the slave's load was caught by the towel that had been laid beneath him.

Trembling with relief and release, the Master and the slave remained in their positions, slave naked on all fours with Master mounting him from behind. When their breathing had finally returned to normal, the Master said:

"You now belong to me. For the first time, call me Master and mean it, with everything you are."

The slave took a deep breath and said:

"Thank you, Master."

WORTH IT

Cari Z

When Jamie grabbed my hand with intent, I knew I was in trouble. I understood his grabs pretty well at this point. There was the insistent "Just-come-quietly" grab, the picky "Pay-attention-to-me" grab, and the ticklish "Let's-go-do-something-fun" grab, among others. This wasn't any of those. This was Jamie's patented "I-need-to-fuck-right-now" grab, with his fingertips pressing hard into the muscles of my forearm. Couple that with the intensity of his gaze and it was a wonder I didn't burst into flames.

Unfortunately this wasn't a good time. We were minutes away from boarding a plane to Germany, where we'd be spending a week with his parents. I'd never met them before, but they were flying both of us out to visit. I didn't want to screw anything up by doing something precipitous, so I shook my head and said, "We can't."

"We so can," Jamie said. He took his earbuds out and brushed his curling brown hair out of his eyes, then gave me the full power of his stare. Jamie's cute when he's not looking at you, a skinny skater kid who looks like a college freshman instead of a first-year graduate student. When he turns his eyes on you, ice blue with flecks of green around the iris, it turns him into a predator. "We can do it, John."

"We board in fifteen minutes."

"Thirteen," he corrected.

"We'll miss the flight."

"We can be fast," he said persuasively, leaning in closer.

"You're crazy."

"I'm horny," he corrected. "You've been so worried about meeting my parents that we haven't fucked in three days, not counting the sixty-nine last night. That was good but it wasn't what I needed." Jamie was the archetype of a pushy bottom. "Once we get to Germany we'll both be jet-lagged, and you'll be all tense with trying to impress the folks, and who knows when I'll get any?"

"Whenever you want it," I said, a little hurt. I never denied Jamie sex; I loved fucking him as much as he loved being fucked, but I didn't react very well to particular types of stress, and meeting his parents qualified as the type that put me out of the mood. "Except right now. Seriously, we're leaving any minute."

"Then we better hurry," he told me, eyes glinting wickedly as he flashed me a smile. I felt myself getting hard and mentally groaned. Jamie had my libido hooked.

"Where?"

"Bathroom. Where else?"

"What about our luggage? We can't leave it here." We each had a backpack as a carry-on.

"We'll bring it with us."

"It's supposed to be in our possession at all times," I objected.

"We'll bring it into the stall, then. Let's hope a handicapped one is free." I opened my mouth to protest again, and Jamie leaned into me, kissed my open lips and murmured, "C'mon, John. It'll be worth it."

That was the thing. Even if we missed the flight, it would still be worth it. Fucking Jamie was always amazing, and if we missed the flight and pissed off his parents and ended up heading back to our apartment, it would still be worth it.

Two minutes later we were in the handicapped stall at the end of the men's bathroom, our backpacks at our feet, and I had Jamie turned toward the wall as I ground my cock against his ass. He groaned and I moved one hand over his mouth.

"Quiet," I whispered in his ear. I traced his lips with my index finger and he sucked it into his mouth, tongue curling around it sensuously. I let him wet my finger as I undid his pants, and he helped me push them down to his knees. After a moment I pulled my finger free and moved my hand down as Jamie gasped, "Back pocket."

I pressed my finger into his hole as my other hand fumbled around for the lubricated condom he'd had the forethought to stick in his pocket. It wouldn't be much, but when Jamie got this way he didn't need much. I loosened him with one finger, then pressed another inside and just held them there while I got my cock out, sighing with relief once the pressure was off.

"Hurry up," Jamie muttered. "*Now.*"

Normally I'd tease him and tell him that patience was a virtue, but under the circumstances it wasn't. I pulled my fingers out, rolled the condom on and moved his feet a little farther apart, then bent my knees just enough and pushed inside.

"Fuuuuck…" Jamie hissed, putting his forehead on the wall and pushing his ass back at me. I brought one hand back up to his mouth and covered it as I began to thrust, not very fast but deep. He was tight and hot and he felt so amazing, and I couldn't believe I had gone three days without fucking him.

"*Now boarding all rows for Flight 837 on Lufthansa to Frankfurt. All rows, Flight 837 to Frankfurt.*"

"That's us," I grunted in his ear, my tension rising again.

Jamie pulled my hand away. "Then you better hurry," he breathed, and began thrusting back at me.

He was right. I picked up the pace, fucking him faster and faster, until our panting had to be audible in other stalls. I was close to coming, I knew it was going to happen soon and it was going to be incredible. I just didn't know if Jamie was there with me. He loved fucking, but he needed a lot of stimulus to come.

It was like he read my mind. "John...please..."

"*Last call for Flight 837 on Lufthansa to Frankfurt. Last call for all rows on Flight 837 to Frankfurt.*"

"Fuck," I groaned. I reached around Jamie's hips and grabbed his cock, and gave him the roughest, sloppiest hand job I'd ever inflicted on anyone. To my surprise he came almost immediately, moaning imperceptibly, catching his cum with a wad of toilet paper he'd had the forethought to grab. I was right there with him, pouring into the condom as he tightened around me. I leaned into Jamie and he leaned into the wall, and we both took a moment to catch our breath before I pulled out.

I threw the condom away, put myself back together and then helped Jamie after making sure he was okay. I grabbed our backpacks, got us out of the stall and we took a second to wash up before I hustled us out the door to the gate. Fortunately it was close, because the flight attendant was shutting the outer door as we hurried up.

"Wait!" Jamie and I passed over our boarding passes. The woman looked us over, taking in our disheveled clothes and Jamie's smugly satisfied look, and hummed to herself before scanning our passes and opening the door for us. We made our way onto the plane and finally settled into our seats in coach, me with a huge sigh of relief.

Jamie buckled his seat belt and then snuggled into my side. "Admit it," he drawled with a grin. "I was right. It was worth it."

"Yeah," I agreed. "You were right. It was."

UNDER THE TUSCAN SUN

D. V. Patton

U nder the heat of the Tuscan sun the artist broke out in perspiration. His hand went to his brow to wipe the sweat from his eyes.

Slowly, methodically, his hands worked the pristine marble. Here the naked breast of the Spartan warrior appeared from the rock. Cold and hard chalk chipped away and a muscular shoulder emerged from the chunk of stone.

An arm appeared, at ease as it lay against the marble warrior's hip. The fingers were surprisingly gentle, feminine almost. Veins appeared on the forearm, a lifetime of muscular ventures released.

The artist felt himself shiver despite the heat. Still his hands worked the stone. He took a step back and looked at the statue. The soldier was half revealed.

The helmeted face looked east, its graceful arm raised

and pointed toward the sun. The warrior's body twisted, accentuating every tone of its midriff. Its chest and body were a valley, contours and sinewy muscle rippling underneath its marble skin.

Still the artist worked, as day became night and then day again. The abdomen was flat and boyish until a forest of pubic hair began. Two *V*-shaped rivers ran down the stone valley ending in the Spartan's manhood, yet here the artist hesitated. Instead his wandering hands chipped lower on the stone, releasing the man's coiled thighs from the depths of the rock.

They were beastly things, powered by tight buttocks that whispered of a constrained power. Soon calves stepped free of the stone, graceful sinewy legs hidden for a million years within this rock.

The old man's sight began to fade but still he worked, as hours became days and weeks. The Spartan's manhood transfixed him and he carved it more carefully and lifelike than his patrons would like. Yet as the end of his greatest creation grew clearer, the man began to weaken and fade until at the last he felt a familiar tightening in his chest.

The old man tottered and fell.

The artist lay on his back, panting and struggling for breath. Something was different. The man known as Carlo gasped as he looked down at his own ailing body. The years had fallen away from him. Gently he stripped his cloth robe from himself, and he viewed his own naked body.

His body had metamorphosed into something it had once been. The years had slipped from him like a fever and now a virile, athletic young man inhabited his skin. His cock lay silently again his thigh, glistening in the candlelight.

From between his thighs he saw the Spartan watching him silently. The helmeted face turned toward him and a pair of keen blue eyes looked into him. Those sky-blue orbs faltered and slipped to the center of his buttocks, staring at the prize offered to the warrior.

Slowly the coiled legs of the warrior stepped from the plinth and the weariness of a thousand years fell away. The warrior seemed to sigh as life sprang into his bones. The manhood between his legs began to sway and then slowly lengthen as blood infused the Spartan's marble-white cock.

How Carlo had labored over that member, smoothing the shaft and curving the beautiful tulip-shaped head. Now it swayed and grew before him, no longer cold marble but infused with life, lust and wanton desire. The battles had been hard but now lay the reward of comfort.

Cold marble hands touched his knees but the artist did not flinch. His eyes grew wide as he sat up, his own cock now rubbing against his belly button. The muscles in his own stomach grew tight, as apprehension fueled his desire. How many years had he toiled? How many years since he had tasted the pleasures of the flesh?

The Spartan's cock hovered inches from his face and,

without hesitation, the artist began to consume the rock-like cock with his mouth. He felt his lips forced apart as the bulbous head forced entry.

He licked and kneaded the shaft and then began to mechanically pleasure the stone warrior come to life. Slowly his mouth fully consumed the marble spear and the artist found his rouge-red lips sliding closer to a forest of black pubic hair.

The warrior bucked his hips and his cock drove down the artist's slick tight throat. Carlo gasped and gagged but did not fight his creation. Instead he felt manly hands placed on his head, locking him in place.

His creation's waist began to tense and release as he forced his shaft methodically into the artist's mouth. Carlo's nostrils flared like those of a horse as he was enslaved by his creation. The motions grew more urgent and now the artist felt the pubic hair slam into his face more frequently. The marble member in his mouth grew ever wider and suddenly began to withdraw. Seed, precious seed filled Carlo's mouth, a taste he had long forgotten. He slurped it greedily as if it were life itself, feeling the slick almond fluid disappearing down his throat.

The artist felt a cool hand on his chest, pushing him flat on his back. The Spartan was not spent, his thick white cock still slick with Carlo's saliva. The artist felt the creation grasp his slim boyish ankles and suddenly his calves were lifted high onto the magnificent soldier's shoulders.

Carlo was open and defenseless, his sweaty smooth manhole an unmistakable invitation between the hills of his buttocks. The warrior did not hesitate; those marble hips arched forward placing the sculpted spear against the slick small hole at the center of the young artist.

Yet there was no pain as he was entered. Carlo felt his center open like a rose peeling apart, his tight, tiny manhole not being forced open, but rather his whole body turned to milk as the veined stone shaft slid past his sphincter. The artist gasped an animalistic sound as he felt the cock impale him.

There was a mastery here he had never felt before, not in his long years on this earth. The sculpted cock twisted his body and found his pleasure point, deep inside, without effort. Each long thrust caused him to gasp and cry out as pleasure mixed with a dart of pain. The throbbing sang from his asshole and up his spine like a bow.

Never had he taken such length and girth inside his tight boyish buttocks and yet there was only pleasure, a sensation of lovemaking he had forever been denied. The Spartan began to pull his bulbous cock head back to his sphincter before slipping its full length deeper inside than before.

Carlo began to cry, gasp and laugh. His eyes grew wide as the morning light filtered in through the window; one beam of sunshine drew ever closer to them as his thighs and buttocks slid up and down the Spartan spear. The light approached as he moaned and screamed in pleasure until suddenly it consumed them both and he was floating in a serene calm sea, his worries and fears forever gone.

When the initiates came to check on the old man that evening, Carlo the artist was gone forever but his creation in marble, the magnificent naked Spartan would live for a thousand years and more.

ONE FOR
THE TEAM

Bob Masters

D ave was walking home one afternoon, slowly making
his way toward his apartment in midtown Atlanta.
The subway had let him off in the middle of the city. He
could have waited for the bus, but it was a beautiful day
in early fall, warm and sunny. Dave liked to get some
sun and exercise his legs instead of sitting in a loud and
crowded bus, so he had decided to hoof the half mile.
Thirty-four, slender and athletic, he kept his hair short
and his body in tip-top shape.

He really wasn't looking to hook up with anyone, but
when he started to pass two slightly paunchy twenty-
year-old guys piling out of a beat-up Japanese car, he
slowed down a little. One of them was rushing back to
the trunk and removing three cases of beer. He smiled,
and they turned and smiled back. They didn't exactly

look gay. Short, stoutly built, they exuded the air of two roommates who didn't know the meaning of clothes beyond jeans and a sweatshirt. Their features were handsome in a boyish way. He expected to keep walking and let them go about their beer business, but their smiles were just a little too lingering and welcoming for that. He broke the silence.

"Hi, guys. What are you going to do with all that beer? Drink it all tonight?"

The guy who was a few steps down the walkway to their apartment answered.

"You betcha. We're gonna watch the football game. You like football? Want to come watch it with us?"

His buddy, the one with the beer, chimed right in.

"Yeah, guy, we could always use another guy to help us down a few brews while we watch the game."

Dave decided that his afternoon was going to be more interesting than he had thought. He liked their innocent enthusiasm and easy, welcoming demeanor. Maybe the beer would lead to something else.

"Sure, when does it start?"

"Well, the first game is going to start in about ten minutes. Why don't you come inside? We got pretzels and potato chips too. Maybe get a pizza later on. Me and Bud here like to have fun when we watch football, don't we Bud?"

"Yes, sir. Me and Jimbo here are from Chicago. Football rules in Chicago. We can tell you anything you want to know about football."

He didn't know the first thing about football, but it didn't really matter. The pretence was sweet. He was their physical opposite, tall and muscular versus their short and somewhat heavy frames. But large and full asses always did something to him, and the thought of having two drunk and horny football freaks on each side of him made his cock jump.

"Well, I am sure up for a few beers. I know a little bit about the game. Maybe you can fill me in on some of the moves."

Did that sound suggestive?

"We can show you every move, if you want," answered Bud, not missing a beat.

"Well, lead on, then. Here, let me help you with some of those beer cases, Jimbo, is it?"

"Sure, and your name?" said Jimbo, handing Dave a case of Pabst.

"Dave."

"Pleased to meet you, Dave," said the dark-haired youngster.

The three young men entered a small apartment, not much more than a living room with an adjoining kitchen, with a bedroom hidden somewhere. They turned on their flat-screen TV, a surprising luxury for what were obviously two twenty-year-olds who barely had money for a decent car. The beers were soon flowing. Dave was seated between the two young men on a none-too-large couch. All of their legs were touching and the amount of friction between them increased exponentially with every exciting play. Bud and Jimbo responded with the enthusiasm of true fans, pounding their feet and standing up to cheer when some player made a touchdown or an interception turned the tide of fortune. The beer was like a lubricant, letting them let go. Dave mostly watched the players' asses. That was the way it went for an hour, two hours, maybe three; Dave really couldn't tell. Yes, there had been pretzels; yes, there had been potato chips; it is even possible that a pizza was involved, at some point. But any food consumed had little chance of counteracting the endless cans of beer the three young men were downing.

It was after sundown and all three were completely drunk. No one leapt up to cheer a successful pass anymore. Bud and Jimbo began to show they had more in mind than just watching sports. The two young men on either side of a drunken Dave had eventually taken to putting their arms around him and lightly slapping his inner thighs. Then their hands started to linger on his thighs a little longer, not that he minded. He softly moaned and laid his head against Bud's shoulder. Jimbo immediately reached over and pulled Dave's polo shirt up over his head.

Both boys began raining kisses all over his chest, pausing to suck his nipples, then licking his abdomen, tonguing his armpits. He trembled with excitement and fell over into Jimbo's lap, while Bud deftly unbuckled his cargo shorts and pulled them down his legs. He was buck naked and drunk between two horned-up, drunken football fanatics. What could be more wonderful? He fumbled with Jimbo's belt, and the large boy helped him by pulling his jeans down his legs. He had beautiful hairy thighs that were bigger than Dave's waist. They were joined to a fleshy and full ass that sent Dave into paroxysms of drunken lust. He could hear and feel Bud struggling with his own jeans behind him. Soon all three were naked, tumbling and wrestling with each other's naked flesh. The previous three hours had been an aphrodisiac, their pent-up desire bursting forth like a water balloon that had reached the breaking point.

Opposites attract, and Dave could feel the two heavyset endomorphs relish his taller ectomorphic body. Bud began rimming him while Jimbo kissed and licked him all over. He yearned to fondle and caress their ample asses, the kind of asses he always wished for himself, being cursed with a "white-boy butt." They both obliged him, and he found himself fucking Jimbo while Bud plowed his own ass from behind. The soft flesh slapping both beneath him and behind him made him feel like he was sandwiched between two hairy teddy bears. They were young and innocent and sweet. The football ceremony strangely made it all seem more personal, more tender. He felt like a twenty-year-old sophomore again. When he felt Bud shudder and shake and empty his sperm up Dave's ass, the sensations made him feel wanton and wild. Soon his own cum was shooting and Jimbo bucked and thrashed underneath him, signaling his own climax.

Dave was pretty sure he would be spending the night. They would hold him between them. Even if it was only for tonight, that would be enough.

NIGHT SWEAT

William Holden

His eyes lingered as I ran my fingers over the soft bristles of the kiwi. I studied his rain-soaked appearance. I could see the hair of his chest through the wet, thin material of his tank top. I wondered if that pelt felt like the ripe fruit. Thunder crashed and exploded outside. He walked toward me. My fingers pressed into the soft flesh of the fruit. He stopped on the other side of the stand and slipped a grape into his mouth. I imagined the cool sweetness exploding down his throat. A smile swept across his face. I could feel him undressing me with his sultry brown eyes.

The silence between us hung heavily in the air. We spoke without words. We touched without hands. Our eyes hid nothing. Our desire grew with every moment. He smiled and walked down the aisle. He looked over his shoulder, tilted his head—inviting me to follow.

He stood by the frozen foods. He held the door open. I walked up next to him. The cold air surrounded us. Thunder erupted again—the lights flickered. In the intermittent light I saw the mass of blond hair that covered his armpit. It was stuck to his skin with sweat from the heat and rain outdoors. I bent down between him and the door and grabbed a box of Popsicles. I could smell his musky overheated scent. I wanted desperately to run my tongue through his armpit, taste his salty sweat. I stood up slowly, moving only inches from his slender body. The heat radiated off of him engulfing me with a mix of scents. Another crash of thunder—then everything went dark.

I stood there without moving, adjusting my eyes to the darkness. We were inches apart. The smell of his body drew me closer. His hot, grape-scented breath brushed across my face—intoxicating me.

I heard a voice in the distance asking people to stay put and not to move. I saw a smile appear on his face. His eyes never left mine as he grabbed the box of Popsicles from my hand and opened it. I heard the paper ripping in the near silence of the darkness, then the sweet smell of raspberries.

Suddenly a biting cold brushed across my skin. A chilling liquid began to run down my neck as the heat of my body melted the icy crystals. He ran it over my neck, then across my lips. I opened my mouth and he slid the frozen stick inside. As he pulled it out a small trail of juice ran down my chin. He moved in closer and licked it off. His tongue moved across my lips. I wanted to kiss him, to suck his tongue into my mouth, but he pulled away too quickly with a teasing grin. He slid the icy stick into his mouth and bit off the tip. I could hear the cold crunching sound of the ice against his teeth. He leaned into me. His lips touched mine. They were warm and sticky. He opened his mouth. I opened mine and sucked the warmed raspberry liquid into my mouth.

I felt his fingers release the buttons of my shirt, as our tongues explored each other's mouths. He pushed the shirt off my shoulders. He pinched my nipples, sending rivers of fire coursing through my body. I broke our kiss and pushed him against the freezer door. Our eyes met in the dim light. I could feel them burning into me. I raised his hands over his head and buried my mouth in his left armpit.

His sweat mixed with a subtle hint of expiring deodorant invaded my mouth and senses. I nibbled on the thick strands of hair, licking and sucking the flavors off every follicle. His body shook against mine. I felt his cock stiffening against me. My hand moved down between us. I traced the outline of his cock with my finger. It pulsed through the fabric of his cutoff jeans.

I spun him around and reached in front of him to release the button and fly. His shorts fell to his ankles, exposing his small, firm ass. I fell to my knees and ran my tongue through the thick, musky scent of his ass. His soft blond hair caressed my nose as I pushed farther into his tightly clenched hole.

My cock, swollen beyond the limits of my underwear, ached. I stood up and quickly released my pants, pulling my jeans and underwear down simultaneously. My cock fell against his ass with a wet smack. I pulled back and let the precome-soaked head sink into the crack of his ass. He moaned against the glass as the head of my cock toyed with his waiting hole.

I grabbed the base of my cock and pushed against him. His ass opened immediately and swallowed my cock whole. It sucked and milked the precome out of me with every muscle contraction. I could feel the beat of his heart deep inside his ass—pulsing against my cock.

I pulled slowly out of him. I felt the warmth of his ass giving way to my thickness, before shoving my cock back inside. The door to the freezer rattled against the force of our bodies. I could hear his moans of painful pleasure. I fucked him harder. I reached in front of him and grabbed his cock. It grew in my grasp. I squeezed and pulled on the thick layers of foreskin as I began to jack his cock to the rhythm of my hips.

Suddenly a light appeared, illuminating our naked bodies. We paused, my cock still lodged deep inside of him. An employee stood down an aisle. A beam of light stroked our bodies in the darkness. He turned the flashlight off. His darkened silhouette didn't leave. He stood watching our movements in the darkness.

I fucked him harder as the thrill of being caught seized

me. My body slammed against his. The cold air of the
freezer chilled our overheated bodies. His cock pulsed
and throbbed in my grip. His moans grew heavier and
louder. Our sex echoed around us and carried down the
aisles.

I could feel the come building inside of me. The
burning heat tightened my hairy balls as I reached my
limit of control. I pushed my face against his back. I
licked the sweat off his skin as my orgasm rushed into
him. My cock continued to swell, shooting several more
thick jets of come into his hungry ass. My body shook
from the final release. I felt his body tighten against
mine. My hand became wet with a hot, thick liquid—his
come rushing through my fingers.

The lights flickered on. We looked at each other but
didn't speak. I wanted to take him home with me—to
fuck him again. He picked up my wallet and shuffled
through the bills. He pulled out fifty dollars then walked
away, leaving me alone with the taste of his sweat still
lingering on my tongue.

FRIENDLY FIRE

Gregory L. Norris

Here, like this…"

Allan moved closer, repositioning my arm, adjusting my shoulder. I caught a hint of his scent on my next sip of breath and my focus wandered further. His skin smelled clean from whatever basic masculine soap he'd last showered with, plus that unmistakable hint of male pheromones leeching through skin, which has always reminded me of summer rain.

"Pay attention, dude," he grumbled, his patience with me clearly wearing thin. The former Navy helicopter mechanic braced my body with his, the warmth of his nearness unleashing a chill down my spine. "The recoil's gonna shoot that stock up and into your chin, you keep holding it like that."

He adjusted the rifle in my grasp. Suddenly, I was

less conscious of the weapon and intimately aware of Allan's musculature. At twenty-six, he was a solid mass of lean maleness, only a year or so removed from military service. He still wore his chestnut hair in a flattop, but had grown a goatee following a very honorable discharge. Adding to the manly scent emanating off his skin was the smell of motor oil. He pressed against me, demonstrating the proper stance, and one muscle in particular registered through his old cammies, whatever he had on for underwear, and my jeans and boxers. My focus evaporated.

"Allan," I sighed.

"Come on, buddy—you can get this."

I pressed back against what he was subconsciously pushing forward. Allan tensed. For another few seconds, we remained together in that position and I swore I felt the pulse of his dick.

"I only wish I could get *this*," I said, rubbing my jeans-clad butt into his thickness.

Allan's throat, so close to mine, knotted under the influence of a heavy swallow. He coughed to clear it and then, one body part at a time, withdrew: strong hands first; arms; chest; the big, booted feet bracing my sneakers; finally his dick.

"So, do you have any more questions?"

"Only one," I said. It was now, or never to be. "You helped me out with my research. Anything I can help you out with? You know, to thank you?"

Letting go of the rifle, I slid my right hand behind me

and reached around. Allan was still close enough. My fingers brushed over his crotch, which turned out to be as tented as I'd imagined. He'd thrown bone and was hard in his cammies.

"Dude," he grunted.

I squeezed the fullness of his cock and groped the loose meat of his balls, which seemed huge beneath my touch.

"I'm not gay."

"No, but you're harder than granite, so how about you let me thank you properly. Interested?"

Allan said, "I'm good, thanks."

My own cock pressed against my zipper, so hard and at such an awkward angle it verged on painful. "I know you're good. The question is, do you want me to go down on you, no reciprocation needed? A little gratitude for teaching me how to handle a rifle properly."

Allan chuckled. "Oh, you sure know what you're doing, that's for fuckin' sure."

I turned around and handed Allan the shotgun. "You hold onto this one. I'll take care of the other."

I stole a brief glance into his gray-blue gaze, saw the last of his hesitation written in and around his eyes, along with his incredible mouth, which had brought so many women pleasure; that goatee adding to his classic, rugged handsomeness. From the periphery, I again recorded the tufts of dark hair poking up from the collar of his threadbare T-shirt.

Dropping to my knees, I drank in the rest of his

magnificence: his toned torso, athletic legs and huge feet. And, of course, that decent bulge, which I worked to free before Allan's twenty-twenty kicked in, and we lost the moment. I popped the four brass buttons of his cammies and worked open his belt and fly. Tented black boxer-briefs waited beneath, with a dot of wetness on the crown. I tugged down the elastic waistband. Allan's cock jumped out, thick and hairy, with a fat head and a pair of fatter balls swinging underneath, all of it ripe with the musty stink of a real man's sweat.

Opening wide, I took his cock into my mouth and sucked.

I knew all about Allan Valico's cock. For months, his girlfriend had told me the intimate details about how its perfect thickness had filled her tightly; how his big, hairy balls had banged her raw from behind, like lead ingots. How—and this was the most telling part—he was always up for a fuck, his nuts swollen and full of come-juice, never going down, no matter how often she threw one at him.

Traci had been clear about this part, too. "He loves head, but I don't like the taste...or the smell. Allan doesn't manscape. His rocks are so hairy and always so sweaty."

She was an excellent photographer at the magazine, which was how she'd met Allan. But she hadn't been the best girlfriend when it came to meeting the man's voracious sexual needs. When I was assigned a story that necessitated me knowing how to properly fire a rifle, I knew exactly who to ask to school me.

Allan now ran a garage out on a remote stretch of Route 13 and had happily offered to show me what he had learned about guns in the service. On my knees, playfully tugging on his balls, I showed him what I knew about servicing a man's needs.

"Oh, *fuck*," Allan growled.

I caressed one of his steel-tough legs, aware of his stiffness all over, not just in the condition of his dick. The cock I'd jerked off to for weeks, replaying Traci's descriptions in my fantasies, was every bit as impressive up close; more so, because while she had rejected it, at that moment it was all mine to enjoy. Allan's nuts were a meaty pair of low-swingers, musky and covered in pelt. I spit out his tool long enough to attend to them. Again, I already knew how much he loved having his stones worked, because she'd bitched about sucking them. I worked Allan's balls, one at a time. This broke his ice. Allan reached down and raked his dirty mechanic's fingers through my hair.

"Fuckin suck my nuts, dude..."

I got both of his jawbreakers into my mouth at the same time, an act that drove him to the tops of his toes. I gobbled Allan's nuts. He rocked on his heels, pulling backward. His cock grew wet and slippery in my hand.

I'd given plenty of head before that afternoon, but I wanted this to be the best ever, because I sensed that if I went the distance, it wouldn't be just a one-time thing.

Allan Valico was the kind of red-blooded, all-American he-man I could get used to having a mutually beneficial relationship with.

I licked his pubes, hungry for a taste of his asshole. In due time, I thought: hole and toes and armpits. But first, I had to show him I was worth thinking outside the norm, outside the *box*. I had to finish what I'd started.

I took his cock between my lips and sucked him down to the root. Allan's balls ricocheted off my chin with mighty weight. Traci hadn't exaggerated on that count, either. I tickled his nuts, pulled back on his bone, plunged down. While I was sucking, Allan thrust in, and the flow of precome quickened. We were in perfect sync. I hummed on Allan's cock. Allan grunted and caressed my skull.

"You want my spunk, pal?"

I moaned an affirmative around his cock.

"You want it? You're a damn fine cocksucker, buddy. Maybe the best I've ever met. I might have to let you worship this big hairy bone again. Yeah, sure, but only if you show me how much you want it. You thirsty, dude? Thirsty for my swimmers? You gonna take it down, swallow Big Allan's seed?"

I ramped things up, and Allan unloaded.

I didn't disappoint, and after I cleaned him up, neither did he with his promise to feed my insatiable hunger in the days, nights and years that followed.

SPIT-BUBBLE
AND SNOT

Larkin

I didn't even ask him his name. It had happened that fast. He was sitting on his bike in Tompkins Square Park.

"What's up?" is always the opening line. We talked about pot.

He was young and not especially pretty. He was a dirty boy with his long hair parted in the middle and a shark tooth earring dangling from one ear. I was fascinated, watching him make spit-bubbles and trying to blow them off his tongue. When he stood up, he looked off in the distance. I watched while he scratched his ass. It took no time to lure him to Eddie's apartment. He knew exactly what was up, and it didn't seem to bother him in the least.

He sat on the couch, undid his pants and pushed them

down. He lifted his legs to pull them off over his Nikes. His asshole was dark and hairless. After he pulled off his shirt, he was naked except for his shoes and socks.

He lay back on the couch and carelessly spread his legs. He had a nice set of big, round balls and a long, uncut cock topped by an early growth of sparse pubic hair. I got down on my hands and knees between his legs. I handled his cock and sucked on it until it got hard. When I was licking his nuts I could smell his ass. It was ripe and slightly untidy. When I was sucking his cock I looked into his impassive eyes. He stared back at me like he didn't give a shit.

While I sucked, the kid dug his finger up his nose. He looked away from me just long enough to study the snot on the end of his finger. Then he rubbed it off on the arm of the couch. Casually, he looked at me as I sucked on his stiff bone.

The kid lifted one leg and pinned it back with his arm, exposing his ass to me. I just couldn't pass it up. I figured it was a valuable part of the experience. I started by giving his ball sac a good lick, both sides and under-neath. Then I moved lower. His cocky untidiness was so fucking thrilling. It was tempting me to come in my pants. I licked all around his hole and then probed its interior with my tongue. The kid started jacking off. He was grooving. He pulled up his other leg so that it spread his ass open and wide. His asshole was expanding and contracting. I studied all of its detail with my tongue. Eating his ass gave me this sick and twisted feeling. It was something like the worshipping of an evil demon. I pushed a spit-covered finger up his dirty hole.

He rested his legs back on the floor. He was standing over me. I looked up and gobs of white cum rained down on my face. I opened my mouth. It was uncomplicated, rude and nasty; definitely worth it.

A few days later I ran into him again. It turned out his name was Phil. I thought Phil was a stupid name for such a hot, nasty punk. Phil never smiled or changed his expression, so it was hard to figure him out. I suggested that we might be able to find some pot, go somewhere and fuck around.

He frowned and said, "Look, I'm not no fag and I don't get fucked up the ass, okay, so fuck off."

I laughed, but Phil looked serious.

I thought of saying, "If you like your asshole licked out so much, then maybe you should try it." But I didn't. "No, no, you know what we did last time and I don't mind if you want to fuck me."

It looked like he was checking me out. I'd like to think that he figured that if he was going to fuck around with a guy, he could do a lot worse.

"Oh, okay, that's cool; I can get into that…" He looked quizzically at me. "You like getting fucked up the ass?"

"Yeah, it feels good, and if it's the right person, it's awesome." Phil shrugged his shoulders.

We ended up back at Eddie's. Eddie had been gone for weeks. I supposed that he could show up at any time.

I liked to imagine Eddie walking in when some guy was in the middle of fucking my ass fast and hard. I really wanted that to happen. I wanted to see the look on his face. I needed Eddie to know that I was desirable even if it meant that he would kick my ass for being a whore.

Phil stood in the middle of the room, hand down his pants, adjusting his cock. This time, I sat on the couch and Phil dropped his pants and climbed on top of me. He fucked me in my mouth.

It seemed like he wasn't interested in me at all, he was just interested in shooting his load.

You know what? I really like it that way just fine.

Standing over me, he pulled off his shirt and threw it on the floor. I managed to kick off my shoes and slide my pants down and off with Phil still straddling me. He got off of me long enough for me to slide into the couch and raise my legs. Phil moved forward and let two huge gobs of spit drop into his cupped hand. He applied the spit to his hard dick and pushed my legs back farther, then, holding his cock in one hand, he pushed it up my asshole and leaned forward to begin the real fuck. He had no choice but to become intimate with me. I looked straight into his animal eyes. I wrapped my arms around him and breathed in the scent from under his arms. In no time, he was fucking me like crazy. He was grunting and growling, going in deep. We were face-to-face. When he gasped, I could smell his breath. It sure made my cock hard and I wanted more. Finally, Phil started huffing in sync with long strokes in and out of my ass. He pushed my legs back farther so that my ass rose up and he dropped in even deeper. Then I felt his cum flooding me. His stiff cock had become suddenly slippery. This was followed by a series of gratifying grunts and short thrusts that eventually petered out.

He lay on me and was still for a moment. When his cock slipped out of my ass, he stood up and swayed there almost out of balance. I rolled forward and began sucking his cock. This surprised Phil, but I thought, *Fuck it*. In a few minutes, he was gone. I thought I could love Phil, because Phil would never love me or anyone for that matter.

The next time I saw him he was in the park with a short, overweight girl who looked pregnant. She had him by the arm and wouldn't let him stray. He had the same impassive look on his face.

GOOD VIBRATIONS

R. J. Bradshaw

His right hand is tightened around the microphone, his lips curled into a smile as he talks. He must be saying something funny; the mostly female crowd is laughing, breasts jiggling and flirtatious eyes attentive. He has creases around his eyes and a dimple between his brows when he smiles; you can tell it's genuine. He loves the music, loves the laughing crowd and standing in the spotlight while wearing a tux. Everybody's confident in a tux; I know I am. The whole band is wearing them, black bow ties to top off the look, no doubt trying to be ironic. They're called Kokomo, a Beach Boys cover band. *He should be wearing a Speedo instead*, I ponder, *or maybe just the bowtie*. I imagine him naked, black bow tie knotted perfectly around his erect dick, the smell of silk in my nostrils as his swollen head slides across my tongue.

Breasts jiggle once more before the vibrations pick up again; I'm standing next to the speaker to catch the full effect. My hands rest on the wooden stage so I can feel the rhythm of his tapping foot as he belts out "Help Me, Rhonda." I watch his lips making love to the song, hot lips that would look even hotter making love to my cock. I scanned over Beach Boys lyrics before coming to the concert so I could follow along with the motion of those lips. "Help me get her out of my heart," he pleads. *I could do that*, I think. *Just give me five minutes alone with you.*

He might actually pass for the surfer Beach Boy type if it wasn't for the tux. His hair is longish, blond, slightly curled in the back. Blond stubble graces his cheeks and chin and the space between his nose and mouth. He must be in his late twenties, early thirties at most. And goddamn, is he attractive. I know I'm not the only one who thinks so; every woman in the crowd is practically in heat. He's got that "I might not be the smartest guy out there, but I can peer into your soul and know exactly how you like it" kinda look. The next song he breaks into is "I Get Around," and I have no doubt that he does. But I bet he's never been with a deaf guy; maybe he hasn't been with a guy at all. I bet I could teach him a few things.

My sight shifts from the edible dimple between his brows to his eyes, and my horniness for him peaks as his eyes lock momentarily with mine; he smiles again, a lyrical smile, this one seemingly meant for me alone. The big-chested woman beside me notices too, giving me a scowl that screams, *What makes you so goddamned special?* Admittedly, I'm wondering the same thing. *There may be two girls for every boy in this room*, I think, *but maybe, just maybe, he's not interested in girls*. I grin at the thought, my eyes peeled for a second sign. There it is: he looks at me again while his foot taps the wooden stage; it's like a heartbeat beneath my palms. His smile is hungry this time. The woman next to me frowns my way again. Still grinning, I shrug at her: sign language for *Eat it, bitch*.

The members of Kokomo take their bows when the show is over, musical vibrations halted. The clapping of hands ensues, a pair of underwear is thrown at the lead man who's still sneaking glances my way. And a crumpled piece of paper is thrown; on it: my name, cell phone number and a few words. He bends over to pick it up, reading it with a wink in my direction. I know it won't be the last time he bends over for me.

The next day, my phone vibrates against my right asscheek: good vibrations.

TALK TO ME

Thomas Fuchs

I guess it's just the life, but it's kind of left me thinking.

I'm standing at the bar and there's this tug at my sleeve, and when I look, there are these beautiful brown eyes and a kind of sly smile. Altogether a very nice-looking guy, a little younger than me I'd say, very early twenties, dark hair, broad shoulders. Not bad at all, and it is getting late.

He's holding a bottle of beer. To be friendly, I offer him another, but he shrugs no, takes a swig. He's still got plenty. I decide on a conversational gambit and say, "My name's Roy."

He presses close to me, coming on very strong, breathing into my ear. He snakes an arm around my waist, his hand brushes my cock.

I say, "I guess you're not into small talk," and there's

still no reply, so I ask, "Are you mute?"

He shakes his head no, kisses me on the ear.

It's kind of a cute game and in any event, he does have me turned on hard, so I ask him if he wants to come over to my place. "I live just a few blocks away. We can walk it." He nods yes, and we're off.

As we're walking, I'm wondering what exactly this guy's into since of course we haven't talked, but things are happening so fast I figure I'll be finding out pretty quick.

Sure enough, as soon as we're in my apartment, he's unzipping my jacket, pulling it and the rest of my clothes off and kissing me, and I'm pulling his clothes off. From this point on, words wouldn't have been necessary, even if he had been talking. He pulls me toward the couch, plops down and starts licking my dick, doing a damn good job of it, I have to say. After a few minutes of this, we move to the bedroom, and when I open the bedside stand and pull out the lube and condoms, he gets onto the bed on his hands and knees, his lovely round ass propped up high and wide for me. We're communicating just fine.

I'll spare you all the details—are you bitterly disappointed? This isn't a porn show, it's something that happened to me—but I did fuck him good. And he was a fine, fine bottom. You know, some guys just lie there and take it, but he pushed back and squeezed me, and I was really giving him my best; I grabbed hold of his dick and pumped him while I was fucking him.

Of course, he wasn't completely silent through all this. When we started fucking, he started making all the sounds you usually hear—grunts, groans and moans, *ohs* and long, drawn-out *ahs*. But still, no words, no talk. He didn't even say anything when I pulled out, stripped off the rubber and gave him my big finish, shooting on his chest. Right after that, he got himself off and then just rolled back and shut his eyes. And still not a word. I was thinking, *Maybe he really is mute or something.*

I guess I fell asleep for a few minutes. When I woke up, I heard the shower. I was going to join him but before I could, he finished and came out, toweling himself off and heading for the living room, where his clothes were. I followed and watched him dress, wondering what kind of a guy he really was and if it might be fun to get to know him.

He got his jacket on, ready to go; he came over and gave me a hug. I really wanted to talk to him, so I told him, "You're driving me crazy with this mute act. Would you please say something?" And this fucker smiled, looked at me and said—and this is exactly what he said—"Hi, you're cute. Have I seen you around here before? Do you live near here? Versatile? Oh, wow, that was hot. Call me sometime? Gotta go. Bye." *Sigh.*

He was out the door a moment after delivering this little speech.

As I said at the beginning, I guess it's just the life, but I'm thinking maybe I ought to take a little break for a while.

WASTE NOT

Troy Storm

G arr strode down the dank stone steps following his first chief, expecting the worst as his drunken minion kicked open a heavy wooden door. Their guest was obviously so incapacitated as to not require guards. *So much for civility.* But this was war, Garr savagely reminded himself, and war was not civil.

The young man hanging with arms and legs stretched wide might not even be alive. The first chief strutted across the stone floor.

"They are beasts, good for nothing but rutting and warring. Yet we touched him not." He hooted. "We flung rotted scraps and garbage at his bulging arms and legs and his disgusting horse cock. Sullen pig. May I return, master?" he wheedled.

"I cannot think in such stink," Garr growled. "Our

shit is no sweeter scented than theirs." He reached for
a nearby bucket of water as his first chief joined in the
dousing. The prisoner lurched to life and gasped for air.
"Return to the mead hall," Garr dismissed the chief.
"Rut at will. We have warred aplenty."

The lean warrior whooped his thanks and bounded
back up the stairs to the boisterous celebration.

"If a beast, a magnificent one," the battle-weary
leader muttered, his eyes roaming the dripping contours
of the splayed prisoner. "What a steed." He gripped the
flaccid horse cock and thrust the heavy skin back from
the massive arrowhead, pink and glowing in the dusky
air. The prisoner groaned, his handsome face barely
aware. Garr firmly pumped his fist. "Could this beget
a race of powerful, perfect animals? Peaceful animals?
Happy in their homes…in their huts?" The exhausted
body tried wanly to protest, but the man's appendage
thickened and rose. "So fucking beautiful. Shower me
with your seed."

There was a cry of anguish and the captive's milk
erupted, splattering the sweating leader, who aimed the
massive cock at his face, his chest, his crotch. His howls
of laughter rang throughout the dungeon. "What cock
sputum to breed, and for those of us not breeders, to
bathe in." His beaming face grew serious as the prisoner's broad chest heaved and his heavy lids blinked
warily down at his captor. "It is senseless to slay such
a being."

He cut the man down and threw him across his

shoulders, mindful of his agonizing cries. "Bear longer. We will now treat your life with respect." One arm circled the slim hips, fingers pressed firmly on the hard, rounded buttocks as Garr's other hand snaked under to grip the solid, still drizzling cock. His smile was wry. "If not your body."

While his alchemist further cleaned and examined the young warrior, Garr washed himself and prepared his chambers with scent, clean furs and lamplight.

"Your ligaments are afire. They must cool and heal." He smiled at the naked body in his bed. "We will strengthen you." Gently he pressed the powerful thighs wide and bent to stroke his tongue from the massive balls up the length of the soft but quickly filling meat.

The deep-set eyes stared at Garr. "Why?" His voice was like a deep rush of summer wind, a crackling winter fire, rich fecund earth.

"I'm sick of war." Garr suckled on the golden knob. "My council disagrees. Perhaps we could buy a pause in this madness with your life. Your death would be a waste." He nuzzled the heavy balls. "Such useful cum." He straightened to preen, sensuously rubbing his face and naked chest. "My skin silkens already."

The wary eyes took their time appreciating the powerfully shaped slim body of his captor. "You would make male love to me? Tamon, son of the great leader? My father is as mad for war as your council. He would sacrifice me in a thunderclap. We are on our own if we wish peace. Now am I so enticing?" His look soured and, painfully, he turned his head away.

"Tamon and Garr. Garr and Tamon." Garr's hands moved over the screaming tendons. "The bards would decide if it resounds." It took both his palms to cup the milk-producing nuts; all his fingers to encompass the insistent python, its thick hood quickly retracting. "Perhaps a cottage in the northern woods. A hearty fire to ward off the cold. Furs to lie on. To sleep on. Ah…" He kissed the head of the python, suctioning from it a bubbling grease. "But *you* do not sleep, great snake."

Garr easily devoured the massive horse cock. His throat opened to the thrust of the huge slab—as Tamon struggled to arch his hips—then closed to encapsulate the beast. The captured warrior gasped. Garr's hands tugged and tossed the giant gonads, explored Tamon's inner thighs and threaded through the dark curls that bedded the python.

"Before, forgive my lack of constraint. I…"

"You are the winner," Tamon croaked. "Take what you will."

"Enough of winning and losing and taking! Your men are slaughtered. Our bravest are rancid meat. What's left crawls in the dirt to survive. Of this, we who lead should be proud? We are idiots. Idiots to decimate ourselves." A final roar. "On both our heads!" He stormed from the room.

Days later the alchemist entered the chamber of his grieving leader. "My master, he is much improved. You have not seen him since your separation. I've taken him to see what's left of his men and our wounded. He seeks to speak with you."

Garr sighed, determined not to abase himself again. *Little cottages,* he snorted to himself. *A horse cock.* How little it took—he could not help but smile—perhaps how *much* it took...but he was over that now.

Tamon bounded into the space, filling it with his healing manliness, his youthful enthusiasm. Garr's heart leaped. With a sigh he realized there could be no constraint. Tamon flung himself at Garr's feet.

"The bards never sing of what comes after. Of how a man must survive with severed limbs, unseeing eyes, incessant hurt." He looked up, his puzzled eyes wet. "But they want to fight anew. It is their destiny, they bleat. Their gods' decree. Their women wail. Our gods' decree. Whose gods are right?" He laid his head in Garr's lap, pressing his face into the roiling mound. "I dream of only us. Am I weak?"

Garr pulled Tamon up and clutched his crotch. "Not that I can tell."

Tamon grinned. "To horse."

Garr smirked. "Aye. Horse cock."

The first chief stood watching the mounted duo disappear into the northern forest. "They're naked?" he questioned the alchemist.

"They wish to commune with the spirits. They have faith."

"The captive is riding backward."

Posted on my former master's not-quite horse cock,

the alchemist mused, rubbing his own rigid rod beneath his robes, thanks to my ointments and salves. And thanks to those same medicaments, the very proud horse cock probably already erupting between them will soon be settled between my former master's begging buttcheeks, digging deep for the happiness and peace I wish them both.

"I have an army to waste!" the first chief chortled. "To arms!" he shouted, turning from the disappearing steed. "We fight...someone...somewhere! For some reason...or none!"

The alchemist's eyes remained on the peace seekers.

"Waste not," he blessed.

AS I LAY

Shane St. John

He spread before me like the land, beautiful but barren, dry but delectable, his nether hills alabaster white, their purity divided by the tempting darkness of the cleft between.

Like the land, he was in need of plowing.

As did Moses, I must strike the hills and bring forth moistness, wetness to gush into the chasm and wash away its iniquitous drought; plant seed within the void, cleanse by defiling, arise and go down. I parted the hills and looked into the dizzying depths where bloomed the one struggling rosebud, opening the width of a breath, closing as if in acknowledgment that it must pay its price, must be penetrated so that from its division would come unification; from the invasion of the fissure would come the fusion between the ravisher and the ravished.

I touched with my staff each hill as if in benediction, then descended the precipice, my intruder in the dust. The rosebud resisted, clinging to its inviolability, its sanctity, then it gave me sanctuary.

I plunged forward, downward. From beneath the hills, from beyond the entrance to the internal eternal verity, came the sound splitting the silence as I split the puckered protesting protector of secrets within.

"Ouch!" he said.

"Yes," I said. "It has always been so."

Then my stranger forged ahead into the unknown, slowly, arduously. The road to redemption has ever been tight. Amidst the cries and the exhalations, the groans and the ohs, the nos and yeses and the agains and mores and the continual inexorable maybe I furrowed farther until I was deep within him. I was deep within him and could no deeper go. We were locked together in the ancient embrace.

"You have to loosen up," I told him.

"Oh," he said.

"Looser," I said. "I need room."

Then began the primordial dance, the retreat the advance the up and the down the redemption of old sins and the commission of new ones, the fever and the fervor the fire in the loin (the one not lost to the bear) and the tortured syntax and the sin taxing and tortuous to the body and the desiccated soul until I burned with lust and my lust burned me like a bush, my bush burning up in flames until I cried out in the heat until I shuddered in the conflagration until my seed burst forth and spent itself within the cavern of his hills.

Later I said, "Was it good for you?"

And he yawned and "A lot of sound and fury," he said, "signifying very little."

THE MASOCHISTS AMONG US

Shaun Levin

The day after I meet Mario at the Queer Film Festival on the South Bank we go for tea at Fortnum's on Piccadilly—peppermint for him, Royal Blend for me— and he tells me about this sex club he went to the night before. I've never been to the Hoist, but I've wanted to go. I'm new to the whole anonymous public sex thing. Mario is handsome, well dressed in the way Italian men seem to be, especially those who live in big cities like Rome, men who travel abroad to find the kind of sex that turns them on. If they don't go to New York, they come here to London.

"But I didn't do nothing," he says.

"What kind of night was it?"

"Everyone was naked."

"No underpants?"

"Just the boots," he says.

"These ones?" I say, touching his leather boot under the table.

And while I undo the laces and stroke his leg—firm and slightly hairy—he talks about the men who pissed on each other, those who knelt at the urinals and waited to drink from the cocks of strangers. He talks of the man who lay in a sling and let a stranger fist fuck him, a stranger who rocked him gently back and forth while his arm went in and out of him up to the elbow. He tells me about an American guy who chatted to him at the bar and asked Mario to watch while he squatted over a plastic sheet and took a dump on the floor. Mario was his audience of one, a witness to the cowboy who rubbed excrement onto his own chest and face.

"That is too much," Mario says. "I walk away at that minute."

"There must have been something you liked."

"I want to be insulted," he says. (Pronounced in-sool-ted.)

"Like what? Like: You fucking faggot?"

He smiles. His face, to use a cliché, lights up.

"Do you like being on all fours?" I say.

"Yes."

"Like a dog?"

"Yes. I would be a dog to somebody."

"Why not at the club?"

"No, no. These are too much faggots," he says. "Disgusting."

"Get up," I say.

* * *

Today should have been the beginning of the war in Iraq. Today was to be the day of bombings and dead bodies, the day that, only weeks ago, we'd marched to avoid, and now, to prove we still cared, we were planning to converge on Trafalgar Square, all one million of us. But I didn't. I went to Fortnum and Mason, purveyors of fine goods and teas, supermarket to the Queen, to have sex with an Italian in a toilet cubicle that seems surprisingly small for a department store that caters to royalty.

Mario does not want to kiss. There is too much love and commitment in such an act. He opens his lips just a fraction and we talk into each other's mouths, his breath warm and clean. As if his shame and guilt and denial have had a cleansing effect on him. His insides smell sweet, but his body trembles. He's been waiting for this moment a long time; so long he can barely contain his excitement.

"I want to be your slave," he says, his eyes closed in prayer.

"And you'll do what I tell you?"

"Yes," he says. "Yes, please."

"You'll be my dog?"

"Yes, everything. I want to be."

"Turn around. Show me your arse."

And he does. Immediately. He leans over the cistern and pulls down his trousers and shows off his smooth arse, cream-colored, tan lines showing. He turns his head to look at me, just a flicker of doubt in his eyes, so tiny, before spreading wider to show off his hole, the kind of hole I like to fuck, smooth and unblemished with a pucker the same color as the skin around it.

"Pull it open," I say.

So I can kneel down and bring my tongue to it. It is soft and clean and odorless, and while I lick I think of the dark warm places on our bodies where the scent of our identity is kept. With him it is perfect, immaculate, as if it's possible to get away with such things as self-loathing and internalized homophobia and be rewarded with a great body, a great job, an untroubled conscience. And there's a part of me, the part that would suck the shit from his arse, would lick at him till my tongue lapped at his insides, that would give up everything I am and everything I believe in to be as simple and smug as him.

"You are making me so *orni*," he says.

"Oh, shut up with that stupid fucking Italian accent."

"Sorry. When I get it wrong, I want you punish me."

When the Inquisitor asks where I was while they bombed Baghdad, the answer will be: Rimming the arse of an Italian tourist in the toilets at Fortnum's. I will say that one protest march was enough for me. If the Government won't listen to the masses, the least we can do is order each other around.

Mario is jerking himself off frantically, oblivious to the fact that his cock is above my rucksack. I'm fingering his arse and licking it and he's got his other hand on the back of my head pulling me harder against his arsehole. I'm getting ready to fuck him, but at the rate we're going, at the speed he's pulling at the cock I haven't seen much of, my own cock isn't going to get anywhere near his wet hole. I don't want him coming on my bag. I don't want him coming at all. I'm worried that when he comes it'll all be over; my desire left hanging in midair, unfulfilled.

But he comes.

"Okay," I say. "Now go."

"What?"

"You're disgusting," I say.

I think we both got off on that final act of malice, surprised by its intensity and spontaneity. He looks hurt; shocked I could say something like that, that I could tell him he's disgusting, no better than the rest of us faggots. But I guess we all have our limits; we're all conflicted. Even the masochists among us need a tender good-bye.

THE MOST UNEXPECTED PLACES

Rachel Kramer Bussel

It's bad enough to run into an ex while on a tropical cruise; even worse to run into your ex's ex, but that's exactly what happened to me. Given the options of going to Minneapolis for Christmas and facing my family for the first time in four years solo, or having fun in the sun with as many gay boys as I could handle, I chose the obvious.

I figured all those strangers would help get my mind off Parker. But one of the first people I ran into was Carlos, Parker's ex. I'd heard all about Carlos, had even met him once, but it'd been a long time before I could even hear his name without wincing. He'd come before me, and I knew he'd always resented the fact that I'd "stolen" Parker away, even though they'd been split up for three months.

"Hey, man," he said to me, slapping my shoulder. I was still getting used to the blazing sun, but there was Carlos, topless; his rippled, smooth chest bared for all to see; wearing red running shorts that hid nothing. If I hadn't known who he was, I might have even found him attractive. Instead, I just gave him a polite smile and quick greeting, and headed to my room. I'd requested a solo, figuring I might want to bring someone (or several someones) back with me.

I took a nap, my subconscious working overtime as I dreamed about me, Parker and Carlos, shiny with grease and sweat, wrestling in an arena while an anonymous crowd cheered us on. I wasn't sure what the point of the match was, but in the dream my dick was hard, and not just the times I managed to pin Parker beneath me. Dream Carlos was smirking at me, and when I finally awoke, I was sweaty and sticky and hard; very, very hard. I stroked my cock, picturing the cute guy with the clipboard who'd checked off my name. I knew he'd been looking at my ass as I walked away. Maybe he'd want to join me later. I finally got up, stripped and stood in front of the mirror. There I was, five-eight, bald, sleek and strong. I preened; I could get a guy for sure.

I took a shower, hoping the water would wash away the dream, but it didn't. There he was again, in my head: Carlos. I remembered every word Parker had ever said about Carlos. Once I'd asked him what Carlos was like in bed. "Oh, he was good. He liked it rough. But I don't want to talk about him...I want to play with you," he'd said, reaching forward to pinch my nipple, the one with the silver stud through it.

I was the bottom in all senses of the word with Parker, and I'd liked it; he knew how to treat me, how to hold me down, how to talk dirty to me, but he took wielding his power over me a little too seriously outside the bedroom. When he tried to dictate what I wore, who I hung out with and even which acting roles I should take, I left him.

I chose a white striped shirt and cargo pants, a step up from the bare chests and surf shorts most of the guys here wore. For some reason, I wanted to impress Carlos. I went to the bar for my complimentary champagne, and while I was perusing the buffet options, Carlos sauntered up to me. He hadn't worried about being over-dressed; his olive skin glistened with what looked like baby oil, his nipples like shiny pearls glistening, and he still wore those shorts that were small enough to hug his body in all the right places. "See anything you like?" he said softly. This was so surreal, but my cock didn't lie: I was turned on.

"Yes," I said, then drained my glass. Carlos took a step closer, running his hand up my arm.

I shivered, and when I dared to look directly into Carlos's dark brown eyes, they were blazing, feral. I'd pegged Carlos for a bottom, but the way he gripped my arm was decidedly dominant. Staring deep into my eyes, Carlos said, "Forget about him. Focus on me." With that, he took my hand and placed it on his cock. I gasped and would've dropped the glass if Carlos hadn't taken it from me.

He silently steered me away from the food and up the stairs. I felt like a teenager with his first older lover, even though I knew Carlos, at twenty-three, was four years younger than me. At his room, he used one hand to reach down my pants and fondle my cock while he opened the door with the other.

He stopped once the door was shut, grabbed a belt from the door knob and tied my hands behind my back. He was so quick I barely had time to respond. My mind was in overdrive. Carlos pushed me to the ground, his hand on my head sending waves of heat through my body. He took out his cock and waved it in my face. "Do you want this?" he asked. I nodded. "I've heard how good you are at swallowing."

I shut my eyes, humiliated but still aroused. Not that being known for my deep-throat prowess was a bad thing necessarily, but I cringed to think that Parker and Carlos had talked about me. "Still want it?" he asked, a teasing note in his voice.

This time I opened my mouth, and he filled it, his dick taking up all the space I'd offered him. I focused on the feel of my lips against his pubic hair, then gliding along his hot, hard skin. When his hand tugged my hair, a shudder went through me. Submitting to him was the perfect antidote to all the moping I'd been doing. The only times I didn't have his hardness between my lips were when he was rubbing it against my cheek, making me kiss the tip or lightly slapping my face. "I'm going to come all over your face," Carlos grunted, and while I loved being bound, at that moment I wished I could touch myself and release all the feelings Carlos was bringing up in me. I savored his last few thrusts, his cock head tickling the back of my throat as he invaded it, before he bathed my face with the warmth of his copious come.

Then Carlos made me stand in front of the mirror, my face covered. He stood behind me and pinched my nipples, then slapped them, before I watched him jerk me off in the mirror. I flinched when he undid the belt, fearing he'd send me on my way. "Want to order room service?" he asked. I smiled. We were inseparable for the rest of the cruise (save for the guys we invited back to the room). When we said good-bye, I gave him a genuine smile. Who knew that I had to go so far away to find a cure for my broken heart so close to home?

GOOD BUDDY

Nick Gilberto Marengo

The following took place just after John and I broke up. I thought my world was coming apart, so I hit the road with a small suitcase and made away with our classic '78 F-100. I figured he owed me. We'd had an old CB radio installed for shits and giggles. It was my dad's and was just collecting dust in the garage. We even learned the lingo and had our own handles. John's was Curly Scruff, mine was Slimy Faucet. Go figure.

Anyway, I was on the 670 in the middle of Missouri. It was hot as fuck and the AC was busted. I had already been on the road for four or five days without much sleep thanks to the heartbreak. It was just that desolate road, me and some big red 18-wheeler. Over the random shit coming over the FM I remembered the games John and I played on the CB and decided to take a listen to help me stay awake. At first all I got was some faint noise, not much.

"Slimy Faucet here on the 670." *Maybe I should've changed my name?*

Static.

"Slimy Faucet with his ears on. Anyone there?"

More static.

"On the 670 too, Slimy. What's up?"

I wasn't prepared for anyone to answer.

"Was just seein' if anyone'd respond. I guess I'm bored. These radio stations aren't much."

Laughter, then, "Yeah, Jesus this and the Holy Ghost that!"

"You got it!" I chuckled a bit. "I didn't catch your name."

"Hefty Hangers."

There was a pause.

"All right, Hefty, where 'bouts are you?"

Another pause.

You wouldn't believe it, but suddenly that giant 18-wheeler pulled up to the passenger's side blaring its horn. There wasn't anyone else on the road so I knew this was for me.

"So, *you're* my bumper sticker, eh?" I chuckled again. Apparently I hadn't forgotten any of the slang.

"That's right; I've been on your ass for a while. Show me what you got, buddy," Hefty replied.

It didn't really seem that I had a choice in the matter.

We were alone on this long stretch and I *had* been horny as hell. John and I hadn't had sex in weeks. It wasn't all that fair, though. This guy could fully see me, but I couldn't even get a glimpse of his face. While I was thinking it over, that tumultuous horn blasted in my ears again.

"All right!" I huffed. Keeping my eyes on the road I unzipped my 501s. The blood was already rushing to the head of my cock. Upon my getting the fly completely down it just flopped out as if it were an overly anxious dog stuck in a kennel for months. While it was slapping against my belly I grabbed hold and pulled the foreskin back, giving my good buddy a full glimpse, and then I tucked it away.

"Why you gotta tease, man? Keep it out," Hefty demanded.

"I can't even see you! Can't we just," I began.

"What I say?" he interrupted. "Keep it out."

Indeed, I hadn't a say in the matter and did just as he said.

"Now play with it. Man, I love the dip you got there." *Was he referring to my heavy foreskin? How could he see such detail from so far up?*

I followed his orders. I shed my wife-beater, which peeled off as if adhesive were keeping it attached. John was supposed to have fixed the AC but never got around to it. Lightly stroking my cock, I saw that I was dripping with precum. I slathered my foreskin with that generous supply and showed it to him using my index finger; I rubbed the head then brought my finger to my mouth. The lengthy stream that followed lightly rested atop my furry torso.

"All right, hammer down. There's a pickle park just a few exits down." Hefty sped off.

It was barren. We really were the only ones on that stretch of road, and not a single vehicle at the rest stop. Hefty was just a little bigger than me. His beer gut complemented his furry, burly arms, thick beard and all. His attire matched him in true trucker fashion: a faded cap that carried the image of an eagle was snug on his head. His Ray-Bans were fairly scuffed, which only added to the aesthetic. I knew this was not going to be just a stroll in the park. There wasn't much of an exchange of words. We both were there for one reason.

I was leaning on the hood of my truck still shirtless with my dick out, waiting. Hefty just hopped out of that massive rig and gestured with a light jerk of his head to the back of my truck. I took his lead.

My cock just slapped against my thighs like a lazy water hose on summertime pavement as I followed. Hefty, gaze locked with full intent, lifted me onto the bed of my truck. His arms felt like steel beams that should be holding a bridge in place. If I'd had any second thoughts about my situation, I was pretty sure I was past the point of no return. Slamming me down and holding me there, he went straight for it. His beard chaffed my inner thigh and got me all worked up. My cock was fully hard again, pounding against the back of Hefty's throat.

With one hand on my throat keeping me in my place, he had the other tugging on my balls. I attempted to push his hand away; no one had ever treated my balls with such steady force. Rather than push *my* hand away he just pulled even harder, his mouth still focused on my cock. I seemed to have no control over what this man was going to do to me. I realized that I was completely helpless. We were in the middle of nowhere. If I did scream for help I was sure I would just get killed by some hillbilly. With that on my mind, walking away after some sex that'd surely leave me black and blue didn't seem so bad. If I *was* going to get killed by Hefty, at least I was getting a killer blow job in the process.

Hefty's hand made its way down to just below my balls. His thumb entered me like he was digging into the peel of a ripe orange. No saliva was needed. I was already dripping in perspiration and Hefty slobber that covered my balls and the thick fur around my ass. I struggled a bit more but those steel beams were holding strong. Taking a taste here and there along the way, he worked his way up. That whopping mouth of his seemed as if it were going to devour my entire head. His tongue made its way to the back of my throat, batting at my tonsils. His teeth ground against my lips and just below my chin. I moaned as he shoved his thumb deeper, just grazing my prostate, while his other hand squeezed tighter around my neck. I gagged. Hefty just gobbled it up and spat it in my face.

"All right, fucker. Enough of this cat-and-mouse shit. Let's do this!" he said, and got up from my truck and removed his belt.

SAFE SEX

M. Christian

I'm gonna fuck you. You know that, don't you? Yeah, you know it. Just look at that pretty pink asshole, all ready and willing. Yeah, it knows. It knows that in just a second I'm gonna feed it—you—my cock. Oh, yes, pretty asshole, so hungry and soft. You want my cock, don't you, asshole? Yes, I think it does—most certainly it does.

"But first I want you to get me really hard. Yes, that's it—put your hand there. See how hard I am already? But I bet you can get me harder. Yeah, that's it, lick that hand. Oh, yes, so slick, so smooth. Stroke me, stroke my cock. Harder. Nice strong cock, isn't it? Nice and long and hard. Your asshole getting itchy, getting those sweet little asshole hunger pains? Oh, yeah, I bet it is; bet it's getting nice and real hungry. Starving maybe…

"But I'm still not hard enough—oh, yeah, I can get even harder, even bigger. Keep stroking me. Keep it up—but I bet I know another part of you that's getting hungry, that needs feeding.

"Yeah, that's right—suck my dick.

"Oh, sweet kisses. Such sweet kisses. Isn't my cock sweet? Sweet to kiss, sweet to taste, sweet to kiss. Take it in your mouth, take it in and really taste it. Isn't that a nice cock? So slick and hard, so tasty. Suck it now, take it all the way down. Taste me nice and deep. Oh, yeah, that's nice. So nice. Take it all the way down—no gagging, no choking. Oh, yeah. Sweet, sweet…

"I could come in your mouth so easy—oh, yeah. But I don't want to do that. I want your asshole. That's where I want to come. I want to fuck you, long and hard, and fill your ass with my come.

"There, that's enough. That's it. Turn around now, show it to me—show me that pretty pink asshole again. Ah, there it is, pink and sweet. Tight I'll bet—nice and tight.

"Ready to get fucked? Oh, yeah, I bet you are. Nice and open and ready. But first a kiss—no, silly, not on your lips, though they are so nice, but right here—yeah, such a nice asshole. A nice, tasty asshole. Just right: pink with that little whiff of old shit. I love that smell, a good asshole smell. Not dirty, but with just enough to remind you what it is. Assholes are so nice, don't you think?

"Yes, a kiss—umm—you taste so good. So nice. Feel my tongue? Feel it pushing in—there—and there again?

You have the prettiest asshole. Just the thing for kissing, licking, rimming, sucking and—yeah—fucking. Just the thing.

"Now I'm really hard. So fucking hard. I want your asshole, want it around my hard dick. Get ready, take a deep breath. Ready—is your asshole ready? Fuck the condom, I want to feel you, want to feel your asshole around my raw dick. That's right, raw: nothing between you and my come, my sweet come. You have a problem with that? Well, fuck you—ha, and that's just what I'm going to do. Stay the fuck where you are. Don't you try and get away from me. Get that asshole up, fuckhead. Get it up nice and high. There—that's it. That's the asshole that's gonna get my dick.

"No use squirming, fuckhead. I'm goin' in. Feel that? That's the tip, and there's this nice little pearl of come just squishing around your asshole. Bet that makes your mouth water, don't it? Well, it's not for that mouth, that nice little drop's going to be my ticket in, my slippery key for your fucking hole.

"There, ain't that nice? Just a little more, a little more cock. Just the tip, just the start of the head. Yeah, I'm going fuck you—fuck you long and hard, and when I come I'm going to shoot right into your sweet ass. More? Fuck, yes, there's more. Feel that? That's the head, just the head of my fuckin' big dick inside you. More? Yeah, that was more—an inch, maybe two now. I'm in you, fuckhead, raw and pure—dick in asshole. More, yeah, fuck, more all the way in now—feel me knocking, fuck-face? Feel that big dick? Yeah, I bet you do—all the way in, every last inch filling up your glorious asshole.

"Fuck you, yeah, fuck you raw and hard—fuck, yeah, in and out, fucking you hard and fast. You got a nice asshole, just right for my dick. Fuck, yeah, fuck you hard and wet, gonna—oh, yeah—gonna fill you with my cream, my nice hot cream. Fuck...fuck you, yeah, fucking...

"Oh, Jesus, yes—oh, fuck, yes. In your asshole, in your hot hole. Fuck, yes," he said, "oh, fucking yes."

When he was done—when he'd come into the tissue—he wadded it up, neat and tidy, and tossed it into the trash. Then he showered, shaved and went out. *Who knows,* he thought, *maybe tonight I'll get lucky?*

MIDNIGHT DECISION

Jay Starre

Jimmy woke just before midnight. The open window above his bed allowed in the night air along with Baxter's loud barking. The barking turned to growls, and Jimmy leaped from bed and stumbled for the door. He snatched his flashlight, shotgun and some shells from the coat closet where he always kept them.

The trailer door slammed behind him as he switched on his flashlight. His collie appeared out of the darkness to whine and pant at his feet. "What's up, buddy? Coyotes?"

Dressed in only plaid boxers and sandals, the blond Texan made a beeline for the chicken coop with Baxter leading the way. The yard was eerily quiet, which meant the hens hadn't been disturbed. Baxter began growling again as he veered off to the left and toward the toolshed.

At the door, the muscular blond hesitated. Being so far out of town and with no close neighbors, he never bothered locking the shed unless he planned on being away for a few days. There was no way to tell if something or someone was in there, except for Baxter's growling.

He'd loaded two shells into his shotgun on the way over and now cradled the weapon in his right arm and his flashlight in his left as he eased the door open. Flashing the light around the room, he saw nothing out of the ordinary. The cabinets were all closed and the workbenches bare, the single window across the room wide open as usual to let in the cool desert night air. The overhead light had burned out a few days earlier and he cursed himself for not getting around to replacing it.

Stepping inside, he closed the door behind him. He didn't want Baxter inside with him in these close quarters if he had to shoot some critter lurking in the corner.

He turned left and nearly tripped over someone.

"What the fuck!"

Sitting with his back up against the wall, the stranger's feet had been sticking out enough so that Jimmy stumbled over them before he automatically raised his shotgun and aimed it.

The barrel pressed against the side of the interloper's head.

"Por favor, señor! Por favor!"

Frightened amber orbs peered up at Jimmy. His hands had come up in a gesture of surrender as quickly as that shotgun had found his head. Jimmy had shot two coyotes and a half-dozen rabbits, but that was it. He'd never had to shoot a person. With his heart pounding in his chest, the young Texan quickly looked over the seated Mexican. He was dressed in a T-shirt, shorts and runners. A small backpack was half-hidden behind his back. He looked about the same age as Jimmy, early twenties.

With the border only a few miles south, it was obvious he was an illegal immigrant gone astray. "What the hell should I do with you?" he muttered breathlessly.

Later, he would wonder why either of them did what they did.

But right then, it happened out of the blue and spontaneously. He could only gasp in disbelief as the seated Mexican reached out with one of his raised hands and thrust it into the fly of Jimmy's boxers.

Fingers squeezed his dick. With a will of its own, Jimmy's cock began to fatten. The Mexican began to pump it with a desperate fervor. "Por favor, señor," the young illegal whispered as he slowly and carefully leaned forward. His face was at Jimmy's crotch.

His cock rose as the man played with it. Jimmy's heart raced. He was as scared as the round-faced illegal.

Flashlight in one hand and shotgun in the other, he had to make a decision. With a gasp, he lowered the shotgun to plant the barrel in the seated Mexican's crotch.

"One wrong move and I blow your balls off," he threatened.

A set of big brown eyes stared up into his as Jimmy pulled his dick out. A wet, warm mouth encased his cock head as velvet-smooth lips smacked over it.

"Oh, fuck," he muttered, and started to face-fuck him.

The beam of his flashlight illuminated the late-night action: the youth's broad cheeks were clean-shaven; his huge brown eyes continued to stare up at Jimmy from under thick, dark lashes and brows; Curly, black hair was cut short above neat ears. His mouth was round and small with full lips.

Jimmy was mesmerized by that face. The look of fright transformed into greed as the man's mouth bobbed deeper on his dick. The young illegal snorted as he gripped the base of Jimmy's cock.

Observing his captive's every move with intensity, still Jimmy did nothing as the man slid his hands around his waist. The Latino pulled the muscular blond's hips forward, forcing his dick to fill his mouth.

That's when Jimmy realized the barrel of his shotgun was pressed against something stiff and solid where it rested in the intruder's crotch: his new friend had quite a boner.

Slurps and smacks echoed as Jimmy drove his cock forward, then pulled it back. The man's hands snatched at the waistband of his boxers, shoving them down past his knees. His ass was bare as fingers dove past his crack to his asshole. Jimmy moaned as the man's finger slid into his hole.

Just then, headlights glared through the open window on their left.

Switching off his flashlight, Jimmy pressed the barrel of his shotgun deeper into the seated Mexican's lap, massaging his stiff cock with it as a blunt reminder of their situation.

With a finger jabbed up Jimmy's snug butthole, the other man kept on sucking.

"Come out and surrender. You won't be harmed."

The loudspeaker blared from the road as the head-light beam moved off slowly: Border Patrol.

There was a moment of hesitation, but the intruder's talented mouth and probing fingers swayed him. He pumped that sweet mouth in the darkness as the loudspeaker's repetitive warning grew fainter and then disappeared entirely.

Jimmy fucked his mouth faster as the man finger-fucked him deeply. Jimmy couldn't hold on and soon came. Cum blasted out over the man's face. As his gasps of release subsided, the silence of the desert night returned.

GROUND-FLOOR BLOW JOB

Shane Allison

All of the stalls were full except the third one because there was no seat on the toilet. Some fucker broke it off. It was the only one vacant, so I took it. Someone wearing black penny loafers sat still in the stall next to me. I knew who it was: this old dude, bald, glasses, who always wears plaid shirts. He didn't stay long. He's not into black dick. I took his stall after he left. The rim of the toilet was hurting my ass. A guy wearing dirty brown boots was sitting on the left side of me. I slid my hand under the partition of his stall. I heard him get up off his toilet. He turned, dropped to his knees and stuck his dick under. It was of average size, cut, but with some foreskin that didn't go all the way over the head. I played with it a little. A pearl of precum stood at ease at the piss slit. I would have sucked him off, but my knees are bad. Without a glory hole, I was in no mood to do all that bending and pushing myself underneath the stall just to get him off. Besides, guys kept coming in and interrupting us. I looked through the glory hole at the set of black sneaks in the stall next to Brown Boots. I had a feeling I knew who it was; this skinny white boy, average height with long brown hair that he keeps mostly in a ponytail. It was the same guy that sucked this guy named Matt off, the same dude who showed me a text message on his cell phone saying that he didn't have time to play because he had to go to class, but now that I think about it, that was probably bullshit. I've wanted to suck his dick for weeks. He sat there pretending to shit. No one stays on the toilet that long. Brown Boots left and took the first stall next to Black Sneaks. They didn't do anything, I don't think. I didn't hear belts dangling against the floor or the rustle of clothes. Black Sneaks ended up leaving. I didn't care. I will get his dick soon enough.

Brown Boots stayed. I stepped outside of my stall and took the stall Black Sneaks had been in. I started to feel like we were playing musical stalls or some shit. I looked over into his to find him jacking off. I knew him. We've sucked each other off in the ground-floor bathroom. He's got nice, red, voluptuous lips. When he kissed me, I could taste the cigarettes. I tapped the door of his stall. He opened it. I didn't think he would. When he let me in, I reached down and started to play with his dick. Brown Boots lifted his shirt up above his stomach.

His dick was warm in my hand. I had my dick out too. I jacked him off until he came, then someone walked in. I jumped in front of a urinal. Brown Boots shut the door quick. I wiped his cum on the wall in front of me.

It was the redhead, this guy I've sucked off dozens of times. He smiled like he knew what was going on. He stood at a urinal pretending to pee. I was sure he was going to get my piece of trade and he did. Brown Boots left his stall to go wash his hands. He and the redhead started talking in front of the sinks. They stood close to each other, and both of their dicks were out—mine too. I jacked off while watching them jack off, playing with each other's dicks. The three of us were startled again when someone walked in. We quickly tucked our dicks away. The guy that walked in took the last urinal at the end of the bathroom. He didn't know what we were doing, or maybe he did, I don't know. But the other two walked out.

I waited a couple of minutes until they were out of sight and followed them. I knew where they were going: the ground-floor bathroom. It's quieter, less traffic, and has two sets of doors that give out this loud squeak when opened, so it allows more time for recovery. When I walked in, they and one other guy were in the bathroom; he was a nerdy brunet with glasses, about five-eight. He was at the sink washing up. I stood next to him checking my face until he left. Brown Boots was in the big, roomy handicapped stall at the end of the bathroom, while the redhead was in the one next to him. I walked over and started looking between the slits of their stalls. The redhead opened his stall door with his dick in his hand. Loose red-orange pubic hair sprouted out of the gap of his open zipper. He gawked at me with those blue eyes as he jacked his dick. I took it in my hand. I got down and started to suck it. Brown Boots stepped out of his stall. I felt him coming up alongside me. I stopped sucking off the redhead. Brown Boots started to jack off his dick still wet with my spit. All three of us had our dicks out. They didn't pay much attention to me. I didn't think Brown Boots had anything left since he had already shot off in the bathroom upstairs. The two of them had nice sized dicks. They started to kiss. It was wet and sloppy. The redhead got down and took Brown Boots's dick in his mouth. I'd never seen him suck someone before. He's never blown me. I bet he's only into white dick. He sucked him for a few minutes before they switched off. Brown Boots took the redhead's entire dick in his mouth. I jacked off watching them. I grabbed Brown Boots's ass and pressed my middle finger between his asscheeks. He sucked until he made the redhead come. It never takes him long. He didn't come in Brown Boots's mouth. He always pulls out right before and comes in his own hand or in the toilet. The redhead came on the floor. It was right on time, too: we heard the doors squeak just then. It scared the hell out of us.

I stepped back into the roomy handicapped stall. I sat on the toilet with my jeans on, but with my dick still out. The redhead unrolled tissue. I could hear the guy that walked in, pissing at the urinal. The redhead left. I stayed put until the bathroom was quiet again. When I stepped out, Brown Boots was gone too. I went back upstairs to the first-floor bathroom. I took a glory hole stall, the side dudes take when they want to suck some dick, but it was after five, so nobody came. I jacked off, talking dirty to myself until I shot off. When I left, one of the lady janitors was coming down the hall with her cleaning cart. I didn't look at her, but could feel her eyes on me like she knew what I had been doing. I thought of the redheaded guy and Brown Boots, knowing I would see them again. These guys always come back. Always.

AFTER HOURS

C. C. Williams

"Coffee, tobacco or tea, BriteWite leaves your smile bright and white!" I delivered the tagline without retching and flashed my cover-model smile.

"Thank you!" yelled the director. "We'll call."

Trying not to look skeptical, I thanked the panel and left the agency's studio. Waiting for the elevator to wheeze down ten floors to the lobby, I examined my reflection in the doors. Who could possibly outdo this—especially for a toothpaste ad? Blond curls framed a tan, all-American boy-next-door face with great teeth. What more could they want? Chiming its arrival, the elevator doors opened and I watched my face ripple as they receded.

On the subway I moped. Usually I people watch—my friends call it cruising. But why not? New York is full of hot guys. Granted, most of us know that we are, but everyone should be appreciated. And I appreciate hot guys. Exiting at Christopher Street, I headed down Seventh and decided to treat myself to Starbucks. Given the imminent demise of my checking account if I didn't find a gig soon, it wasn't a prudent thing; but a caramel macchiato would soothe my ego.

Starbucks was quiet; a few NYU students sat hunched over laptops. I ordered my drink and eyed the shorts-wearing barista—he had sexy legs with a cool tattoo around his calf. I considered passing him my number, but the hot Italian guy walking in distracted me. Tall and dark, he oozed masculinity with curly hair filling the open collar of his shirt and covering his muscular forearms. Oakley sunglasses that had easily set him back a bill and a half hid his eyes. Disappointingly his glance passed right over me; although a blond coed got a twice-over for ten seconds—or at least her tits did.

Not above a little stalking, I followed him as he left. We headed up Grove toward Fourth; he walked confidently, striding among the pedestrians; I followed secretively, lusting after his butt. Past Waverly he crossed over what was now Christopher Street and entered a storefront beneath a red awning with TRATTORIA LOUISA in black script. Dodging a cab, I went after and pretended to read the menu posted in the window. Unable to see into the dark interior, my eyes glimpsed the handwritten sign below the menu—SERVER NEEDED. APPLY WITHIN. Bingo!

* * *

Louisa, née Lois Mitcham, was a big-busted, loud-laughed, bottle-dyed mountain of a woman with a soft spot for stray animals—most of whom she had hired to work at the restaurant. We were a motley crew: Jayzee, born Jakob Zuchowski, the tattooed, skater-wannabe busboy; Adamo, the hot Starbucks guy, the bartender and only real Italian in the place; Carlie, the cocktail waitress who was screwing Adamo; and Axel, the dark-haired, elfin, blue-eyed cook.

Two weeks had passed and I felt right at home: everybody bitched, just like family. Saturday night was finished. We'd been shorthanded, so Louisa had belted down two Tanquerays with dribbles of tonic and tossed the keys to Adamo, telling him to lock up, as she lurched out the door.

Stocking fell to me, and I moved around the restaurant refilling supplies. At the prep sink I closed the door of the first-aid cabinet and did a double take at its attached mirror. With the proper angle I could see around the corner into the storage room—where Jayzee and Adamo were making out!

Mesmerized, I watched as Jayzee unbuttoned Adamo's jeans and pulled out a breathtaking length of dark cock. Rolling foreskin between his fingers, Jayzee coaxed the bartender's dick to full attention. Running his fingers down the shaft, the busboy combed through the curly bush to cup the bartender's balls and roll them on his palm. Adamo groaned. His plum-colored cock head peeked out past the retreating foreskin. Jayzee dropped down, taking the head in his mouth. Amazed, I held my breath as he swallowed the entire length, finally burying his nose in the black pubes.

Adamo gripped the back of the busboy's head and began to fuck Jayzee's throat, gaining rhythm and speed. With one hand tugging Adamo's nuts, Jayzee used the other to pull out his own cock. His meat, cut and blue-veined, bobbed free, rising immediately. Wiping precome on his palm, Jayzee stroked the length of his hard-on; all the while his lips and tongue were working Adamo's cock.

Trapped in my slacks, my dick swelled uncomfortably. Adjusting my half-hard cock, I forced myself to breathe quietly, not wanting to gasp and betray myself. Nervous, but unable to look away, I gripped my erection through the fabric of my pants. I had never considered myself a voyeur—I wasn't even that big on porn—but watching them excited me.

Suddenly a hand closed over my mouth. Axel's voice whispered, "Enchanting, aren't they?" I caught my breath, unsure of his intentions. "They've got you turned on." His other hand landed atop mine, pressing my hand harder against my groin. Electric tingles shot up my arm. "Can I help you with that?"

I nodded against Axel's hand as his cock pushed against my hip. Rather than releasing me, he pulled my head to the side and ran his lips along my neck. His breath tickled, sending shivers down my spine. The shivers met the tingles and sparks exploded in my chest. My heart raced, hammering against my ribs.

Axel's tongue traced a burning cold line along my collarbone as he undid my belt and pants. His mouth never left my skin. Keeping one hand over my mouth, he pulled me back against him, supporting my weight as his left hand grasped my throbbing cock.

"Watch them. Imagine you're there."

By now I was more aroused by Axel's control than by Jayzee and Adamo's show. Usually I'm in charge, but Axel's sure dominance gave me little choice. The enforced submission fired my cock. My pulse beat in my ears, competing in intensity with my panting breaths.

Axel stroked me, moving down across my balls and between my legs. My cock twitched, sending spasms through my abs. Rubbing up, his fingers traced the edge of the corona. My dick was so hard it ached. Faster and faster he stroked. Tension built in my gut. All the while he nuzzled me, licking and nipping at my neck.

Orgasm washed over me, exploding outward from my groin. My body shook as Axel held me even closer.

"Yeah," he cooed. "Come for me."

Semen coated his fingers as he drained me. I slumped against him; releasing my jaw, he caught me under the shoulders.

"Shit!" I whispered. "That was hot!"

Axel steadied me. "Not as hot as you, Ryan." Licking his fingers, he grinned, moving away. "I've wanted to taste your sauce since I first saw you."

Zipping up, I followed after. "And?"

"I want more."

"I'd go for more too." I reached for him, turning his face so his gaze met mine. "You always take charge like that?"

"Why? Did you like it?"

My face grew warm. "Well...yeah."

Axel grabbed my neck and whispered, "Good." He pulled me close.

Our lips met, wet and hot; our tongues dueled.

I surrendered.

THE SWIMMER

Mike Bruno

Stretched tight across acres of shoulder, his skin glitters orange in the glow of the slowly sinking sun. Swimmer's shoulders, after all, buttressed by wide, strong lats and proud, plush pecs. Unwieldy and clumsy on land, his is a body to be reckoned with in the water, and I scoot my erect, naked self closer to the edge of the rock—Our Rock—for what the sunset insists must be our good-bye.

I don't live in Hawaii, and I don't know if he does or not. But it was in these wild and moody waters off the Big Island that we first met, and it is to this spot, out past Pualaa, that we return every year. It's an unspoken, undeniable pact that pulls me across the water every July, whatever the cost. My life at home unfolds without him, as his must without me. My job is challenging and

rewarding, my boyfriend charming and romantic; to
feel a need for more than I have is avarice in its basest
form. But he is in my mind every day, no matter my
circumstances, and he is only in my arms once a year;
there is nothing—no appointment, no career, no relationship—that I wouldn't risk for our annual afternoon
of passionate union.

I don't know how far he travels. I have no idea what
he might risk by coming. I don't care. I care only to taste
his lips on mine, and the way he greedily drinks from
them, it seems that he returns each year with the same
ambition. We never speak. *Never*, and it's been eleven
years. I don't even know if he understands English. It
doesn't seem to matter. We get one afternoon a year, and
the list of things we enjoy doing together leaves little
time for small talk.

No matter how early I clamber down to the beach,
he's always there, waiting for me out by Our Rock, and
he greets me unfailingly with five kisses: a goofy-happy
one on each cheek, the tenderest whisper of one on both
of my eyelids and a kiss on my mouth that knocks me
senseless. It knocks my knees right out from under me,
truth be told, but he's always ready for that. Once I slide
into the water, he's got me where he wants me, and we
loll in the sea, sometimes for hours. We splash around;
we bodysurf; we dive alongside sea turtles, the *humuhu-
munukunukuapuaa* painting the seascape, darting hither
and yon. And he offers his body wholly up to me; in the
water, he is mine to do with what I wish. I grope and

nibble at the brick shit house that is his chest, warm and welcoming for all that it seems to be a mere miracle of masonry. I embrace him in the waves, pressed against his broad, ridged abdomen, squashing the pillow of the belly that I'm trying not to grow and that he won't let me be ashamed of. And always, because it is this more than anything that keeps me awake nights, that makes my body call out for his in the quiet darkness when I am at home, I revel in the still-astonishing length of him. With my eyes. My hands. My greedy, gratified mouth. He's not one inch under seven feet tall, and I drink in as much of him as I can, engraving every inch of him onto my memory, knowing that these delirious hours will have to see me through many desolate months to come.

Eventually I tire in the water, and he lifts me onto Our Rock, where my languorous body is his plaything. With those sparkling, spectacular shoulders he lifts himself from the water to take ownership of me, marveling at all the ways we are different. He is tickled at the way I am soft and plump where he is hard and lean, fascinated by the thick and ubiquitous coat of hair where he is slippery-smooth. I stir just looking in his eyes, and at the first whisper of his lips against my neck, my cock jumps. There is no part of my body that he does not kiss; no curve on which he does not playfully nibble or hungrily slurp. By the time he is deep in the thrall of my feet, sucking at each toe like a calf at a teat, never breaking eye contact, my dick stands tall, solid and proud. This pleases him—he smiles and teases it with kisses—but it will be a while, sometimes it's hours, before he will heed my wordless, moaned entreaties and drink my climax as the sea behind him drinks the last few shimmering drops of sunshine.

It always happens, desperately though we might wish that it wouldn't. After a glorious moment of Hawaiian twilight, the air itself glowing pink, the sun begins in earnest to make preparations for its inexorable departure. This year there are tears, and he licks each one away, slowly and purposefully, as if protecting each one, the better to carry it with him as a keepsake, before he slides noiselessly back into the golden water and helps me find a perch at the edge of Our Rock. He teases me for just the most deliciously agonizing moment, allowing nothing but the trade winds to caress my rigid, supplicant cock, before he takes me in one gulp into his huge, hungry mouth.

He sucks me practically numb, my dick banging against the back of his ravenous throat. I have to lie back on Our Rock, light-headed as every droplet of blood in my body rushes to the scene. He takes me deeper than any other man could, then slides back, grazing the top of my erection with his teeth, electrifying the underside with his dexterous tongue, stopping to tickle the dripping tip of my dick before sliding down my shaft anew. I rally and sit up because I know I am close, and the ecstasy in his eyes when I explode, howling, in his mouth is so stark and genuine that it spurs me to reload and shoot again. He spits me out at the last of all possible seconds and I shoot my second load in ropes across his face. He grins up at me and slathers my cum all over his face, up into his hair; licks it from his fingertips before submerging himself in the ocean and splashing himself clean.

Nothing remains of the sun but its fiery tip, which quickly plops into the water with what you'd swear was a splash. I reach out for a last touch—of his hand, his face, whatever I can reach. But he has already turned to go. He lifts his mighty arms up out of the water, brings them together over his head and leaps to follow them through the air and into the hole that they part in the waves. The gauzy, orange fluke of his magnificent tail unfurls, and then, with a snap, my merman is gone.

SOCK FUZZ

Gregory L. Norris

A friend of his brother's, Zach had come home with Conner for the holidays and was snoring in the den, his bare feet kicked up. Eric snuck into the room for a look at their weekend guest. The dude was as magnificent as Eric had suspected when he heard the news that they were having company: a long, athletic succession of muscles, passed out in a classic male pose on one of the two recliners in front of the massive flat screen, which was tuned to a sports channel. Zach had short, dark hair and the face of a sleeping angel, which Eric guessed was equal parts devil when awake, being that he was Conner's buddy. Dress shirt and skinny tie, khaki pants and those big naked feet completed the picture. Fluffy sweat socks sat discarded atop shoes at the side of the recliner, a new pair of socks, judging by the bits of white fuzz stuck to the dude's toes.

The cadence of snores sent Eric's heart into a gallop. Seeing those feet—easily size twelves, the feet of a college jock—made his pulse race even faster. Zach had passed out with one hand tucked under his belt, his fingers presumably clamped around his junk. Eric couldn't tell if the dude had thrown wood beneath his grip but imagined that he had, which added to the growing flush of excitement.

Conner was always bringing home fellow teammates and buddies for the holidays, strays with nowhere else to go. The image of Zach left Eric struggling to breathe. He was, without question, their handsomest visitor since Conner won a full ride on a football scholarship. Suddenly, all he could think about was getting up close to those feet being aired out, stealing a whiff of their scent, and extending his tongue for a taste. He sighed Zach's name and snuck a hand into his shorts. Much as he imagined the current state of Zach's dick, Eric's was stiff. Reaching the recliner, a distance of several yards across the den, seemed more like bridging a gulf of miles. Eventually, he made it. Lowering, Eric drew a deep breath.

The masculine odor of Zach's toes triggered such intense chemical impulses, Eric worried he'd nut on the next squeeze of his dick. A shiver tumbled down his spine, hotter more than chilly. He boldly extended his tongue and licked the sweaty underside of Zach's right big toe. The college jock, who probably played baseball, hoops and ice hockey as well as football with Eric's big brother, snorted in response. Eric froze. Zach resumed snoring.

Licking his lips, Eric savored the buttery taste of the dude's foot-sweat. He wanted more, but a sound from the staircase sent him scrambling. Conner caught up to him in the kitchen.

"Dude," his older brother said.

Hoping to conceal his guilt, Eric turned away, shielding his front. "What's up?"

Conner's eyes sized Eric up through narrowed slits. "It goes without saying—keep out of the den."

"What's that supposed to mean?"

Eric knew, but Conner only growled in response before uncapping the orange juice and gulping down a mouthful, right from the jug.

"You're Conner's kid brother," Zach said, his voice a manly baritone.

"Guilty," Eric said, extending his hand. Zach accepted the offer and shook with enough strength to shatter bone if he'd wanted, Eric guessed.

Zach's grip lingered. So did his gaze. Eric felt the dude's eyes wandering over him, a look similar to the one his brother had lobbed, the kind that addressed the meat of the matter without the need for actual words. Awake, Zach was even handsomer.

"Come on boys, sit down and eat," a voice from the dining room beckoned. They did, and throughout the meal Zach's deep baby-browns kept wandering across the table in Eric's direction.

He was a single child, Zach revealed, twenty-two, like Conner—two years older than Eric. His parents had gone away from their empty nest for the holidays, some-place warm, so Zach would otherwise have spent the weekend alone in the family home, probably starving to death, he joked.

"Well, we can't have that happening to one of our son's friends," their dad said.

"I appreciate it."

"So, Zach, do you have a girlfriend?"

Around a mouthful of meat and gravy, Conner said, "He's got *several*, Dad."

More laughter ensued, and Zach came clean. "No, sir, not at the moment."

And then his eyes again rolled toward Eric.

The men were downstairs watching hockey. The disem-bodied voice of the wind moaned around the eaves. Eric tried to ignore the ache in his nuts, the knowledge that so handsome a stranger was staying under their roof, and that he'd stolen a forbidden taste, however brief, of the dude's body.

Knuckles wrapped on the bedroom door. Eric jolted in place and pulled the covers over his erect cock, which three previous bastings hadn't satisfied.

"Yeah," Eric called.

The door opened. He expected Conner to be standing there, waiting to deliver another warning about not messing around with one of his buddies, as had happened the last time he'd brought a stray jock home. But it was the buddy himself, Zach.

"Hey, dude," he said.

Eric choked down a heavy swallow, his mouth suddenly as dry as a desert. "Hey."

Zach lingered at the door. "Can I come in?"

The okay was past Eric's lips before he could stop it. Zach plodded in and closed the door. The thin tie had been loosened and his shirttails hung out, framing the meaty bulge of the young man's crotch. He looked strangely awkward for a dude in such great shape, nervous and sweaty. Some unaffected register in Eric's dazed thoughts imagined how wonderfully male Zach's toes would smell now, following an afternoon and part of the evening spent back in those socks. He imagined Zach's feet, his nuts, his pits and asshole.

"Nice room," Zach said. It was conversation meant to fill a void.

"Thanks. How's the hockey game?"

Zach's throat, quite hairy with five o'clock shadow at ten p.m., knotted. "They're all passed out down there. So, Conner said…"

Here it was. "He said that I'm his gay younger bro? He also told you that he caught me messing around with one of the guys he brought home over Thanksgiving?"

Zach's hands went fishing in his pockets. "He never said who. Did you hear the part about how I don't have a girlfriend?"

Their eyes met. The dopey grin fell off Zach's face,

his expression becoming all business.

"I haven't met a lot of gay dudes, not even at school. But I want—"

Eric reached up and groped the obvious bulge at the front of Zach's pants. Stiffness pushed against his palm and fingertips. "I can guess."

"Oh, fuck," Zach moaned.

Eric tore back the covers and shifted on the bed. Sitting up put him in the perfect position: his mouth level with Zach's dick, which he freed from confinement with a few deft moves. Pants and tight whites dropped down to the tops of hairy ankles. Zach's cock snapped up, an above-average column thickest at the middle with an arrow-shaped head and plenty of veins and dings along the shaft. Two bloated nuts in a hairy sac spilled beneath it. The musty ripeness of male sweat filled Eric's next breath. He sucked Zach in. The dude's bone lay warm and rubbery on his tongue.

"Yeah," Zach huffed. "Fuck, *yeah!*"

Eric tickled his nuts. Without asking, Zach reached down and fondled the thickness between Eric's legs. An uncoordinated tumble onto the bed followed as the last of their clothes came off, including Zach's sweat socks.

Eric lowered his head for a taste of the dude's big jock feet. Zach seized in place.

"What are you doing?"

"What do you think I'm doing?" Eric countered, gripping Zach's closest foot by its furry ankle.

"My *feet* dude, seriously?"

Eric licked between Zach's toes. "Seriously," he answered. "Clearly, you've got a lot to learn about the fun you can have with another dude's body. Luckily, you're gonna be around here for the long weekend."

Zach flashed a smile and nodded. Then, while the rest of the house slept, they returned to enjoying each other in the bedroom at the top of the stairs.

ABOUT
THE EDITOR

SHANE ALLISON is the editor of the Gaybie award-winning collection *College Boys: Gay Erotic Stories*, along with *Hard Working Men: Gay Erotic Stories*, *Afternoon Pleasures: Erotica for Gay Couples*, *Back-draft: Fireman Erotica* and *Hot Cops: Gay Erotic Stories*. His debut book of poetry, *Slut Machine*, is out from Queer Mojo Press. His work has appeared in more than a dozen anthologies including five editions of *Best Gay Erotica*, *Best Black Gay Erotica* and *Ultimate Gay Erotica*. He received his MFA from New School University and lives in Tallahassee, Florida. He loves chubby, hairy men.

More Gay Erotic Stories from Shane Allison

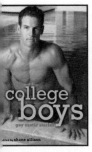

Buy 4 books, Get 1 *FREE**

College Boys
Gay Erotic Stories
Edited by Shane Allison

First feelings of lust for another boy, all-night study sessions, the excitement of a student hot for a teacher... is it any wonder that college boys are the objects of fantasy the world over?
ISBN 978-1-57344-399-9 $14.95

ʜot Cops
ʜay Erotic Stories
ᴇdited by Shane Allison

ꜰrom smooth and fit to big and hairy... ꜱ like a downtown locker room where ʀeryone has some sort of badge."—*Bay ꜱea Reporter*
ꜱBN 978-1-57344-277-0 $14.95

Backdraft
Fireman Erotica
Edited by Shane Allison

"Seriously: This book is so scorching hot that you should box it with a fire extinguisher and ointment. It will burn more than your fingers." —*Tucson Weekly*
ISBN 978-1-57344-325-8 $14.95

More of the Very Best from Cleis Press

ꜱest Gay Erotica 2010
ᴇdited by Richard Labonté
ꜱelected and introduced by Blair Mastbaum
ꜱBN 978-1-57344-374-6 $15.95

ꜱest of the Best Gay Erotica 3
ᴇdited by Richard Labonté
ꜱBN 978-1-57344-410-1 $14.95

Skater Boys
Gay Erotic Stories
Edited by Neil Plakcy
ISBN 978-1-57344-401-9 $14.95

A Sticky End
A Mitch Mitchell Mystery
By James Lear
ISBN 978-1-57344-395-1 $14.95

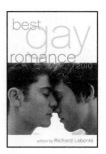

Ordering is easy! Call us toll free or fax us to place your MC/VISA order.
You can also mail the order form below with payment to:
Cleis Press, 2246 Sixth St., Berkeley, CA 94710.

ORDER FORM

QTY	TITLE	PRICE

SUBTOTAL _____

SHIPPING _____

SALES TAX _____

TOTAL _____

Add $3.95 postage/handling for the first book ordered and $1.00 for each additional book. Outside North America, please contact us for shipping rates. California residents add 9.75% sales tax. Payment in U.S. dollars only.

★ **Free book of equal or lesser value. Shipping and applicable sales tax extra.**

Cleis Press • Phone: (800) 780-2279 • Fax: 510-845-8001
orders@cleispress.com • www.cleispress.com
You'll find more great books on our website

Follow us on Twitter @cleispress • Friend/fan us on Facebook